# of *Merlot* and MURDER

# of *Merlot* and MURDER

## A Tangled Vines Mystery

# JONI FOLGER

MIDNIGHT INK
WOODBURY, MINNESOTA

FIRST EDITION
First Printing, 2014

Book design and format by Donna Burch-Brown
Cover design by Kevin R. Brown
Cover Illustration: Ken Joudrey

Midnight Ink, an imprint of Llewellyn Worldwide Ltd.

This is a work of fiction. Names, characters, places, and incidents are either the product of the author's imagination or are used fictitiously, and any resemblance to actual persons, living or dead, business establishments, events, or locales is entirely coincidental.

Cover model(s) used for illustrative purposes only and may not endorse or represent the books subject matter.

**Library of Congress Cataloging-in-Publication Data**

Folger, Joni.
  Of Merlot and murder : a Tangled Vines mystery / Joni Folger. — First edition.
      p. cm. — (A Tangled Vines mystery; #2)
    ISBN 978-0-7387-4076-8
1. Vineyards—Fiction. 2. Murder—Investigation—Fiction. I. Title.
    PS3606.O44O4      2014
    813'.6—dc23                                              2014011641

Midnight Ink
Llewellyn Worldwide Ltd.
2143 Wooddale Drive
Woodbury, MN 55125-2989
www.midnightinkbooks.com

Printed in the United States of America

*This story is dedicated to my cohorts in crime—you know who you are—and to BFFs everywhere. We all have them—those special friends who'll have a glass of wine with you during good times and wade right into the melee beside you in bad times. Here's a toast to you all. Party on…*

## ACKNOWLEDGMENTS

There are several folks to thank, so please bear with me. To family, friends, and the above-mentioned BFFs, thanks for providing support at every turn. I'm very thankful, and I love you all.

To my beta-readers: Recca Maze and Robin Pearsall, thanks for your patience and encouragement. You're the best. To long-time buddy and BFF Natalie Bellissimo: words cannot convey how grateful I am for your presence in my life, your eagle eyes, and your level-headed suggestions. Love ya, my friend!

And finally to Liz Lipperman, my fabulous critique partner and valued friend: you keep me honest, are always there to listen, and are a continuous source of support—no matter what I write. I'm so proud to call you friend.

# ONE

SHE WAS GOING TO be late—*again*. Elise Beckett worked her bottom lip between her teeth as she flew down Highway 71 in her little red sports car. How did this always happen to her? Time and again—no matter how hard she tried—she usually ended up late for something.

She'd lost track of time in Austin this afternoon, dazzled by the most fabulous designer-brand shoe sale. Her grandmother would have her hide if she was tardy for yet another Sunday family dinner.

Unfortunately, this time around Abigail DeVries, her maternal grandmother, wouldn't be the only one on Elise's case if she arrived at the family vineyard too late. Today's dinner was more than the usual Sunday family gathering. It was her Gram's seventy-third birthday, and the rest of her family would eat her alive if she was late for *that*—especially since Elise was bringing the family's gift with her. This birthday gift was special and had been Elise's main reason for going into Austin in the first place.

Just west of Bastrop, she flipped on her blinker and turned north onto FM969, the Farm-to-Market road that would take her home to River Bend Winery and Vineyard. The vineyard had been in her family for several generations and as she got closer she could feel the tension in her shoulders begin to drain away.

The weather over the last couple of months had been unseasonably hot, with July being especially nasty, but they'd managed to escape the horrors of last year's fire season, which had been one of the worst in memory. The Bastrop State Park fire had destroyed over fourteen thousand acres and three hundred homes before firefighters managed to shut the beast down.

That tragic event had hit very close to home. Too close.

They'd been lucky that the vineyard lay on the west bank of the Colorado River and the wind was blowing to the south. Still, it had been a terrible thing to witness.

Now, in late October, the slate gray of the overcast sky added a stark element to the landscape. The live oaks and blackjack oaks had dropped their leaves weeks ago, and the deep evergreen of pine and cedar stood out in harsh relief against their skeletal trunks.

Even this late in the year, they'd enjoyed a stretch of sixty- to seventy-degree weather over the past weeks. Perhaps they'd be in for a mild winter, which would make the dry season just that much dicier come summer when the temperatures once again soared into triple digits.

Elise smiled as she rounded the next bend in the road and acres of grape rows with their bare vines came into view.

Regardless of the weather, the vineyard always had a way of lifting her spirits, but moreover, it stirred something deep inside her. Like her father before her, Elise had an immense love and respect for the fertile land that stretched along this part of the Colorado River. Those emotions had been passed down to her through generations.

Tradition.

With her master's degree in the field of horticulture, Elise was in charge of producing hybrids, as well as coming up with other innovations that would hopefully keep River Bend highly competitive for years to come. Though she no longer lived on the property—choosing instead to live fifteen minutes away in downtown Delphine—River Bend would always be home.

When her cell phone rang, she scrambled to dig it out of her purse with her free hand. *What a surprise* she thought as she read her brother's name on the screen.

Ross was two years older and lived in a cottage on the vineyard with his wife, Caroline, and two young sons, Ethan and Caleb. At thirty-one, Ross was the financial manager for the property. He was also a pain in the neck with his constant bitching about her perpetual state of tardiness. This was no doubt his *where-the-hell-are-you* phone call.

"Hey, Ross," she said, putting the phone to her ear. "What's up?"

"*What's up*? Are you joking? Where in hell are you, El? We're about to sit down to dinner."

She had to stifle a giggle at how right on the money her thoughts had been. "Cool your jets, big brother. I'm on 969 and almost home."

"Geez, of all days to be late."

"Oh, for the love of mud, it's not going to ruin Gram's birthday if I'm five minutes late to dinner, so take a breath." She loved Ross dearly, but sometimes he and his almost manic punctuality could work every last nerve she had.

"Did you get it?"

"Of course I got it. Don't be a dork. Gram's present is right here on the seat next to me."

"How does it look?"

Elise could hear the excitement in his voice and couldn't help her own smile from spreading, but that didn't stop her from needling him a bit. "I guess you're going to have to wait and see, aren't you?"

"*Elise.*"

He whined her name so pitifully that she laughed out loud. "Okay. I will say that it looks awesome. Maddy's suggestion of a framed generational photograph was inspired."

Their younger sister, Madison, lived on the property as well, sharing the main residence with their mother, Laura, and grandmother, Abigail—Miss Abby to most who knew her. Maddy was the driving force behind Lodge Merlot, the vineyard's event venue, and always had the most creative ideas.

"Anyway, you're going to have to stall another ten minutes."

"*Stall?* How am I supposed to do that? We're all about to head for the dining room."

"Oh, please. Pull out one of your spreadsheets," she suggested. "I've heard you drone on for hours over one of those boring things. Ten minutes ought to be a snap."

"Ha, ha. Very funny."

"Seriously, dude. You're down to eight minutes, better get on it. You know I don't like to talk on the phone when I'm driving, especially when I don't have my headset with me, so I'm hanging up.

See you in a few." She hung up before he could start in again—which he definitely would have if given half a chance.

Only a few moments later she was turning through the gates at River Bend and winding her way past The Wine Barrel, the vineyard's retail outlet. Here her gram ruled the roost, running the store smoothly with precision and charming customers with personality and wit.

As she rounded the bend, she smiled as she passed Lodge Merlot. Her sister had organized the most spectacular wedding and reception for the mayor's daughter there at the end of August. That event had added a nice chunk of green to the vineyard's bottom line and paved the way for several more reservations. Things were starting to look up after a pretty rough summer.

Yes, tradition ran deep at River Bend—as did emotions.

Elise's father inherited the vineyard when his father passed, even though her uncle Edmond had been the older of the two sons. And Edmond had been bypassed in her grandfather's will altogether.

This had caused hard feelings between her uncle and the rest of the family and sparked a small feud. The touchy situation only escalated when her father died two years ago and left the whole she-bang to her mother in *his* will.

Edmond had been furious about that, making terrible threats and accusations. He'd even resorted to browbeating her mother in an effort to get his hands on at least a portion of the vineyard.

Elise shook her head at the thought. For all his posturing, everyone knew he'd had no use for the property other than to sell it to feed his gambling and other habits of debauchery. Sadly, through his antics, poor Uncle Edmond had succeeded in alienating every bit of family he'd had left.

The little sports car kicked up a small cloud of dust as Elise pulled into a spot next to the police cruiser parked out front. Climbing out and shaking away depressing thoughts, she looked toward the porch where Deputy Jackson Landry sprawled in one of the wicker chairs with his long legs stretched out in front of him.

Jackson was Ross's best friend and had practically grown up on the vineyard with them. He'd also been the lead investigator on her uncle's homicide case during the summer. Poor Jax had been forced to walk a very fine line during those tense few weeks. Elise thought he'd done an amazing job of working a thorough investigation, yet protecting the family at the same time, though she was certain he would have said that he was just doing his job.

"Good afternoon, Officer." Leaning on the open car door, she tilted her head and gave him a considering look. "You expecting trouble?"

She watched as Jackson unfolded himself from the chair and strolled over to the top of the porch steps. "Yes, ma'am. And looks like it just arrived, late as usual."

*My-oh-my but the man is a sweet piece of eye candy.*

Elise spent a moment admiring the way he filled out his uniform as he started down the steps toward her. She'd had a thing for Jackson Landry as long as she could remember, but their timing had never been any good. When she'd been free to date whom she pleased, he'd been in a relationship, and vice versa. As it turned out, the feeling was mutual, which was handy now that they were both unattached. It seemed she and Jackson had finally found their stride.

Turning, she leaned into the car to retrieve her gram's gift and her shopping bags. When she straightened, he was right behind her.

Checking out the gift and her purchases, he raised an eyebrow. "Did some shopping, did we? I figure the wrapped frame is for Miss Abby. What's in the bags?"

"Shoes," she said with a grin. "I found the most incredible sale."

"More shoes? Geez, El, you already have enough shoes to fill a warehouse. What do you need more for? If memory serves, you only have two feet. You can only wear one pair at a time, right?"

"Oh, sweetie," she began with a shake of her head. "It's not a question of *needing*. I swear, Jax, we practically grew up together, but sometimes it's like you don't know me at all."

Glancing over to the other side of his cruiser, she noticed her friend C.C. Duncan's car. C.C. was taking several days off from her day job at the Extension office to help them with the details for this year's Lost Pines Food and Wine Festival. "Anyway, I thought I'd bring them in and watch Maddy and C.C. weep with jealousy."

"Uh-huh. And then you can take them home so Chunk can swipe 'em and hide 'em from you."

The mention of her sixteen-pound Snowshoe Siamese with his unexplainable shoe fetish had her narrowing her eyes. "Oh no. That little twerp so much as drools anywhere near these shoes and he's dead meat. Besides, he won't have the opportunity. I intend to keep them in their boxes. And after wearing them each time, they'll go right back into said boxes."

"Oh, sweetie," Jackson replied, mimicking her. "And you think that will stop him?" He shook his head sadly. "El. You've had him for what? Almost a decade? It's like you don't even know him."

"Very funny." Biting the inside of her cheek, she struggled not to smile at his clever imitation. Shoving the wrapped frame at him, she realized he was staring at her head. "And what are you looking at?" she asked, running her free hand over her new layered cut. "Do I have something in my hair?"

"No, but what did you do to it?"

"What do you mean? I got it cut yesterday. Why?"

When he just stared at her with an annoyed look on his face, she shrugged. "What?"

"I realize that it's shorter, darlin'," he said and gave her shoulder-length tresses a quick tug. "What I *mean* is what are those streaky things you've added?"

With a hand on her hip, she flipped her recently highlighted summer-blonde hair and gave him a bland look. "They're called *highlights*, Jackson. And what's with the sudden obsession with my hair?"

He slid his free arm around her and snatched her up close in one smooth move. His bright-green eyes twinkled with mischief as he grinned down at her. "Who says your hair is all I'm obsessed with?"

The next moment he was kissing her senseless. And boy-oh-boy, this deputy could kiss, she thought as she melted against him.

When he finally let her breathe, he touched his forehead to hers. "I gotta tell you, I've been waiting for that all damn day."

"Some things are just worth the wait, I guess," she said in a voice gone breathless.

"And by the way, I like your *highlights*," he added with a wiggle of his eyebrows.

Elise would have pulled him in for another taste, but Ross's shout interrupted the beginnings of a fine moment.

"Are you *kidding* me with this?" He yelled from the open front door. "We're in here waiting on you and you're playing kissy-face out in the front yard? Get your butts in here. You can do that crap on your own time."

"Good Lord, he's so romantic." Elise heaved a sigh. "My sister-in-law is such a lucky girl."

Jackson chuckled. "Guess we better go in before he has an aneurism."

They started up the steps, and when they reached the porch Ross eyeballed the shopping bags she carried. "What's in the bags?"

"Shoes," Jackson replied, which she felt earned him a dirty look for his indiscretion.

"*Shoes*?" Ross sputtered. "You went *shopping*? That's why you're late for Gram's birthday dinner?"

"Stuff it, Ross," she told him as she shoved past him into the house. Honestly, men just did not get the importance of a good shoe sale.

Throwing a glance over her shoulder, she started down the hall. "Jax, would you put Gram's gift with the others in the living room, please?"

"Will do, darlin'," Jackson said before turning to Ross with a stone-serious face. "Shoes, bro. There was an incredible sale."

"I heard that, Jackson," she said as she swung into the dining room.

"There you are, baby girl!" Abigail said, coming in from the kitchen carrying a bowl of piping hot string beans. "I was beginning to worry."

"You were beginning to *worry*?" Ross followed Elise into the room with an incredulous expression on his face. "Geez, Gram, that's all she gets when she's late to your birthday dinner? If it was me, I'd be catching all kinds of hell."

Elise turned and gave him a sorrowful look. "That's because Gram has never really liked you. I know it's hard to hear, but Maddy and I have always been her favorites." She followed the statement up with a flutter of her eyelashes.

"Bite me, El."

"Ross Alexander, watch your mouth in my house," Laura Beckett spoke up as she came into the room. "That's a terrible way to speak to your sister."

Jackson arrived on the heels of the conversation and pointed a finger at Elise. "And *I'm* sorry to have to tell *you*, darlin', but your statement isn't exactly accurate."

He took the bowl Abigail carried and set it on the table, then swept her into his arms and gave her a loud, obnoxious smack on the cheek. Looking up, he grinned. "Sure, Miss Abby's never cared for Ross much, and she likes you fine, but I happen to know that *I'm* Miss Abby's favorite. Always have been."

Elise made a face at him. "Doubtful, law-boy. She only tolerates you because you hang around and make a nuisance of yourself."

Abigail barked out a laugh and patted Jackson's cheek. "Jackson Landry, you are cute as a bug's ear. I tell you, if I were thirty-five or forty years younger I'd give my baby girl there a run for her money."

Elise made a gagging sound, and Jackson looked over and nodded. "See? Better watch your P's and Q's, darlin'."

"Baby girl, my butt," Ross spoke up in a grumble. "More like spoiled brat."

"Now, Ross, Elise has had a couple of rough months," Abigail said with a stern look for emphasis. "What with Edmond's murder and her finally getting rid of that rat-bastard of a boyfriend."

The mention of her uncle's death had anxiety flooding Elise's system. Of course, the mention of her ex-boyfriend, Stuart Jenkins, didn't help either.

"Mother! For crying out loud," Laura admonished.

"Well, she's right, Mom," Ross added. "Stuart *is* a rat-bastard. But come on, Gram, Uncle Edmond's homicide investigation is over. How long does El get to ride that horse?"

"For a while longer, I'd say," Abigail replied with a nod. "We could have lost her so easily. And I will remind you, with her quick thinking that day at Kohler's winery, she not only saved herself, but you and Jackson as well. Things could have turned out so much worse than they did."

"Yes, but she's out of the life-saving business now," Jackson said, sliding a calculated glance her way. "And she won't be doing any more amateur sleuthing, either. Right, pal?"

Though there was a smile on his face, it didn't quite reach his eyes, and Elise had no trouble recognizing Jackson's shift into police mode. "Absolutely, Deputy. All done with that now. Cross my heart."

To be honest, she was more than ready to bring this particular conversation to an end. Any discussion on the horrible events of the summer, not to mention her "rat-bastard" ex, was something she was keen to avoid. Plus, she hadn't told Jackson or anyone in her family about the nightmares she continued to have over her uncle's murder.

Looking around the room, she suddenly realized there were people missing. "Hey, wait a minute. Where's Maddy? And isn't C.C. here? Her car's out front."

Abigail waved a hand toward the ceiling. "They went upstairs while we waited for you to get here. Something about a new outfit that needed to be ogled."

As if conjuring them out of thin air with her words alone, the two women entered the dining room as Abigail finished her sentence.

"Hey, El, you finally made it. Perfect timing, because I'm starving." Madison sat down at the table before pointing to the shopping bags Elise still held. "What's in the bags?"

"Oh no. We're not getting sucked into *that* vortex," Ross said as he snatched the bags away from Elise and turned toward the door. "You can waste time on these later—after we've eaten and Gram's had her birthday party."

"What a buzz-kill he is," C.C. said, sliding into the chair next to Madison.

Once Ross came back, they all sat down to eat, and Elise was relieved when the topic of conversation moved on to the upcoming Lost Pines Food and Wine Festival.

Patterned after the larger Hill Country Food and Wine Festival, the LPFW was still in its infancy, but growing fast. Vintners from all around the country were already taking notice.

River Bend was one of several sponsors, which was a big deal for the vineyard. Her gram was contact person and also in charge of their booth this year. Everyone would have a specific area of responsibility, but Elise, Madison, and C.C. would be assisting Abigail with everything from set-up to tear-down.

By the time they'd finished dinner and moved to the living room, Madison had pulled out one of her enormous planning folders.

"I finally got a complete list of entries for this year's food and wine booths," she said. "I swear, Marlette Casper is the sweetest woman alive, but her organizational skills are sadly lacking in so many ways. Anyway, it looks like we'll have a great turnout this year."

"Does that include Garrett Larson and his Third Coast Winery?" Ross asked with a twinkle in his eye.

At the mention of her high school sweetheart and his south Texas winery, Abigail made a face. "Yeah, they're on the list, all right."

"You don't sound happy about that, Miss Abby," Jackson said. "I thought Third Coast was owned by your old beau."

Ross laughed. "Garrett Larson isn't the problem. Gram doesn't like the hussy he married after his wife died."

"Ross, please don't get her started," Laura said with a sigh.

"Hussy is right!" Abigail growled. "That woman is a self-absorbed, gold-digging terror without a shred of decency or the common sense the good Lord gave a goose. I don't know what in the world Garrett was thinking when he took up with her."

Madison glanced up from her planner. "She *was* pretty ugly at last year's festival. I felt so bad for Mr. Larson. He looked mortified."

"*Ugly?*" Abigail folded her arms and made a *pfft* sound. "She sashayed up to our booth in her short skirt and baubles. Then, she proceeded to make a damn fool of herself with her poisonous comments, all the while smiling like a hyena. It was disgusting. All I can say is that Garrett better have a muzzle on her this year or somebody may take her out."

"Mom!" Laura said, shock lacing her words. "After all the violence we endured over the summer, let's refrain from using that kind of rhetoric, shall we?"

"I'm just sayin'."

"Well, I wish you wouldn't. Please make an effort to keep those kinds of thoughts to yourself."

Silence reigned for a moment and the discomfort in the room was palatable. Elise felt a change in subject was in order. "Gram, why don't you open your birthday presents? Then we can cut into that fabulous-looking cake C.C. brought with her."

Elise gave a sigh of relief as the focus changed and the mood lightened. She sent up a quick prayer that this year's festival wouldn't be marred by the likes of Divia Larson.

# TWO

Elise awoke early Monday morning to the sound of crinkling paper. Really *loud* crinkling paper. With a sigh, she rolled over and tried to block out the noise with her pillow. When that didn't work, she pried one eye open and glanced at the alarm clock on the night stand, and uttered a groan when she realized it was eight minutes *before* her alarm was set to go off. Eight minutes she could have used after the restless night she'd had.

Yawning, she pushed back her sleep-tousled hair and tried to clear her brain long enough to zero in on where the annoying racket was coming from.

That's when she saw him.

"Chunk!" she yelled, leaping from the bed. "Get out of that bag right now."

True to Jackson's words the day before, her fat devil-of-a-cat had found her new shoes. He'd tipped over one of the bags and was buried halfway inside with his butt in the air and his tail switching back and forth as he dug for buried treasure. She knew she should've put her purchases away the minute she'd walked in the door last night, but it had been late and she'd been exhausted.

"I don't know what on earth is wrong with you," she muttered. "You've got a huge basket of toys in the living room, yet you can't seem to leave my shoes alone."

Reaching into the shopping bag, she grabbed him around the middle and hauled his sixteen-pound butt out. Then, turning him around, she tried not to laugh at the disoriented look on his face or the way he blinked up at her and meowed as if to say, *"But I really want them, Mom."*

"You are in dire need of some kind of therapy, you know that?" When he gave up another pitiful meow, she cuddled him close and kissed the top of his scruffy head. "I know, buddy. Life is so dang hard, isn't it?"

Setting him down on the bed, she quickly stuffed both shopping bags into the closet and securely closed the closet doors. At least that would keep him from doing any damage or making off with a shoe until she could store her purchases properly.

When her alarm began to blare she turned it off and shivered. Her apartment wasn't as cozy as she normally liked and the chill quickly seeped through her thin pajamas. Although the outside temperature had been unseasonably warm lately, it had taken a tumble over the past few days.

Elise adored her little retro apartment. Built in the 1940s, it had grabbed her imagination the minute she'd clapped eyes on it—like a snapshot in time. Unfortunately, the walls weren't all that well insulated, and the ancient radiator was a relic of that bygone era. She had a feeling it would be in need of attention again very soon. It seemed they went through the same routine every year. She'd have to remember to give Mr. and Mrs. Powers a heads up.

Her landlords, Lila and Avery Powers, owned and operated the Delphine pharmacy downstairs, which was handy when she required something fixed or wanted to drop off the rent check. They'd been very good to her, allowing her to put her own unique stamp on the space when she'd moved in.

Though the apartment hadn't been used in years, once she'd scraped away the dust and grime, she'd found a gem waiting for her. By the time she'd finished with it, her apartment had become a fresh, unconventional mix—a kaleidoscope of color that suited her right down to the ground.

"Come on, you great, furry lump. Let's go get you a proper breakfast and a stiff belt of caffeine for me."

Pulling on a sweatshirt and a pair of lavender fleece-lined house shoes, she headed for the kitchen. Her spoiled bundle of fur followed close behind. The mention of food obviously took precedence over shiny new shoes, at least for the moment.

She was going to need an infusion of caffeine to jump start her system for the long day ahead. The Lost Pines Food and Wine Festival would commence on Thursday, and today was organization day out at River Bend. Elise, along with C.C., Madison, and the rest of the Beckett family, would be assisting her grandmother with getting everything ready for transport to the venue on Tuesday and Wednesday. They had a lot to accomplish in a short amount of time, but they'd been planning this weekend for several months and were well prepared.

By the time she'd fed the cat and downed half a bottle of icy-cold diet soda, she was feeling much more like herself. Grabbing another bottle from the fridge, she showered, dressed, and was walking out the door in just over an hour—which she thought might be some kind of record for her.

"Do not make a mess while I'm gone," she told Chunk from the doorway as he sat basking in the Papasan chair in the living room. Of course, she had no illusions that he was actually paying a bit of attention to her, but at least her new shoes were now safely tucked away out of his reach. Giving up, she closed the door behind her and marched down the stairs.

The frigid north wind slapped her in the face and nearly stole her breath when she stepped out onto the sidewalk, making her glad she'd listened to the weather report this morning. Flipping up the collar on the red, knee-length wool coat that she'd thrown on over her jeans and a thick, cobalt-blue sweater, she scurried around the corner to the pharmacy door as fast as her feet would carry her.

The little bell over the door cheerfully announced her presence as she entered, and Mr. Powers looked up and smiled from the back counter. "Hello, Elise," he called. "You're up and out early on this chilly morning."

"Hey, Mr. P. You got that right. It is downright *brisk* out there. I have a meeting about the festival at the vineyard first thing; otherwise, I'd be tempted to go in a little late and stay home out of the cold a bit longer."

Mr. Powers laughed. "Those blue northers really know how to put an ache in your bones, don't they?"

"You can say that again."

"What can I do for you today?" he asked. "Besides turn up the temperature, that is."

"Well, actually…"

"Let me guess," he said with a twinkle in his eyes. "The radiator's not pulling its weight this morning, right?"

It was Elise's turn to chuckle. "Man, you're good. You got it in one. Do you think you could have someone come out and check it?"

"Already done, darlin'. Charley Hawks from Claymore Heating should be out later this morning. I'm sorry that old thing has such issues. I wish we had the extra cash to change the building over to a more efficient and reliable unit."

Elise waved a hand in the air. "No worries, Mr. P. You know I love antiques, but I guess a little more efficiency and reliability would be nice, too."

He nodded and leaned on the counter. "How are the preparations coming for the festival? The missus and I are looking forward to spending our Saturday afternoon doing food and wine tastings."

"Plans are moving right along. That's what this morning's meeting is about—where we're at and what we have left to do by Thursday. I think Maddy has some ideas for decorations that she wants to share. Our little festival is gaining steam and some much-needed recognition."

"Yes, I know. My cousin over in Beaumont is coming. He and his wife are foodies and belong to some wine club. Likes to think of himself as a connoisseur." Mr. Powers made a skeptical face and Elise giggled. "Anyway, they should be here sometime tomorrow. They're coming in a day early to visit and sponge off my hospitality."

"Great. The more word of mouth, the better."

"Easy for you to say. You don't have to feed them." He laughed and Elise joined him.

"Well, I'd better head out. Make sure you and Mrs. P. stop by the booth on Saturday."

He nodded and waved. "Oh, you know we will."

She hurried out the door and got into her vehicle. Starting the car, she pulled out her day planner and made a few notes while she waited for the heater to warm up the interior. The upcoming wine festival would take place out at the Delphine fairgrounds located just on the outskirts of town. This year's festival theme was *Bountiful Fall Harvest,* and she'd been tasked with putting together a quick presentation on grape varieties and their hybridization for Friday afternoon.

Elise disliked public speaking in just about any form—preferring to work in the solitude of her greenhouse—but this was for the vineyard and she would give it her best shot. Although a "quick presentation" on that particular topic would be near to impossible, she was sure she could come up with a brief overview that would satisfy the requirements in a simple yet interesting way.

The vehicle was finally warmed up twenty-five minutes later when Elise pulled onto the vineyard property. Parking outside the residence, she shut off the engine and glanced at the digital clock on the dashboard.

And then did a double-take.

She'd arrived a full fifteen minutes early for the meeting. *Geez, Ross will have a stroke,* she thought with a grin as she got out of the car and climbed the porch steps.

Entering the house, Elise went directly to the dining room, where all the family meetings took place. There she found her grandmother and C.C., the only ones in attendance so far.

Abigail greeted her with a smile. "Morning, baby girl."

"Hey, Gram. Where is everyone? I know I'm early, but I can't be the first one here."

"No. *I* was the first one here," C.C. said with a smirk.

Elise rolled her eyes and shrugged out of her coat. "You don't count, girlfriend. You're always early for everything you do."

Cackling, Abigail shook her head. "Your sister was here for a minute, but she got a jumbled voicemail from Lita Washington—something about the booth arrangements. She went to call her back and see what the hubbub was about. I've yet to see Ross, though, so you're one up on him at least."

Ross hadn't shown up yet? The thought made Elise smile. The man had an obsession with punctuality that bordered on OCD and was usually ten minutes early for everything. He was always ragging on her when she was running behind, which was more often than she cared to admit. It would be very satisfying indeed to rub it in his face that his perpetually late sister had arrived for something before him.

"Sorry that took so long." A little out of breath, Madison breezed into the room and dropped her planners on the table. "What a mess."

"What now?" Abigail asked, pouring herself another cup of coffee from the pot on the warmer. "With Lita, it's always something, and the something is regularly a crisis."

Madison frowned and scribbled in one of her notebooks before looking up. "Well, this time it seems it really *is* a bit of a crisis. And I guarantee you're not going to like it much."

Elise slid into the chair next to C.C. and took a blueberry muffin from the basket on the table. "Well? Spit it out already," she said when her sister didn't offer any further information. "What's got Lita's undies in a wad this time?"

"Give me a minute, wouldja? I'm getting to it. It's just that it involves... Divia Larson," she replied, then winced when their grandmother spoke up.

"Oh for the love of mud!" Abigail shouted. "What's the wicked witch of the South done now? I swear, if she does anything to ruin this year's festival, I just might wring her scrawny neck with my bare hands. And I'll enjoy every minute of it."

"Time out," C.C. said, making a T with her hands and looking back and forth between Madison and Abigail. "Just to be clear, we don't like Divia Larson, right? She's the hideous gold-digger you were talking about last night, the one who married Miss Abby's high school sweetheart?"

Madison began to laugh, and then abruptly sobered at the look on her grandmother's face. "Yes. Garrett Larson married her several years ago, and they own Third Coast Winery in south Texas."

Elise nodded. "Divia tends to think she's an expert on just about everything and will tell you so in the most civilized yet cutting fashion. She is *extremely* difficult to take."

"Duly noted," C.C. said and waved a hand in Madison's direction. "Proceed."

"Okay, it seems Divia, the diva, is less than pleased with the placement of their booth. She's demanding that Third Coast be moved to a better location."

Abigail growled. "What in hell is wrong with that woman? She's a prima donna with no damn good reason to be. Worthless chit."

"Where is she wanting us to move them? And are there even any open booths left?" Elise asked. "Because we are *not* shuffling around any other group just to pacify Divia Larson."

"As of two days ago, we were completely full." Madison sighed and tapped her pen on the table in frustration. "However, we had a cancellation yesterday, so technically, we could move Third Coast to that now open booth. But…"

Elise narrowed her eyes at her sister. "But what?"

"The cancellation was Cactus Flats Winery."

"*What?*" Abigail shouted.

"No way." Elise shook her head. "Absolutely not."

"I don't see that we really have a choice," Madison said with a sigh. "I mean, we'd do it for anyone else."

"What?" C.C. asked. "What am I missing?"

Madison sighed. "Moving Third Coast to Cactus Flats' vacated spot would put them on the main thoroughfare kitty-corner to River Bend's booth."

"That's all we need is that horrible woman just across the aisle taking verbal potshots at us all day long," Elise said with a frown.

"This festival is so new, El. It's only a few years old and already competing with the larger food and wine festivals around the area. And there's been talk of Delphine hosting it again next season."

"So?" Elise asked. "What does that have to do with not wanting Third Coast just across the midway from us?"

Madison sighed. "As a sponsor and co-organizer of this year's event, River Bend can't afford to get the reputation for playing favorites. The festival is just now receiving some great, much-needed press. And I've been approached about us doing it again next season, should this year's festival be a success."

Abigail set her cup down with a clatter. "Okay, while I'm not happy about having that woman within spittin' distance of our booth for the entire weekend, Maddy's right. We're going to have to pull on our big-girl panties and get over it. Jackson may have to arrest me when I fail to restrain myself and do that woman some serious bodily harm, but we're going to have to let 'em move."

"Let who move?" Laura asked, coming in from the kitchen with Ross following close behind.

"And where are they moving to?" Ross added.

"Divia Larson," Elise replied, as if that should be enough said.

"Uh-oh," Ross commented, sitting down at the head of the table. "What's she done now? The festival hasn't even gotten underway. How can she be causing trouble already?"

Elise wrinkled her nose. "Please. What part of 'it's Divia Larson' did you not get? The woman can cause trouble without breaking a sweat."

Madison pulled out the booth chart from her humungous planner and explained the dilemma to Ross and their mother as she had the rest of the group.

When she'd finished, Laura nodded and put a hand on Abigail's shoulder. "You're right, of course, Mom. We're going to have to let them move if there's an open spot. As unpleasant as it might be, we'll just have to take the high road and make the best of it."

Ross nodded, but his look was skeptical. "And maybe she'll be so focused on her own booth that she won't have time to harass anyone else."

"Ha! When pigs fly," Abigail replied. "That woman will *make* time to harass everyone else." When Laura gave her shoulder another squeeze, she relented. "But like you said, we'll just have to try to ignore her and concentrate on having the best booth at the festival. Speaking of which, let's get this meeting started. Maddy, you take point and give us the rundown of where we stand."

Madison nodded and flipped several pages in her planner. "Okay, following the theme of 'Bountiful Fall Harvest' we're going all out this year with a rustic makeover for the booth. I've got dried corn stalks and pumpkins for the stand. We'll decorate with baskets filled with ears of corn, gourds, dried flowers, that sort of thing. And of course, River Bend wine."

"That sounds like fun," C.C. said. "Very country fair chic."

"Yeah, that's what I was thinking," Madison said with a smile. "We'll do tastings, too, and we've got six cases of those small plastic cups for that purpose. That should be plenty. We've got River Bend cocktail napkins to go with them. I tried to make sure our brand was on display as much as possible."

"That's excellent, sweetheart. The new River Bend brochures and postcards came in last month. We can hand those out to everyone who stops at the booth," Laura added. "It'll all be good advertisement for the winery. Sounds like we've got a workable game plan. So, let's start boxing everything up for transport."

Their mother was right, they did seem to have a workable plan and a good handle on the details, Elise thought. So why couldn't she shake the vague feeling that things were about to go south?

# THREE

By the time Thursday morning rolled around, they'd gotten everything packed up and transported out to the festival venue, and River Bend's booth was now decked out in the finest country chic. Elise eyed the front of the booth as her grandmother filled the wine racks at the back of the stall. She thought the quaint effect they'd achieved was sure to draw in a steady stream of customers.

The gates opened and the festival officially kicked off at eleven a.m., just a little over two hours away. All that was left to do now were some minor adjustments and a few finishing touches. Closer to showtime, they would start opening bottles for tasting and be ready to rock and roll when the first wave came through the door.

Standing in front of the booth, she looked up and down the bustling walkway. She was pleased to see that River Bend had been given a decent location halfway between the entrance and the corner at the other end of the midway where restaurant row began.

Just about all the vendors at this end of the thoroughfare had arrived, with the exception of a few late-comers. Third Coast Winery was one such straggler. The Larsons had yet to turn up, but Elise was certain that they'd be arriving shortly. There was no way Divia Larson would miss a chance to preen and bad-mouth the competition, especially after the fit she'd thrown over the placement of their booth.

"For the first round of tastings I chose the Lenoir, Syrah, and the Cab for the reds," Abigail said, bringing Elise's attention back to business. "I thought for white, the Blanc du Bois and the Semillon. Which do you think would be best for the third pick? The Chenin Blanc or the Riesling?"

Elise wandered over and leaned on the counter. "Since the Semillon is fairly dry, I think the Riesling instead of the Chenin Blanc. We can always open something else if there's a request. I see you brought a few cases of the Private Reserve, too. Good thinkin', Gram."

"Well, I always say, put your best foot forward. Just in case."

"Yes, ma'am."

"Hey, El."

Hearing her name called, Elise looked up the midway toward the entrance and watched C.C. approach with another woman.

"Sorry I wasn't here right away," C.C. said as they walked up to the booth. "I had to go to the Extension office first thing. Got hung up there longer than I'd planned. I swear those yahoos I work with wouldn't know what to do without me. Oh, El, do you know Grace Vanderhouse?"

Elise looked at the other woman and smiled. "No, I don't think we've met, have we?"

"No, I don't think so," Grace replied. "Nice to meet you. I love your wine, by the way. We serve it at my restaurant."

"Grace is executive chef at The Plough in Austin," C.C. added.

"Oh, yeah? I love that restaurant," Elise said. "I've eaten there several times. The last time I was there I had a very tasty game pie, and the summer pudding I ordered for dessert was to die for."

Grace laughed, obviously pleased with the compliments. "The owner is a Brit and very persnickety about his menu. I'm glad you enjoyed it."

"Grace, this is Miss Abigail DeVries, Elise's grandmother. Miss Abby, this is Grace Vanderhouse," C.C. said, making the introductions.

Grace shook Abigail's hand. "Pleasure to meet you, Miss Abby."

"Likewise."

"The restaurant's booth is about halfway down the food aisle." C.C. nodded in that direction, before turning back to Elise and wiggling her eyebrows. "I thought we could head over for a taste around the lunch hour."

"Absolutely. I look forward to it," Elise agreed with a nod, then looked up the thoroughfare and frowned. "Oh, crap. Here come the Larsons. I'd started to hope that they'd decided not to come."

As a group, they watched Divia Larson strut toward them wearing a skirt a couple of inches too short for a woman of her age and a blouse showing ample cleavage. Fortunately, the weather had warmed up since Monday's norther had blown through or she'd be freezing her butt off in that outfit. The woman was too tan, too thin, and wearing way too much makeup, in Elise's opinion. With her husband trailing in her wake, she worked both sides of the midway like a pro.

"Guess we couldn't be that lucky, huh?" C.C. shook her head at the spectacle.

"Guess not."

"And would you look at that fake smile?"

"Who are the Larsons?" Grace asked with a curious glance.

Elise made a face. "Garrett and Divia Larson own Third Coast Winery down south."

"*Divia*?" Grace repeated in a surprised tone, and watched the Larsons draw near with an odd look on her face.

"Do you know them, Grace?" C.C. asked, noticing her friend's intense reaction to the couple.

"Huh? Oh, no. No," Grace said, shaking her head and dismissing the Larsons. "Divia is just an unusual name, that's all."

"Yes, it is. And I should probably apologize. You must think we're terrible, talking that way about the competition," Elise said with a laugh. "Mr. Larson was Gram's high school sweetheart and Divia is his second wife. She's not the most … pleasant person."

"You can say that again," Abigail muttered.

"Oh, you don't have to apologize," Grace said, waving away the explanation. "I understand completely. The restaurant business is just as competitive, believe me. And we have our share of unpleasant restaurateurs, too."

As the Larsons neared, Divia zeroed in on River Bend's booth with the accuracy of a homing pigeon and detoured in their direction.

"Crap. She's spotted us. It was nice to meet you, Grace, but you'll have to excuse me. I don't think I can stomach that woman this early in the day." Abigail turned and began pulling wine from the cases, obviously hoping Divia wouldn't notice her at the back of the stall.

"It was a pleasure, Miss Abby. And I should probably be going anyway," Grace said, checking her watch. "Doors open in less than two hours and I've got a list of things to get done before then. It was nice to meet you, Elise. I'll talk to you later, C.C. Y'all come by the booth, okay?"

"Definitely." Elise watched Grace hurry away as Divia Larson descended on them like a vulture in drag.

"Oh, good Lord, Garrett. Would you have a look at this? Isn't this just the *cutest*? River Bend's gone with a country bumpkin theme this year," the woman drawled, and her tone was sugar-coated vinegar. "Abigail? Is that you hiding back there?"

The bright smile on Divia's face was so obviously forced that Elise had to resist the urge to gag.

She watched her grandmother's spine stiffen at the sound of Divia Larson's voice and when Abigail slowly turned an equally false smile blossomed.

"Well, hello, Divia. Garrett." She nodded in Mr. Larson's direction before addressing his wife's question. "I'm not hiding, Divia. I'm just finishing our set-up in keeping with the festival's theme." Tilting her head, she pinned the younger woman with a glare. "And just to be clear, it's not country bumpkin. It's country *chic*."

"Hmm, if you say so, sweetie," Divia said with a skeptical look and an underlying layer of snark.

"Divia, please," Garrett Larson said in a warning tone. "Don't start."

"What?" She gave him a wide-eyed look. "All I did was *agree* with her, darling."

Abigail gave the woman another hard stare and then took a breath before changing the subject. "Are you two just now getting here?" She clucked her tongue. "The doors open in less than two hours. Cuttin' it kind of close, aren't you? Third Coast isn't participating in this year's theme?"

Elise bit her lip in an effort not to snicker at her gram's subtle dig that it wasn't River Bend but Third Coast that was somehow lacking, or the way Divia's eyes narrowed slightly at the remark.

"Oh, we have plenty of time," Divia returned, slipping her arm possessively through her husband's and gazing up at him with a sultry look. "Our *staff* will have us up and running in no time. Right, lover?"

*Staff my ass* Elise thought, and by the set of her grandmother's shoulders, knew she was thinking the same thing. Exchanging looks with C.C., she rolled her eyes.

But Abigail just smiled. "Well, good for you," she said with a nod. "And your *staff*, too, for sure."

"Of course, we won't have the need for an *adorable* country theme like y'all have. We'll do just fine without all the fluff."

Elise wanted to smack the woman for her ugly tone and the insinuation that River Bend needed all the help they could get, but before anyone could respond, Mr. Larson spoke up.

"Darling, it looks like Toby has arrived. Why don't you two go see how things are going at the booth, and I'll be right along."

At the mention of her son, Divia gazed up at him for a moment before her smile spread when she looked past him toward the entrance. "Oh, and look, the Toussaints are here as well. Their winery is just a short hop from ours." Her tone clearly implied that the rest of them had no idea who the French vintners were. "I'll just go say hello to Alain."

As they watched her go Elise noticed that the Toussaints didn't look all that jazzed to see her either, especially Alain's wife, Monique.

When Mr. Larson turned back, he only had eyes for Elise's grandmother. "I'm sorry, Abby. Divia doesn't always think about how she comes across. She didn't mean—"

"To be snide and belittling?" Abigail said, then sighed and quickly put up a hand before he could respond. "Forget I said that, Garrett. I didn't mean it. It's been a long, stressful week."

As Mr. Larson stared at her grandmother for a moment, Elise could clearly read the sadness in his eyes.

"Yes you did, but it's okay," he said with the ghost of a smile. "You always say exactly what you mean, Abigail—always have. It's one of the things I admire about you."

He glanced back up the midway where his wife was obviously fawning over Alain Toussaint. "She has a real insecurity where you're concerned."

"There's no need," Abigail returned softly. "That ship sailed a hell of a long time ago, Garrett."

Turning back, he gave her a full grin this time. "I know, but it still makes her behave badly. And that's not an excuse, just an explanation."

After a brief uncomfortable silence, he spared a glance at his watch. "Well, times a' tickin'. I should go help at the booth. I'm sure I'll see you later."

As they watched him cross the aisle and head toward Third Coast's booth, Elise let out a breath. "Wow. *That* was fun. Not!"

"I'll say," C.C. agreed.

"Isn't his fault that his wife's a small-minded, superficial tart," Abigail stated matter-of-factly and then shrugged. "Besides, her kind doesn't show their true colors until it's all over but the sufferin'. Garrett will just have to live with the choices he's made."

"Better him than me," C.C. said and gave a mock shudder. "I can't imagine living with that day after day, can you? It's got to be exhausting."

"Be that as it may, I think we've wasted enough time and energy on the likes of Divia Larson," Abigail remarked. "Let's get this finished up and take a walk around, check out the venue before showtime."

———

If Elise had entertained hopes that the earlier encounter with Divia Larson would be the extent of the unpleasantness associated with the woman, she was disappointed later in the afternoon. Walking back from a break, her attention was snagged by raised voices coming from the direction of Third Coast's booth.

"What's going on over there?" Stepping back behind the River Bend counter, she looked over at C.C., who was watching the scene with avid interest.

Her friend shook her head. "Not sure yet. We had a lull for ten minutes or so. Then the French chick came by, and what looked like a bit of an argument broke out—a little pushy-shovie between her and Divia. But it was all on the down-low and I hadn't been able to hear what they were saying until now. You got back just in time, my friend. It's starting to get good … well, at least it's louder so we can hear what's happening."

As if to reinforce the sentiment, Monique Toussaint stepped right into Divia Larson's bubble and poked the older woman in the chest.

"And I'm telling *you*, stay away from Alain or I will make you sorry you didn't," Monique told Divia in a heated French accent.

Divia burst out laughing and shoved Alain's wife back a few paces. "Really, Monique. If you can't keep your husband in line it's not my problem."

"No? And what about Toby? Would you consider him and his financial funny business your problem? Does Garrett know what's going on with the books at his own winery?"

Monique's words sobered Divia in a blink, and Elise thought the French beauty may have said too much.

"You leave my boy out of this, do you hear me?" Divia yelled before advancing on Monique.

In the next moment, the two women had jumped at each other, and an out-and-out catfight ensued.

"Oh my *Lord*! What the hell is *wrong* with them?" Abigail said in disgust as she flew around the counter and ran toward the scratching, hair-pulling hullabaloo.

Elise didn't really want to get involved but felt she had no choice. She and C.C. quickly followed her grandmother over to Third Coast's booth to provide backup. But before any of them could intervene, Alain Toussaint's brother Philippe was there to help Divia's son, Toby Raymond,break up the row.

"Mom! For God's sake, calm down," Toby said, trying to hold a struggling Divia back. "Will you get a *grip*? People are watching."

Slowly, Divia seemed to realize what a spectacle they'd made of themselves, and she quit resisting.

"Come, Monique, *ma petit*, let's go. This woman is not worth our time and Alain will be back soon." Philippe had Alain's wife around the waist, but by the look of fury on his sister-in-law's face, Elise wasn't sure that was sufficient restraint.

"I am warning you for the last time, you filthy, worn-out *bitch*," Monique spat as she shoved away from Philippe. "You'd better back off and watch your step or you just may end up dead!"

*Well, that's a lovely sentiment*, Elise thought.

With that parting shot, the French woman turned on her heel and stalked away with Philippe hurrying after her.

In the silence that followed, Abigail stepped over and laid a hand on Divia's arm. "Are you all right, Divia?"

The other woman looked around at the crowd that had gathered before turning her attention to Abigail.

"Like you give two shits if I'm okay or not," she sneered. "I'm sure you enjoyed the floor show, Miss Goodie-Two-Shoes DeVries, but it's over now. So why don't you take yourself back to your country *bumpkin* booth and leave me and *my* husband alone?"

By the time she finished, Divia was yelling and attracting even more attention—this time sucking Elise's grandmother into the display as well. With a cry, Divia pushed away from her son and ran up the midway toward restaurant row.

"I apologize for my mother's behavior, Ms. DeVries," Toby said after a moment. He watched his mother disappear into the crowded corridor. "I don't know what else to say."

Abigail shook her head and patted the man's shoulder. "Not your fault, Toby. Not your fault."

She looked over at Elise and C.C. "Come on, girls. Like the woman said, show's over. Let's get back to our country bumpkin booth, shall we?"

"Well, that was dramatic and exciting," C.C. said when they got back to the booth. "Although, if I was Divia, I don't think I'd be messing around with anything that belonged to the French chick. Did you see the look of loathing on her face? I almost expected Divia to drop dead from just that one look."

Elise nodded and glanced back at Third Coast's booth. "I know what you mean. Sounds like the situation in south Texas is somewhat volatile. I just hope they left the powder keg at home. After the summer we just had, I'd like to keep the explosions to a minimum."

# FOUR

PULLING INTO THE FAIRGROUND parking lot on Friday afternoon, Jackson parked the big motorcycle and turned off the engine. It was his only day off this week, and he was feeling pretty damn pleased with himself at the moment. And the reason for his pleasure was sitting directly behind him on the bike.

It had taken quite a bit of cajoling, but he'd managed to talk Elise into riding out to the festival with him this afternoon, then having a nice, quiet dinner together later. Though the dinner had turned into a group deal, at least he'd have her to himself for the day.

She'd been more than a little reluctant to—as she put it—go any-where on the back of his "monstrous death machine." At which point he'd felt obliged to point out that considering the way she drove her little red sports car, riding on the back of his bike ought to be cake and pie.

Unfortunately, that response didn't have the desired effect. So, in the end, he'd reminded her that being his "motorcycle momma" would give her the opportunity to wear that fancy leather designer 'biker' jacket she'd only worn a handful of times. To his amazement, she'd pounced on that idea almost immediately, deciding that she could pair the jacket with her spiffy knee-high suede boots as well. It still baffled the hell out of him how fashion had won out over any safety concerns she might have had about the bike. Of course, she'd say that he just didn't get it … and she'd be correct.

When she climbed down, he pulled off his helmet and then sat watching as she did the same. She bent at the waist, shaking out all that gorgeous, highlighted hair—and he supposed—any possible remains of what she would perceive as helmet head. When she stood up, he couldn't help the grin that spread across his face—or the desire that shot through his belly.

"What?" she asked with a tilt of her head.

Knowing that the thought zipping through his mind at that precise moment was inappropriate, he chuckled. "Nothing. Just enjoying your transformation from hot horticulturist into super-hot biker chick."

She fisted one hand on her cocked hip and fluffed her wild hair with the other. "I am a woman of many facets, Deputy Landry, and don't you forget it. You are extremely lucky that I even hang around with you."

"Oh honey, trust me, I'm aware." He laughed out loud before pulling her up close and giving her a quick kiss. "You make me look good, darlin'."

"Yes. Yes I do."

He climbed off the bike and took her hand. "Come on. Let's go make all the other boys jealous."

The festival was already doing a brisk business, which astounded Jackson, it being just shy of two o'clock on a Friday afternoon.

*Didn't anybody work on Fridays anymore?*

The crowd at River Bend's booth was three and four deep, and he could see Ross, Caroline, and Laura feverishly working the group, with Miss Abby opening more boxes at the back of the stall.

"Geez, they're really busy. Makes me feel kind of guilty," Elise said, eyeing the frenzy as they strolled by. "It wasn't half this crazy yesterday. Of course, I didn't expect it to be since it was a Thursday and opening day. And I know I don't have any control over it, but still, it makes me feel like we were slacking."

He watched closely and could almost see her train of thought before she spoke up. "Maybe I should go back there and help them out for a while."

"Huh-uh. No way."

"But Jax—"

He stopped in the middle of the midway and turned to her. "Did y'all not decide on a schedule last week?"

"Well, yeah. But—"

He nodded. "And why did you do that?"

She folded her arms and blew out a breath in a huff, then just stared at him with a mutinous look on her face.

"I'll tell you why you did it. So that everyone would work their fair share at the booth. That's why." He took her hand and started walking toward restaurant row, pulling her along behind him at a brisk clip. "This is my only day off this week, El. With all the festival prep, we haven't spent but a handful of hours together over the last month."

"Come on, that's a bit of an exaggeration, don't you think?" When he gave her a narrow look over his shoulder, her eyebrows shot up and she relented. "Well, okay, maybe not, but this time of year is busy, Jax. Anyway, I just hate seeing them getting hammered like that when I could help."

He shook his head. "They'll just have to suck it up, because you promised to spend the day with me, and let me remind you that I've already compromised on dinner. It was supposed to be just you and me, remember? Now there's a whole damn gang going."

"Yeah, yeah. Take a breath, wouldja?" Tugging on his hand to slow him down, she slipped her arm through his. "After this weekend, things will ease up and get back to normal. I promise. Then we'll have plenty of time for just us, all right?"

As they rounded the corner, they ran into Madison and Toby Raymond standing in line at The Plough's booth.

"Hey, you two," Madison said with a wave and then introduced Toby—whom Jackson had heard about but never actually met.

If Elise thought it was odd that her sister was hanging out with the son of the woman who'd caused such a ruckus with the family, it didn't show. Jackson tried to follow her lead, but he still thought it was damn weird.

"What are you guys up to?" she asked, as if seeing them together was an everyday event.

"We're taking a break," Madison replied, casting what Jackson saw as a very flirty look toward Toby. "Toby was nice enough to help me haul a few crates of wine from the truck to the booth."

"A few?" Toby asked with a charming grin for Elise's younger sister. "Felt more like we moved a stockroom full."

That response earned him a light punch in the arm and another saucy smile from Madison. "It wasn't that bad and you know it."

Toby laughed and tucked a wayward strand of hair behind her ear. "I'm joking, gorgeous. I was happy to help."

Madison literally beamed at him before looking over at Elise and Jackson, as if just remembering they were there. "Anyway, we're about to have a bite to eat. Have you guys eaten yet?" she asked. "If not, the food here is awesome."

"Yes, C.C. and I had lunch here yesterday," Elise replied. "I've actually eaten at the restaurant in Austin a couple of times and the food *is* amazing. I met Grace Vanderhouse yesterday, too. She's the Executive Chef for the restaurant and a friend of C.C.'s."

"I'm sorry, did you say *Grace Vanderhouse*?" Toby asked with an intense look, and Jackson thought he even paled slightly.

*Weirder and weirder…*

Elise nodded. "Yes, do you know her?"

When the man didn't answer right away, Madison put a hand on his sleeve. "Toby? Are you all right?" she asked with obvious concern. "You don't look so good."

After a moment, Toby blinked and seemed to come to his senses. "Wha—? Oh, I felt a little light-headed for a minute, that's all. Must be the humidity. No matter how long I've lived in the sticky heat of south Texas, I've never really gotten used to it."

"Well, our weather here *has* been pretty wacky lately," Madison said with a shake of her head. "Monday was freezing, and today we're back to the upper sixties and muggy."

"Are you sure it's just the weather, Toby?" Jackson asked, thinking the man looked like someone had just walked over his grave.

"Yeah, I'll be fine. But maybe I'll go back to the booth, get a bottle of water, and try to cool off. Wouldn't want to embarrass myself in the middle of the walkway. And I suddenly don't feel like eating."

"Do you want me to go with you?" Madison asked, her eyes full of distress.

"No. You go ahead and eat, Maddy." He smiled down at her and patted her hand. "And don't worry about me. Enjoy your afternoon. I'm sure this will pass. I'll meet up with you later. Toucan's On Main, right?"

Madison searched his face again before nodding. "Seven thirty."

Jackson watched the man walk away and thought something about his demeanor appeared off. Maybe he really wasn't feeling well all of a sudden, but it seemed more like something had spooked him—and spooked him good. But what? Was it something as simple as hearing Grace Vanderhouse's name? And why would that cause such a strong reaction?

"Okay, did anyone else find that really odd and a little awkward?" Elise asked. "Or was it just me?"

"Oh no. That was peculiar," Jackson replied.

Madison frowned. "What do you mean?"

Elise stared at her sister with her mouth open. "Well, Maddy, geez. Did you see his face when I mentioned Grace's name? And what the hell are you doing hanging around with Divia Larson's son, for that matter? Did I hear correctly that you invited him to dinner with us tonight?"

"You're always making something out of nothing, El." Madison pointed at Elise before crossing her arms. "And yes, I did invite him to dinner with us tonight. Just because his mother is hard to be around doesn't mean Toby is the same way. He's actually very sweet and hates that his mom treats the people around her so poorly."

"That may be true, Maddy," Jackson said in a gentle tone. "But it sure did look like it was the mention of Grace Vanderhouse that upset him rather than the humidity."

42

"I know, right?" Elise turned to him and nodded. "And here's the really weird thing. Yesterday Grace had a similar reaction to Divia's name."

Madison rolled her eyes. "Come on, El. What is this? Some kind of conspiracy theory?"

"No, I'm serious," Elise insisted. "And she had the same stunned look on her face, I kid you not."

"Did you ask her about it?" Jackson asked.

Elise nodded. "Yes. But she passed it off as Divia being an unusual name. Said she didn't know the Larsons."

"Well, maybe she *didn't* know them." Madison sighed. "And Divia *is* an unusual name. What's so odd about remarking on it?"

"So you think they know each other and she didn't want to say so?" Jackson asked.

Elise shook her head. "I don't know. I asked C.C. where Grace was from; if she came from south Texas, thinking there might be a connection. But C.C. said Grace is from Georgia originally, so I don't know how they would know each other. I didn't think much about it until seeing Toby's reaction just now."

"Again, you're making a huge deal out of what is probably nothing. Maybe Toby simply wasn't feeling well." Madison gave her sister a dirty look. "You know what? I think I'm done listening to you two. I'll talk to you later."

They watched her disappear into the crowd before Elise turned to him and asked, "Do you think we were making too much out of this?"

Jackson scratched his head and thought about it for a moment. "I gotta say—though I don't want to be one of those guys labeled as a 'conspiracy freak'—no matter what Maddy says, that whole thing had a very strange vibe to it."

A sexy smile slipped across Elise's face and she patted his cheek with the palm of her hand. "This would be why we make such a good pair, sweetie. Great minds, same plane."

"Yeah, well your sweetie here is feeling very peckish and needs to eat. So, let's get to it."

———

It took them a couple hours, but after they'd perused every booth and tried every sample offered, it was finally time to head back into town. The late afternoon sunlight was waning, and Elise was talking about taking a nap before dinner with the group later that evening. Jackson would normally be fine with that scenario, but they'd had so little time together lately he didn't want to waste the rest of his afternoon sleeping.

Plus, he had to admit, the thought of napping during daylight hours worried him some. He had an idea that was how the decline began. One minute you were a vital young man, full of piss and vinegar. The next thing you knew, you were a doddering old fool who couldn't keep his eyes open in the afternoon. And it all started with napping during the day. Of course, if he was watching *ESPN* while she napped, that would be a different kettle of fish.

When they wandered back along the midway toward the exit, he gave Ross a smug nod when they passed River Bend's booth. It was still packed with customers, and Jackson could read the nasty comment on his friend's face as they continued on down the thoroughfare. God help him, he couldn't help but snicker to himself. He loved the Becketts dearly, but he'd contemplate putting a bullet in his own head before manning a booth at the festival. Some individuals just weren't cut out for that kind of customer service.

As he and Elise headed out into the parking lot and the specialty parking area where he'd left the bike, a loud argument caught their attention and could be clearly heard from a few aisles over. He glanced in that direction, and by the looks of things, Toby Raymond, miraculously recovered from his sudden illness, was having a heated conversation with his mother.

"That's not what you told me back then. Shall I remind you what you said at the time?" he shouted.

"Would you lower your voice, please?" Divia Larson snapped in a sharp tone, and even from a distance Jackson could tell that she was not happy. "You were a child back then, Toby, barely ten years old. What you remember from that time would be hazy at best and probably fit in a thimble."

"My recollection is just fine, Mother. I need you to tell me what's going on. Why someone you said was dead—someone important to me—is actually alive and well."

"Toby, sweetheart, I don't know what you're talking about, or what you think you heard or saw, but all I can say is that it must be some kind of coincidence."

Toby laughed out loud at that, but it didn't sound to Jackson like he was all that amused. "Really, Mom? A coincidence? That's what you're going with here? You really are a piece of work."

"You watch your tone, son."

Jackson stepped up his pace, guiding Elise to the motorcycle, and they exchanged looks. He so did not want to get involved with anyone else's squabbles right now. This was supposed to be his day off with his girl.

On the heels of that thought, it seemed like the argument came to an abrupt end with Mrs. Larson having the last word. "You need to calm down. This is absurd, and I am not going to continue this conversation."

She spun around and walked away from her son. Toby took a deep breath, and then scrubbed his hands over his face. He stood staring out over the parking lot for another moment or two before following her back into the venue.

"Well … that was illuminating," Elise said as she twisted her hair up into a knot at the top of her head. "What do you think that was all about? Grace Vanderhouse, perhaps?"

Jackson shook his head as he watched her pull on her helmet. "Don't know and don't really care." Swinging a leg over the motorcycle, he put on his own helmet and flipped up the visor. "None of my business."

"Come on, Jax," she said, climbing onto the bike and settling in behind him. "Aren't you at least curious?"

"Not even a little bit," he replied before firing up the engine. "Hang on, darlin'. We're gonna motor out onto the highway now and go really, really fast."

Revving the engine, he popped the clutch and the bike lurched forward. He probably took more pleasure than he should have in the way she squealed and grabbed him around the middle when they shot out of the parking lot onto the road, but damn if he didn't enjoy it.

In the end, they opted for a long ride in the country instead of a nap and sports on the tube. Jackson dropped Elise off at her apartment at a quarter to six and ran home to shower and change vehicles.

When he came back a little over an hour later, she still wasn't ready, which was no surprise to him. He'd known her most of his life and had accepted long ago that Elise Brianna Beckett just wasn't made for punctuality. And he was okay with that.

She let him into the apartment with a flurry of chaotic energy. "I'm almost done. Go keep Chunk company in the living room for a minute while I finish up. He's pouting because I locked up the new shoe purchases in the closet and he hasn't been able to even get a good whiff of 'em yet." She waved a hand in the direction of the living room, then quickly disappeared down the hall.

Jackson sauntered into the other room and squinted down at the fat cat in the Papasan chair. "So … thwarted in your pursuit of fabulous new shoes?"

When the cat stared back at him with the inscrutable look all cats seem to innately possess, he shook his head. "Dude, you do know this shoe fetish thing is, like, so unmanly, right? And it's a little creepy. Chicks don't dig creepy."

"You got that right, pal," Elise said, entering the living room in a swirl of perfume that made his mouth water. "Are you ready to go?"

He walked over and stared down at her gloss-slicked lips. "Will be in just a sec." Before she could protest, he grabbed her up and kissed her thoroughly, enjoying the way she melted against him after a moment and kissed him back with abandon.

"Jax," she said with a sigh when he'd satisfied them both. "I just put on my lip gloss. Now you're wearing half of it and the rest is mushed all over the lower half of my face."

Wiping his bottom lip with his thumb, he wiggled his eyebrows at her. "Well, darlin', it's your own fault. You smell like heaven and taste like dessert." He took her arm and herded her toward the front door before she could backtrack to the bathroom. "And I gotta tell you, I kinda like you a little mushed up."

The walk to Delphine's premier Mexican restaurant Toucan's On Main was short, and they were only ten minutes late arriving, which was probably a record where Elise was concerned. Ross, Caroline, C.C., and Madison had already procured a table and were sipping drinks while they waited.

"Hey, buddy," Jackson said, sitting down next to Ross. "You and Caro having a night out free of parental responsibilities, I see."

"Yeah." Ross nodded and slid a wry look at his wife before continuing, "It doesn't happen very often, so we like to take advantage when it does."

"It's nice to have a night to ourselves," Caroline agreed. "Don't get me wrong, I love my boys, but sometimes I just want to spend time with adults."

C.C. laughed. "Well, I'm not sure we qualify, but I know what you mean."

"I thought Grace was coming, C.C." Elise said.

"She sent me a text to say she had a last-minute meeting and would have to take a rain check on dinner."

"That's too bad." Elise frowned and sent a quick look to Jackson.

He figured he knew what she was thinking and casually turned to Madison. "Is Toby still coming?" he asked. "We saw him in the parking lot as we were leaving the festival. He looked like he was feeling better."

"I haven't heard from him, but I'm sure he'll be here. He's probably just running late, too. We've already decided not to wait on him to order."

"Good, because I'm starving," Jackson replied.

"For the love of God, Jax," Elise said with a roll of her eyes. "You're always starving. I don't know how you can eat like you do and not gain an ounce."

"Good genes, baby. Good genes."

The waitress came by then, and they ordered. Thirty minutes later their food had been delivered, and Toby Raymond finally arrived in a flurry, looking a bit disheveled.

"Sorry I'm late. I got hung up," he said, taking off his coat and slinging it over his chair before sitting down next to Madison with a smile just for her. "I see y'all ordered. Good. I wouldn't want to hold up your dinner."

"It's not a problem," Madison said and made a grab for his coat before it hit the floor when it slipped off the back of his chair. "Hey, you're missing a button," she told him good-naturedly, as she handed the garment back to him.

"Thanks," he replied, and his face turned scarlet. "I must have gotten caught on something."

Madison grinned at him and made the introductions, while Ross flagged down the waitress. Toby glanced at the menu she brought him and had just given her his order when Jackson's cell phone rang. Pulling it out of his pocket, he looked at the readout and quickly answered. "Hey, Miss Abby. You looking for Elise?"

"No, Jackson. I'm looking for you," she said on the other end of the line.

He didn't like the sound of her voice and the cop in him immediately went on alert. Something was wrong, that much was obvious. "Well, you found me, sweetheart," he replied, trying to keep his tone light. "What's the matter?"

"I need you to come, Jackson. And I mean, right now."

"Of course I'll come. If you need me, I'll head out now. Where are you?"

"I'm at the Lost Pines Motel. Divia Larson's room. Please, you need to come right away. She's dead, Jackson."

# FIVE

JACKSON HUNG UP THE phone and could literally feel all eyes at the table on him.

"Jax?" Elise laid a hand on his arm. "Was that Gram? What's wrong?"

How on earth did he explain the situation, especially to the man sitting across the table from him? There was a very good possibility Toby's mother was dead. Of course, he didn't know that for certain, and until he did, he wasn't about to pass on unconfirmed information and cause a panic.

On the other hand, if Mrs. Larson really was deceased—and he had no reason to believe Miss Abby was mistaken—he was going to have to tell a family member as soon as he finished inspecting the scene.

*So, what was Miss Abby doing in the woman's motel room? Wasn't there a mutual dislike between the two of them? And just where was Mr. Larson?*

"Jax?" Elise prompted when his mind began its investigatory rabbit-trail. "You're scaring me. What's happened? Is Gram all right?"

Taking her hand, he looked around the table at the expectant faces. "Miss Abby is fine. She's out at the Lost Pines Motel. Sound's like there's been an incident and she wants me to come."

"What? The Lost Pines Motel? What's she doing over there?" Ross asked with a frown, before glancing down at his watch. "It's almost nine o'clock, for God's sake."

"I don't know anything yet, other than the fact that Miss Abby is okay."

"We're staying at that motel, along with a lot of other festival attendees," Toby said. "It didn't seem like a place where there'd be trouble."

"Come on, Jax. You have to know more than what you're telling us," Madison said, shooting him a skeptical look. "What kind of incident?"

At that point the conversation began to deteriorate and everyone started yammering at once. Jackson finally had to raise his voice above the din to get control of the situation before it got out of hand. The last thing he needed was unsubstantiated rumors flying around town before he even got out to the potential scene.

"Enough, y'all! Geez, we're in a public place. Act like rational adults, would you? Like I said, I don't have any of the facts yet. Hell, I just got off the damn phone. I am not, repeat, *not* going to speculate on anything until I get out there and see for myself what's what."

Standing, he took out his wallet and threw down a couple of twenties. Looking over at Ross, he nodded at the bills. "That should be enough to cover me and El."

"Now, wait just a minute, Jax—"

Elise spoke up and cut her brother off as soon as he started to object. "Don't worry, Ross. I'll ride out with Jackson. I'll stay with Gram until you guys finish up here."

"Toby, I'm gonna need you to follow us out there as soon as you're done eating as well," Jackson said. "Sounds like your mother might be involved in whatever has transpired." He didn't want to say too much, but to leave the man here at the restaurant without saying anything at all seemed wrong and somewhat heartless.

"Oh, God. What's she done now?" the man asked with a shake of his head. "With my mom, it's always something."

"Again, I don't know anything for sure, so I'd rather not speculate about what may or may not have happened."

Toby nodded. "All right. I'll have the waitress box up my order and be along as soon as I can."

"I'll wait with Toby." Madison turned to the man. "If that's okay with you."

Toby gave her a shy smile. "Sure. That'll work."

Jackson pulled out his keys, thinking that his one day off was probably about to end very poorly. "Come on, El. Let's get a move on. I don't want to keep Miss Abby waiting any longer than necessary."

They left the restaurant and hadn't gone half a block before Elise started grilling him. "Are you gonna tell me what's really going on?"

"Not out here on the street, I'm not."

They walked the rest of the way to his pickup in silence, but she didn't waste any time after they climbed in and he'd fired up the engine.

"Okay. Give. What is Gram doing out at the Lost Pines Motel? And what aren't you saying?"

"Evidently she went out to see Divia Larson," he said as he headed the vehicle out of town.

"I beg your pardon? Gram can't stand the woman. Why would she go see her?"

"No idea. I'm more interested in the reason Miss Abby called me."

"Well, spit it out. What did Gram say?"

Jackson slid an annoyed look her way. "Impatient much?"

"Jax!"

"Okay, okay. She called me because she says Mrs. Larson is dead."

"*What?*" Elise shrieked. "Divia's dead? When? For the love of God, how?"

"Well, geez, El. I don't know any of that yet, do I? That would be why we're presently driving out there."

"Nobody likes a smart ass, Jackson." Blowing out a breath, she shook her head. "This is all so shocking. I mean, we just saw her earlier today. Toby is going to be distraught. Why didn't you tell him?"

"What *could* I tell him, Elise? Nothing has been confirmed. I trust that if your grandmother says Divia's dead, then she probably is, but at this point it's all conjecture—hearsay. That was one of the reasons I didn't want to say too much in the restaurant. God, El, the guy was sitting right across the table from me."

"I know. This is terrible. I don't understand what Gram was doing out there, Jax. And at this time of night."

"I guess we'll find out soon enough."

And he was right. It didn't take long before they were pulling into the motel parking lot.

The Lost Pines Motel was your run-of-the-mill small town lodging establishment. The 1950s style building was L-shaped with a large parking lot and a covered walkway that ran the length of the structure.

It was owned and operated by Theo and Harriet Wilson, and they ran it in a squeaky-clean fashion. To Jackson's knowledge, there'd never been more than the usual calls of excessive noise or disturbing the peace here, and those had been few and very far between.

A death at their motel would devastate Mr. and Mrs. Wilson, especially if that death was anything other than natural causes. He hated to think about an alternate possibility, but he couldn't get the sound of Miss Abby's voice out of his head. And he had a very bad feeling in his gut.

He spotted Elise's grandmother before he'd even pulled the truck into a parking spot. She'd taken a chair from the room out onto the walkway and was sitting in it with her back to the door. He grabbed a pair of latex gloves out of the console between the seats, which earned him an odd look from Elise.

"Just what are you expecting, Jax? A homicide?" she asked with a bit of sarcasm. "I mean, Divia was a piece of work, but I doubt someone did her in out here at the Lost Pines Motel."

"You never know, darlin'. Regardless, I have to follow protocol."

"Jackson," Abigail acknowledged when he climbed out of the cab and walked toward her, "thanks for coming."

"Gram, are you all right?" Elise asked as she followed him over and squatted down in front of her grandmother. "What's going on here?"

"I'm fine, baby girl. But unfortunately, Divia Larson is not." Abigail stood up and removed the chair blocking the door before turning to Jackson. "The minute I found her I called you. I pulled this chair out of the room, but I didn't touch anything else, other than to check for a pulse, that is."

Jackson nodded. "I need you two to stay out here while I go in and have a quick look."

Abigail had stuck her purse in the jamb so as not to get locked out of the room, which was smart. He put on the gloves but was still careful not to touch the knob. Giving the door a shove, he did a quick scan of the room before entering and partially closing the door behind him.

The first thing he noticed was Divia Larson's body lying between the foot of the bed closest to the wall and the adjacent dresser.

Carefully, he walked over to her body and checked her vitals himself, verifying Abigail's claim that the woman was indeed deceased. She had a deep gash over one eye and the cherry-red blood that had run down her face had not yet dried, telling him the wound was fairly fresh. A closer look showed that the color in the victim's face was noticeably pink.

*Bright red blood, pinker than normal skin tone.* Warning bells were beginning to peal in Jackson's head.

Looking around the room, he noticed an open bottle of Merlot—River Bend Reserve—on the cabinet next to a solitary empty glass. Leaning over, he gave the glass a sniff.

And those warning bells got louder.

Stepping over Divia's body, he glanced into the bathroom. Everything seemed normal, with the exception of a glass that looked to be recently washed and left to drain on a damp towel on the counter next to the sink.

Pulling out his cell phone, he called the station. "Hey Jim, this is Jackson Landry," he began when fellow Deputy Jim Stockton answered the line. "I've got a situation out here at the Lost Pines Motel."

"You and everyone else, it seems. What is it tonight? A full moon or something?" the deputy asked. "We've had all sorts of wild calls tonight. Dub Pendergast drank a boatload of his homemade mead and went berserk out at the Rum Pot, and Rusty Falcone shot out his neighbor's tires, evidently because said neighbor had the audacity to park on the street just a smidgen too close to Rusty's driveway." Jim chuckled on the other end of the line. "And the best call? Sam Gordon got his johnson stuck in a knot hole in the fence between his property and Willard Nelson's yard. Fortunately for him, he had his cell phone on him. Don't know what Willard would've done had he found his nemesis stuck in the fence like that after pissing in his yard."

"Sounds like it's been a busy night." Jackson sighed. "I hate to add to the craziness, but I think I can trump all of it. I've got a dead body out here."

"No shit?"

"Yeah. I've done a preliminary, but for reasons I won't go into on the phone, I'm calling this a suspicious death. I'll tape off the room as soon as I hang up and then wait for the team."

"Okay. Sounds good. Can you give me the basics?"

"Female, Caucasian, mid-fifties. The victim's name is Divia Larson. She was here with Third Coast Winery for the food and wine festival. And after a cursory look at the scene, I've got more questions than answers at this point. Elise's grandmother found the body, and I'll be taking her statement directly."

"Uh … okay. I'll get a team out there ASAP."

"Thanks." That was the easy part, Jackson thought as he hung up. Now came the hard part.

Stepping out of the room, he pulled the door closed behind him, taking care in case there were prints to be found. The door would lock behind him and effectively block off what he was beginning to think of as a crime scene. He'd get a key from the office for the crew in a minute, but first things, first.

Elise and her grandmother stood close together just outside the room and one look at their faces told him they were both worried.

"Jax?" Elise began the moment he closed the door. "What did you find?"

Abigail gave a grunt. "He found Divia Larson's dead body, that's what he found."

"Gram. That's not helping."

"Well, he did. What else did you find, Jackson?"

His gaze locked onto Abigail's, and there he saw understanding. "I figure you know what else I found, Miss Abby. I've called it in and Deputy Stockton has a team on the way."

Abigail nodded, but Elise was obviously confused and impatient. "I'm glad you two seem to be on the same page, but could one of you fill me in?"

"Sweetheart, what Jackson found is a probable crime scene. Poison, if I'm not mistaken."

"*What?*" Elise gasped. "How do you know that, Gram?"

"Ha! From all those damn mysteries I read. That and the smell."

Elise shook her head. "Smell? What smell?"

Again, Jackson's gaze met Abigail's. "The smell of bitter almonds."

"You could smell it, too?" Abigail's eyebrows shot up. "I wondered if you would. Not everyone can, you know."

"Yeah, I could smell it, but there were other clues. Like the bright red blood and pink skin tone. I'm thinking cyanide, but we'll wait for the tox screen."

"Oh my God!" Elise cried. "Are you *kidding* me? Cyanide? You think someone *murdered* Divia?"

"I don't know what happened yet, El. All I've got is first impressions, but I've tagged it as a suspicious death. From here, I'll have to follow the evidence."

"I guess you're gonna want my statement," Abigail said with a nod.

"Yes, ma'am, I do." Stepping over to the truck, he pulled off his gloves and got a notepad and pen out of the glove compartment. "Miss Abby, some of the questions are going to be hard. But you understand I have to ask, right?"

Abigail gave him a grim look before nodding again. "I know. Ask your questions, Jackson. Let's get this over with."

"Jax, what are you talking about? You make it sound like Gram is a suspect when you don't even know for certain there was foul play."

"Elise, I have to make sure Miss Abby is in the clear before this *becomes* a murder investigation."

"And you think that's where this is going?"

The frightened look on her face went straight to his heart. He didn't want to scare either of them any more than he had to, but his gut was telling him murder was exactly where this scenario was going to end up.

"Let's just get Miss Abby's statement out of the way before Toby or Mr. Larson get here. Then we'll wait for the CSI team's findings, okay? Now, Miss Abby, what were you doing out here in the first place?"

"I got a text from Divia in the late afternoon, which I ignored." Abigail heaved a beleaguered sigh. "It's no secret that we weren't the best of friends, to say the least."

Jackson made some notes. "And what time did you get the text?"

"I left the festival for home about half past five, so it must have been closer to five, maybe just before."

"That would have been thirty or forty minutes after we saw Divia and Toby having that argument in the parking lot," Elise said. "Remember, Jax?"

"Yes, that would fit the timeline so far. Go on, Miss Abby. You ignored the text. So, how did you end up coming out here anyway?"

"Well, she called me a couple hours later. Must have been a little after seven. Said she knew I didn't think much of her and that we'd never be friends, but could I come over right away."

Abigail ran a hand through her hair and shut her eyes briefly. When she opened them again, her sorrow was evident. "Jackson, she begged me to come. She said she was afraid and needed to talk to somebody."

"How did she get your cell number? Like she said, it's not like you were friends."

"I don't know how she got my personal number." Abigail sighed and shook her head. "Perhaps she got it from Garrett, or maybe from one of the festival organizers like Lita Washington."

"No offense, but why do you think she called you?" he asked. "I mean, why not call her husband or her son?"

"I asked her that as well. She said Garrett had gone into Austin for a meeting and wasn't due back until late. Toby was still out at the festival." She shook her head. "I advised her to wait for one of them to get back, but she was adamant. Said she needed someone she could trust—someone who wasn't connected."

"Not connected?" Jackson repeated. "What did she mean by that? Connected to what?"

Again, Abigail shook her head. "I don't *know*. She wouldn't say any more over the phone. She plain wore me down and I finally said that I would come, but God help me, I didn't want to." Abigail's voice broke as she continued and Jackson's heart went out to her. "Oh, Jackson, I putzed around and didn't get out here until after eight. Maybe if I'd gotten here sooner Divia would still be alive."

Elise hugged her grandmother close. "You don't know that, Gram. We don't even know what happened yet, but Jackson's going to find out, right?"

"That's the plan," he answered, then addressed Abigail. "Miss Abby, tell me the rest. Take me through what happened when you got here?"

She pointed toward the parking lot where her Buick was parked. "I pulled in, parked, and walked straight here. I wanted to get whatever this was over with quickly and get back home. When I got closer I could tell the door was slightly ajar—I could see the purse stuck in the jamb. That didn't seem odd to me, though. People do that all the time, right? Stick something in the jamb to keep from being locked out when they run to the car or go get ice."

Jackson pointed to the purse that he'd moved to a spot beside the door when he'd gone into the room. "You mean that's not your purse?"

"Hell no, it's not mine. I wanted in and out as fast as possible, so I left mine in the Buick."

In that case, he figured it probably belonged to the deceased, but he'd have the crew bag it when they got here. "Okay, go on."

"Well, I did pretty much what you did. I pushed the door open and saw her immediately. I called out to see if anyone else was inside and when I got no answer I went in as far as her body. After I checked for a pulse and realized she was dead, I called you, grabbed a chair, and came back out the way I went in. Then I sat down and waited. That's it."

"One last question, Miss Abby. Did you bring anything else into the room with you?"

"Anything else?" Elise asked with a frown. "She just told you she left her purse in the car, Jackson. What else would she have had?"

"Miss Abby?" he repeated, ignoring Elise's testy outburst.

Abigail shook her head in response. "No, Jackson. I had my keys in my hand, and that's all I had with me. I didn't bring the wine."

"What wine?" Elise asked in confusion. "What are you two talking about now?"

Reluctantly, Jackson answered. "There's an open bottle of Merlot sitting on the dresser. It's River Bend Reserve."

"Really, Jackson! Anyone could have gotten that bottle at the festival, or at the Wine Barrel, for that matter," Elise pointed out. "How many cases did we take out to the venue at set-up, Gram?"

"We had four cases of the Reserve: two of the Cab and two of the Merlot when the festival opened yesterday. And before you ask, Jackson, as of today when I left, we'd sold almost a case of the Merlot."

"See, almost a case," Elise said, jabbing a finger in his direction. "Anyone could have purchased that bottle and brought it out here."

"Okay, okay." He put up a hand in surrender before she really got going. "Calm down, would you? I had to ask."

Just as he was about to send them home, Jackson looked up to see a couple of vehicles pulling into the parking lot. One was the CSI SUV, and the other one was Toby Raymond's Mustang. Jackson was not looking forward to telling the man that his mother was dead.

"I haven't had time to tape the door," Jackson said to Reggie Martins, the lead CSI, as he approached. "But I've been standing right here since I came out of the room. The door's locked now, so you'll have to get a key from the office."

As the man headed off in that direction, Toby Raymond hurried over, followed closely by Madison. "What's going on here?" he asked, his voice starting to rise. "Where's my mother? And why is the CSI vehicle here?"

Jackson stepped over to the man and put a hand on his shoulder. "Toby, I'm sorry to have to tell you this way, but your mother is dead."

# SIX

To say Toby Raymond had a meltdown after hearing the news of his mother's untimely death would have been an understatement. Elise's heart ached for him as she watched him go from shocked disbelief to emotional denial, and on to accusatory anger, in a matter of minutes.

In his angry phase, he did his best to bully Jackson into allowing him access to his mother's motel room. When that didn't work, he dissolved into a pool of hysteria right there on the sidewalk outside the room.

It was incredibly hard to watch.

Of course, Elise had no idea how she would react to such news and sincerely hoped she never had to find out. That left her unqualified to judge anyone else.

She had to give her sister credit, though. Madison and Toby hadn't known each other long, but she'd sat down next to him on the sidewalk and held him as he wept, murmuring softly and rubbing his back in a soothing manner. After a time, Toby seemed to compose himself a bit, and her sister had helped him back to his room.

Jackson called Doc Nagle down to the scene to get his opinion and clear the body for transport into Austin. Since Bastrop County had no coroner, the Travis County Medical Examiner's office would conduct the autopsy and run any tests needed, as it had on her uncle a few months back.

Realizing Divia's son was in distress and needed help, the physician had given Toby something to calm his nerves and help him sleep, before heading into the Larson's room with Jackson.

Josiah Nagle looked like your typical sixty-ish, small-town country doctor, but looks were often deceiving. He was actually a country doctor-turned-author who had an avid fascination with death by poison. He'd written and published several works of fiction—all featuring murder with this main theme—and it was an area in which he excelled. Somewhat of a local celebrity, the doctor was sharp as a blade and never missed a trick.

"I agree with your initial assessment, Jackson," Nagle said when they came out of the room fifteen minutes later.

He and Jackson were keeping their voices low. Elise tried not to be too obvious as she strained to hear the details of their conversation.

"The telltale signs are there for cyanide poisoning, but the wound over her eye is substantial," the doctor continued. "Either could have caused her death, but until an autopsy is conducted I won't speculate. You'll have to wait for the reports from the M.E. to be certain."

"I figured as much. Thanks for your assistance."

"There are definitely questions to be answered. I'll be interested in what the tests reveal about the wine spill on the carpet."

"Yeah. Like if the spill contains cyanide, who put the glass back on the dresser next to the bottle?"

The doctor nodded. "That would be one question. Another would be who washed out the other glass and left it on the towel in the bathroom?"

"I know," Jackson replied with a frown. "I'll have the team bag that one, too. But I doubt we'll get anything from it. It seems like someone did a good job of covering their tracks."

Elise found that last tidbit disturbing. The Lost Pines motel was a throwback to a simpler time, using drinking glasses that were actually made of glass. In the room, one had been left sitting in plain sight on the dresser along with the open bottle of Merlot. Evidently another glass had been found washed and left to drain on a towel in the bathroom. If someone had murdered Divia, then this could have been the killer's glass.

In any case, it suggested Divia had known this person, perhaps had a glass of wine with her killer. That this person would clean-up before leaving the room—with the woman's freshly dead corpse lying right there on the carpet—suggested a coldness that was too gross for words.

Elise was still mulling over this new information when Ross showed up alone a few minutes later.

"The look on Jackson's face in the restaurant was a dead giveaway that there was something seriously wrong out here. I figured it would be better to take Caro home first," he told Elise. "I also stopped and told Mom what I knew, which of course, isn't much. She wanted to come with me, but I talked her into staying home. I told her we'd call when we knew anything, and I'd get Gram home as soon as I could. I'll check in with her in a bit."

He paused to point to the CSI vehicle. "So, what's up with that?"

A part of Elise wished Ross would have brought Laura with him. Their mom was a rock during stressful situations and usually knew just what to say to keep everyone calm. And this definitely qualified as a stressful situation. While they waited for more information, Elise used the time to take her brother aside and fill him in.

"Somebody killed Divia Larson? With cyanide?" He scratched his head and blew out a breath. "That's incredible."

The motel was an L-shaped building with all the room doors opening onto the covered walkway and the parking lot beyond. He nodded toward the other end of the building. Though they kept their distance, a number of people had come out of their rooms to see what was happening. "Lookie-loos. Everyone loves a show."

Elise shrugged. "Human nature, I guess."

"Looks like Jax really has his work cut out for him. I mean, there were quite a few folks that would've delighted in spiking Divia Larson's drink with a little poison if they thought they could get away with it."

"That's true," she replied in a hushed tone. "There's no shortage of murder suspects. Gram included."

"What the hell are you talking about, El?" he said before dropping his voice and taking her arm. He nudged her farther down the breezeway, maneuvering her away from where Jackson and Abigail stood on the sidewalk. "What do you mean Gram is a suspect? She couldn't murder anyone and you know it."

"I agree. But think about it, Ross. Divia's husband is Gram's old high school sweetheart. It's no secret what Gram thought of the woman, and she had words with her just yesterday in front of witnesses. The bottle found at the scene—which may or may not have been tainted—was River Bend's Private Reserve. Whether the cyanide was put in the bottle or just her glass, it was probably how she ingested the poison. And finally, Gram found the body and was here by herself until we showed up."

"Come on, El. You're taking it all out of context, making it sound suspicious. At this point, it's all circumstantial. So Gram didn't like the woman. None of what you just said adds up to a strong enough motive for murder."

"Maybe not. And you're right, it *is* circumstantial, but Jax will have to consider everyone a suspect until he can positively rule them out. And that includes Gram. Remember how it was with Uncle Edmond's murder? All those little things by themselves might not be enough to establish motive, but when you put them together, it doesn't look good for Gram, either." Elise glanced back toward Abigail and sighed. "What we need to do is give Jax a little help in eliminating her from the suspect list. And the sooner, the better."

Ross narrowed his eyes at her. "I thought Jax made you promise to butt out of his police investigations."

"He did." She gave an indifferent shrug. "And I won't put myself in that kind of danger again, but he didn't say anything about helping to clear a family member's name. It's bad enough that Gram got caught up in this and was the one who found Divia's body. I'll be damned if I'm going to stand around and see her name dragged through the mud as a suspect, too." She folded her arms and glared at him. "So, are you going to help me?"

"Fine. But where do we start? We don't have much to go on."

"We start by keeping our eyes and ears open. Somebody knows what went on here tonight, and they'll slip up at some point. We just have to be ready when that happens. I'm gonna call C.C. and get her on board, too. The more eyes and ears we have out there, the faster we'll find the information we're looking for."

They walked back over to where Jackson and Abigail stood just as the EMTs carried Divia's body out of the room on a gurney and lifted it into the waiting ambulance. Jackson went with the CSI team and lingered while they did a thorough sweep of the Larsons' room.

In the light from the open doorway, Elise watched over his shoulder as Jackson pulled out the contents of the purse that had been used to hold the door open, not surprised to find that it had indeed been Divia's.

After taking a quick inventory, he bagged it. Elise couldn't say if anything was missing, but important items like the woman's cell phone, checkbook, and wallet were all found inside. And the wallet still held several credit cards and a little over two hundred dollars in cash, which seemed to rule out robbery.

But then, what thief took the time to poison their victims after robbing them?

Ross did what he did best in stressful situations—he paced—while Elise and Abigail watched the investigators continue their work. That is, what they were able to see. The team kept the room's curtains closed, but every time Elise saw the flash light up the window, she knew they'd snapped another photograph. Toward the end of their sweep, the techs made several trips to the SUV with sealed brown paper bags containing potential evidence.

All through the nearly two-hour process, one question kept circling around in her mind. Where was Divia's husband? The woman had told her grandmother on the phone that Garrett had gone into Austin for a meeting and wouldn't be back until late. But it was going on eleven o'clock at night and he still hadn't returned. Madison had tried to contact Garrett with the mobile number Toby had given her earlier, but the calls had gone straight to voicemail.

Abigail continued to worry that her former beau would get back to the motel after everyone had gone, only to find his wife missing and their room blocked off with crime scene tape. It was a terrible situation and Elise hated seeing her grandmother so upset.

For the past twenty minutes or so, Jackson had been gently pressuring them all to go home and just when they were about to do that, another vehicle pulled into the parking lot.

Garrett Larson had finally come back from Austin—or wherever he'd been.

Elise watched the older man get out of his car and come toward them with a worried look on his face. Then he zeroed in on her grandmother.

"Abigail? What are you doing here?" His gaze went from the motel room door, to Jackson, and back to her, as if she alone held all the answers he needed. "Why is our room blocked off? Where are Divia and Toby? Has something happened?"

When Jackson tried to step in, her grandmother stopped him with a shake of her head and a pleading look.

"Garrett," Abigail's tone was soft as she reached out to take the man's hand. "I'm so sorry, but yes, something terrible has happened. I don't know how to soften the blow, so I'll just say it. I'm afraid that Divia is dead."

The man blinked several times as if trying to understand a complicated foreign language. "That … that can't be," he finally said.

"I ... I just talked to her this afternoon. She said they were doing brisk sales out at the festival and she probably wouldn't come back to the room until after dinner. There must be some mistake."

Abigail shook her head and looked him in the eye. "Garrett, there is no mistake. I found her myself. Again, I'm so sorry."

The man paled then and looked like he might drop at any second. Abigail guided him to the chair that was still sitting off to the side where she'd moved it. "Sit here a moment and get your breath. I know this is dreadful news and a lot to take in. Toby gave Maddy your cell number and she tried to call you several times but got no answer. I think she left a couple messages."

Garrett looked up at her with a vacant look, and his eyes filled with tears. "I ... uh ... I was in a meeting and turned my phone off for the duration. I guess I forgot to turn it back on."

"It's okay. That's not important right now."

"What happened, Abigail? What happened to my Divia? And what were you doing in our hotel room?"

Jackson stepped over and knelt down next to Garrett's chair. "Mr. Larson, I'm Deputy Jackson Landry. I'm sorry for your loss, sir. Miss Abby called me when she found your wife. We don't have a lot of information to go on yet and are still trying to piece together just what happened. You said you were in Austin at a meeting. I'm going to need the particulars, as well as anyone that can confirm your presence there."

"I'm sorry. I don't understand," Garrett said, his face showing genuine confusion. "Why would you need to confirm information about my meeting? And where is Toby? None of this makes any sense to me."

"Jackson, do you think this could wait until morning?" Abigail asked with a pointed look. "He's had a tremendous shock and needs time to absorb what's happened."

After a moment, Jackson nodded. "Of course. Your stepson is in his room, Mr. Larson, but he was very upset. Doctor Nagle gave him a sedative. We've secured another room for you, and Miss Abby took the liberty of moving some of your things there. Maybe she could show you the way."

"Yes. That's a good idea, Jackson. Thank you," Abigail said.

"Gram, do you want us to wait for you?" Elise asked. She didn't want to leave her grandmother here alone. Garrett Larson *looked* devastated, and although he *said* he was at a meeting in Austin, until Jackson confirmed that, Elise wasn't willing to give him the benefit of the doubt. At least not where her grandmother was concerned.

"No, baby girl. You and Ross go on home."

"But Gram—" Ross began before she cut him off.

"Ross Alexander, I'll be right along as soon as I get Garrett into his new room. I'll call you when I get home. Now go." She turned to Mr. Larson and helped him to stand. "Come on, Garrett. I've got your room key right here. Let's get you settled."

Abigail took Mr. Larson by the arm and guided him down the breezeway toward his new room, passing Madison as she came out of Toby's room.

"Mr. Larson finally got back?" Madison asked when she reached them. "I'm glad he got here before everyone left. That would have made a terrible situation even worse."

Slipping an arm around Jackson, Elise took comfort from him when he enfolded her into his embrace. "Oh Jax, this is all so sad. I mean, Divia may not have been the most well-liked person in town, but why would someone intentionally poison her?"

"I know. And not to sound callous, but it's a really crappy way to end my one day off." He gave her a quick squeeze. "Unfortunately, I'm going to be awhile longer, so I'm going to have Ross drop you, okay?"

She nodded. "That's fine, as long as you promise to stay until Gram heads home as well. I don't want her out here on her own."

"Will do." He leaned in and kissed her. "I'll talk to you tomorrow."

"Toby's finally asleep," Madison said. "I am so ready to go home. This whole thing has been too stressful for words, especially after going through everything with Uncle Edmond's homicide just a couple of months ago."

"Do you want me to drop you at your car, Maddy? Or do you just want to ride home with me?" Ross asked.

"You can drop me at the car since you're taking El home. My car is parked just up the street from her apartment."

As the three of them headed for Ross' car, the wheels began to turn in Elise's mind. "I think the first thing we need to do is make a list," she said as Ross pulled the car out of the parking lot and onto the highway.

"A list? What kind of list?" Madison asked from the back seat.

"An inventory of all the people who had a problem with Divia Larson."

Ross chuckled. "I hate to speak ill of the recently dead, but considering the kind of person she was, that *inventory* could be pretty lengthy, El."

"Well, we have to start somewhere, right?"

"What are you two talking about?" Madison asked. "You're not butting into Jackson's police business again, are you?"

"No." Elise said. "We're just going to make sure that Gram is cleared of any suspicions." She gave her sister a run-through of her earlier conversation with Ross. When she was finished, she turned and looked over the seat at Madison. "So? In or out?"

Her sister sighed and rolled her eyes, but in the end relented. "In, of course. Where do we start?"

# SEVEN

Good news travels fast. At least, that's what Elise had always heard, but what she found was that bad news usually ended up winning the race. By the time the festival gates opened on Saturday morning, it seemed reports of Divia Larson's death were common knowledge.

And it wasn't pretty.

While River Bend's booth was experiencing a lull in customers by mid-morning, Third Coast across the way was jam-packed.

"I'm sorry, but don't you find it just incredibly ghoulish the way people will flock to a tragedy like maggots to a carcass?" C.C. asked as they watched the frenzy from the other side of the midway. "It's positively macabre."

Elise leaned on the counter next to her friend and made a face. "Well, speaking of macabre, I find your analogy gross and completely inappropriate, but I get your point. Yesterday, they were having a hard time giving their wine away over there. Today everybody wants to say they bought their vino from the dead woman's booth. It's pretty repulsive, but typical."

"I guess."

"You should've seen the rubber-neckers pouring out of their rooms last night at the motel trying to get a glimpse of the action. With some of the festival vendors staying at Lost Pines, it's no wonder the news of Divia's death has spread like a brush fire."

C.C. turned to her with a sour look. "I say again, ghoulish."

Elise laughed at her friend's expression. "Yes. Very."

"Hey, aren't we supposed to be making some kind of list? With so many people around here having a beef with the victim, we should probably get started, don't you think? Might take us a while."

"Right again, my friend, and I've already started it." Elise pulled a notepad out of her bag before nodding up the midway toward the entrance where the Toussaints could be seen coming their way. "And speaking of suspects ..."

"Yeah. Scary French chick alert," C.C. muttered. "I think she should go to the top of the list after that cat fight we witnessed on Thursday."

"Agreed."

"And didn't Frenchie actually say something about Divia ending up dead if she didn't leave her husband alone?"

"Yes. Loud and clear. I'd venture a guess that Monique wouldn't think twice about poisoning Divia if she thought she could get away with it. She'd probably enjoy it. And I think a woman would do a better job of cleaning up after killing someone than a man, don't you?"

"Well, yeah. Men can be such slobs," C.C. said with a grin. "But that doesn't mean that Mr. *Handsome* Toussaint there couldn't have done the deed. After all, the scuffle between those two crazy girls *was* about a little sumpin'-sumpin' supposedly going on between him and Mrs. Larson, right?"

Elise pointed the pen in her friend's direction. "You make an excellent point. But we're going to have to get some evidence to support the allegations. Just because Monique thought there was something going on between Divia and Alain doesn't necessarily mean there actually was."

"True," C.C. said with a naughty gleam in her eye. "But I have to say, it's quite salacious to think about."

"Maybe so, but if Divia and Alain *were* having an affair, and Monique already knew about it or at least suspected, then what would be his motive?"

"Hmm. That's a good question. To which I have no answer … yet."

Monique Toussaint had her arm through her husband's and looked like she hadn't a care in the world as she strolled beside him. When they got closer, the couple veered over to River Bend's booth, and Monique was all smiles.

"*Bonjour*, Elise," the French beauty said. "Have you heard the ghastly news about Divia Larson?"

*Well, for crying out loud. Let's get right to the gory details, shall we? And with a smile on your face.*

"Good morning." Elise nodded and heaved a sigh. "It's really terrible, isn't it?"

"Mmm." Monique clucked her tongue. "I was thinking this must be quite unsettling for you and your family."

"I beg your pardon?" Elise couldn't keep the shock from her voice. "What do you mean by that, Monique? I should think this would be *unsettling* for everyone here at the festival. You included."

"*Mais oui*, of course. A tragedy such as this is dreadful for all of us in the vineyard community. I did not intend to cause offense, I only meant that with your uncle's grizzly murder not so long ago, this horrible news must be doubly upsetting to you." The French woman gave an exaggerated shudder. "And of course, with your *grand-mère* being the one to find poor Divia. Very distressing, is it not?"

"Yes. Very," Elise replied in a cool tone.

"I heard somewhere that Garrett and your *grand-mère* were once sweethearts. Is this true?"

The question was posed innocently enough with just the right amount of concern in her voice, but Elise wasn't fooled. Monique knew very well the history between Garrett Larson and her grandmother. She read the underlying implication Monique was obviously trying to make with crystal clarity. "Yes. Gram and Garrett were high school sweethearts. But that was ages ago."

The other woman gave her a sympathetic pout. "Ah, yes. But one never forgets a first love, *n'est-ce-pas?* I'm certain it was difficult for her to see him in a loveless marriage with a woman who thinks only of herself and what she can take."

"Monique," Alain Toussaint spoke up in a warning tone. "That is only your opinion. You should not voice things you can't know as fact."

Monique's mouth dropped open and she looked like she would object, but then seemed to catch herself. "But you are correct, of course, *mon cher*. Sometimes my mouth runs away with me."

"I suppose the police will have questions for everyone who—shall we say—had issues with Divia." Elise suggested in a mild tone. "Have they contacted you yet?"

Monique blanched and began to sputter. "Me? Why on earth would they want to contact me? We aren't even staying at that terrible little motel. I know nothing about her death. Other than what I've heard this morning, of course."

"How did you find out? About Divia's death, I mean," C.C. asked.

The woman seemed to stumble for a moment before regaining her momentum. "Alain and I first heard it at the bakery in town. But again, the police have no reason to contact either of us. We had nothing to do with that woman."

"Well, no offense, but that's not entirely true, is it? I mean, after the little scuffle between you two on Thursday, I would think they would at least want to interview you." Elise exchanged looks with C.C. before continuing. "Of course, we would never say anything, but there were quite a few spectators that day who heard everything that was said. I should think it's only a matter of time before the police hear about it as well."

The look on Alain Toussaint's face was priceless when he turned to his wife. This was obviously the first he'd heard about the incident between the two women. "What is she talking about, Monique? What *scuffle*? What have you done now?"

The Frenchwoman threw Elise a nasty glare before turning to her husband for some damage control. "It was nothing, *cher*. I simply wanted to have a word with her, and the woman acted in a most hideous way. She attacked me, and I merely defended myself. It was over in an instant," she said, snapping her fingers for emphasis.

"Really, Monique," Alain said in dismay. "After we'd talked about this? I told you to stay away from Divia. It was finished."

Monique's nonchalant façade cracked wide open then, and she seemed to forget for the moment that Elise and C.C. were avidly listening to the conversation. "Finished? Don't be such a naïve fool! And *we* talked about nothing, Alain. You issued orders as if I were a wayward child." The woman shook back her hair and poked her husband in the chest. "As if *I* was the one who'd strayed, instead of you. You say it was finished, but did you really think I would sit by and let that woman ruin everything?"

Alain's expression hardened and he leaned in close to his wife's face. "I expected you to act with a small amount of dignity. But I can see that my expectations were perhaps too high. Now you may have involved us in a murder investigation."

With an oath, Alain turned on his heel and stormed away, leaving Elise and C.C. to deal with a fuming Monique.

"Well, I hope you're happy with the little scene you caused."

Elise gave the woman her most innocent look. "I'm so sorry, Monique. I truly didn't mean to cause trouble between the two of you. I had no idea that you hadn't told Alain about your run-in with Divia, or what the fight was about."

The woman took a deep breath and stared at Elise for a long moment as if trying to control her emotions before responding. Finally, she waved a hand in the air and shook her head. "Forget it. The whole incident has been blown out of proportion. This is the reason I said nothing to Alain about the horrible scene in the first place. He has a tendency to overreact, as you just witnessed."

"Men, huh?" C.C. gave the woman a congenial smile, then shook her head. "So dramatic. Besides, I'm sure you both have an alibi for

Friday night, right? You and your husband were probably out to dinner or something, like everyone else. So you won't have a thing to worry about when the police get around to questioning you about it."

C.C.'s comments were sheer genius, Elise, thought, and she wanted to laugh out loud. By the look of sheer panic that briefly crossed Monique's face, Elise was pretty sure no alibi would be forthcoming anytime soon, which was an interesting development. If the Toussaints weren't together on Friday night around the time of the murder, Monique would be scrambling to come up with something plausible. It also led to the question of where they each were during that crucial hour.

But she had to hand it to Monique. The woman recovered quickly.

"Yes, of course you are correct. Alain and I have nothing to worry about." She sniffed before adding, "Well, I really should catch up to him, smooth his ruffled feathers. Otherwise, he will brood. You understand."

"Yes, yes I do," C.C. said under her breath as they watched the Frenchwoman hurry away. Turning, she gave Elise a low five.

"*O-M-G!* That was awesome!" Elise said with a grin when Monique was out of hearing range.

C.C. returned the smile. "You bet. Scary French chick doesn't like it so much when someone else is dishing it out."

"She sure doesn't. Conniving wench."

C.C. batted her eyelashes and effected an awful French accent. "*Oh, Ele-e-ze. Zees must be quite unsettling for you and your fam-i-ly. Oh, no, I did not mean to cause offense.* Please. What a crock. She knew exactly what she was doing."

81

Elise laughed out loud at her friend's antics. "And did you see the look on her face when you mentioned the bit about having an alibi? I thought she was gonna pop a vein. That was a stroke of genius."

"Yeah. I got the feeling that perhaps Mr. and Mrs. Toussaint weren't enjoying each other's company on Friday night. I also think she had more on her mind than her husband off brooding somewhere when she hurried away to find him."

"And if they weren't together, it will be interesting to find out where they were and what they were doing."

C.C. nodded. "Perhaps one of them was drinking wine with the late Mrs. Larson?"

"Could be, but let's not get ahead of ourselves."

"Do you think Alain would lie for her? I mean, if neither of them has an alibi?"

Elise pursed her lips in thought. "I don't know. He seemed pretty pissed off, but then again, she is his wife. And to give himself an alibi I think it would be a necessary evil—something he would do whether he liked it or not."

"Oh, to be a fly on the wall when *that* conversation takes place."

"But if they weren't together and they try to say they were … well … there's always someone watching. Somebody will have seen something. We just have to find that somebody."

C.C. paused and narrowed her eyes in Elise's direction. "Are you going to tell Jackson about this?"

Elise nodded, and then heaved a sigh. "I'll have to be careful about it, though. He's so touchy about his investigations, especially after the fiasco with Uncle Edmond's murder inquiry."

"Well, yeah. That and you almost getting yourself killed over the whole thing. Our Jackson didn't take too kindly to that, either."

"I know, I know. But this is different. I'm just asking a few questions here and there, and it's all to make sure Gram is in the clear."

"Correct me if I'm wrong, but isn't that how your uncle's deal started out? Just asking a few questions? Then it was just checking out his house?"

"Geez, C.C., whose side are you on?" Elise asked with a frown.

"I'm always on your side, girlfriend. I'm just saying that you need to watch your back."

"Okay, okay," Elise relented. "But it's not just me snooping around this time, you know. There are four of us in this little sleuthing club. Remember?"

"Absolutely." C.C. nodded vigorously. "So, where do we go from here? And how do we get the dirt on the Toussaints?"

"I don't know. I guess we'll just have to keep our eyes and ears open. Now, let's look at the rest of the list."

The two women huddled over Elise's note pad for a moment before C.C. spotted her first problem. "Hey! What's Grace's name doing on here? She wouldn't hurt a fly. And she already said she didn't even know the Larsons."

Elise laid down her pen and faced her friend. "All right, now I realize that Grace is a friend and that she *said* she didn't know the Larsons, but come on, C.C. Did you see the look on her face when Divia's name was mentioned on Thursday afternoon?"

"She explained that, Elise."

"Yes, she said that Divia was an unusual name, and it is. But her look of recognition is why I asked her about it in the first place. I'm sorry, but her answer didn't quite cover it for me. And," Elise said, putting up a forefinger when her friend started to argue, "Toby Raymond had the same reaction to Grace's name Friday when Jackson and I ran into him and Maddy at The Plough's booth. And I have to say, his response was much stronger. The man turned positively white."

"Did he say why?"

"No. He blamed it on the heat. But if you'd have seen his face, C.C., trust me when I say that it had nothing to do with the weather and everything to do with name recognition. The question isn't if they know each other, but how."

"Well, you'll never convince me that Grace had anything to do with Divia's death. She's not that kind of person."

Elise didn't reply, but she knew from personal experience that the last person you expected could surprise you in the most hideous fashion in the blink of an eye. In any event, she thought it best to let it go, and the two spent the next thirty minutes concentrating on the other names on the list.

"Hey, you two."

Looking up, they watched Madison make her way around Third Coast's long line to River Bend's booth. "Geez, Divia's death has sure beefed up sales at Third Coast's booth."

"I know. It's crazy," Elise said. "Where've you been? And where's Ross? C.C. and I would like a break. It's been pretty slow and I'm starting to get hungry. Plus, we have some snooping to do."

"That's exactly what I've been doing. You'll never guess what I just witnessed."

C.C. went on high alert. "Yeah? What? Something juicy?"

Madison gave them both a sly smile. "Judge for yourself. I just saw Monique Toussaint and Alain's brother Philippe having a heated rendezvous behind one of the public buildings. And even better, I heard quite a bit of the conversation—and it wasn't pretty."

# EIGHT

"WELL, FOR CRYING OUT loud. Spit it out! Don't leave us hanging," Elise said as she and C.C. leaned in to hear the details of Madison's news.

"Yeah," C.C. added. "What were Monique and Philippe talking about?"

"Did it have to do with Divia's death?" Elise asked.

"And what do you mean by heated?" C.C. questioned further.

"Probably some kind of argument," Elise said turning toward her friend.

Frowning, Madison put up her hands, seeking to gain their attention. "Whoa, if you'd both shut up for a minute and let me get a word in, I'll explain. Geez!"

"Sorry, we got carried away," Elise said with a grin. "Go ahead. Tell us."

Her sister gave her a dirty look but relented and began her tale. "Okay, so I'm down on Restaurant Row getting coffee about twenty minutes ago when I look up and see Monique coming around the corner. She has this really intense look on her face. You know, like she's looking for something or someone."

Elise smiled to herself as she watched Madison unconsciously acting out the story she was telling them.

"Then she stops and waves toward the other end of the midway and calls Philippe's name. I look the other way and see him hurrying toward her. So they meet and have this brief conversation that I couldn't hear, and then they disappear between the booths in the direction of building D, which I thought looked really suspicious—"

"Wait," C.C. said, interrupting Madison's storytelling frenzy. "I thought you said you heard what they were saying?"

A slow smile spread across Madison's face. "I did—when I followed them back behind the building."

"Ohmygosh, Maddy!" C.C. exclaimed. "Did they see you?"

Madison rolled her eyes. "Please. Give me some credit, wouldja? I can be very stealthy when I want to be."

Elise laughed out loud and nudged C.C. "I can attest to that. More like sneaky, if you ask me."

Madison folded her arms and gave Elise a stubborn glare. "Do you want to hear the rest of this or not?"

Still chuckling, Elise gave her sister a go-ahead gesture with a sweep of her hand. "By all means, proceed, oh stealthy one."

Her sister made a face, but continued with her story. "Anyway, I followed them at a discreet distance and watched as they headed around the corner of the building. When I got to the corner myself, I took a quick peek and saw them disappear behind a copse of mesquite and cedar shrubs. Since it provided a fairly good screen, I snuck up as close as I could get."

"Wow. Look at you, little secret agent girl," C.C. commented, giggling. "I think I hear the producers of the next Bond movie calling your name."

"Laugh it up all you want, my friend, but I got results," Madison insisted. "They couldn't have moved much farther away because I could hear their conversation pretty clearly."

"Okay, but what was the conversation about?" Elise asked eagerly.

"Impatient much?" Madison replied with a smirk.

"Maddy!"

"All right, all right, keep your panties on. So, while I stood there on the other side of the makeshift screen, the two of them started to argue about Friday night and *alibis*. Well, it wasn't so much arguing, I guess. It sounded more like a frantic scramble to get their stories straight."

"I *knew* it!" Elise shouted and pointed a finger in C.C.'s direction. "Didn't I say Monique would be looking for a plausible alibi for the time of Divia's death? She's trying to get ahead of the game for when she's questioned."

C.C. nodded and replayed their earlier conversation with the French woman for Madison. "It seemed like a pretty good bet from her expressions and attitude that she and Alain weren't together Friday night. Instead of catching up with Alain like she said she was going to, she must have high-tailed it to Restaurant Row to find Philippe."

"Their conversation makes perfect sense now. I thought at the time that it seemed like something had happened to get Monique really fired up, but didn't know what. From the sound of things, Philippe was mostly wringing his hands during the whole thing and trying to calm her down."

Elise turned to her sister. "What exactly was said? Did you hear where they were Friday night?"

"Did they say anything incriminating?" C.C. asked.

Madison shook her head. "No, they didn't say anything about Friday night, but Monique said that they 'were in trouble', and if Alain 'found out' he wouldn't be inclined to cover for her. To which Philippe assured her that no one, least of all Alain, had any proof of what they'd done, so she needn't be too worried."

"Ah-ha!" Elise turned and gave C.C. a high-five. "What did I tell you? That sounds suspicious for sure. Did they give any details? Did you get an idea of what she meant or if it was connected to Divia's death?"

"Unfortunately, no," Madison replied.

"Crap," C.C. said with disappointment. "I guess it was wishful thinking to have expected them to out-and-out confess. It couldn't be that easy."

"They actually never mentioned Divia's name at all, but Philippe alluded to her when he said that Monique had been 'unwise' to engage 'the Larson bitch' the way she had—that it would only come back to bite them in the end."

Elise laughed. "And how did Monique react to that?"

"She sure as heck didn't like it, I can tell you," Madison said with a shake of her head. "She doesn't seem to take criticism very well. Anyway, he spent the next few minutes backpedaling and trying to make amends. 'I'm sorry, *cheri*. I'm just trying to be the voice of reason, *ma petite.*'" She giggled. "It was pretty pathetic the way he became this simpering doormat for her rampage."

"Though it's not a clear confession, it could definitely be what they were talking about," C.C. said. "It sounds pretty incriminating."

"What does?" Ross asked as he came up to the booth to stand next to Madison.

The three women spent the next fifteen minutes filling him in on the morning's events to bring him up to speed.

"Okay, I'll admit it does sound like Monique and her brother-in-law were up to something shady," he said when they wound down. "But to be honest, it seems more like a lovers' spat to me."

"What?" C.C. asked in a doubtful tone.

"Well, think about what was actually said," Ross continued. "If Alain 'found out'? 'No one, least of all Alain, had proof of what they'd done'? They could easily be talking about an affair."

"Man, that would take some stones to give your husband and his married lover grief while you were doing the horizontal mambo with his brother," C.C. replied with a sour look on her face.

"Be that as it may, and I hate to say it, but Ross is right. Their conversation doesn't really connect them to Divia's death in any way, at least not from what Maddy heard."

"Well, Philippe did say something else that was promising," Madison said. "He said he'd kept her secrets and protected her up to this point, and that he'd do whatever it took to make sure the truth wasn't revealed."

"Wow. That's a little more like it, but until we know for sure what they were up to, we keep digging. We also have more suspects on the list to check out."

Ross leaned down onto his elbows on the booth counter. "Look, I don't want to be the wet blanket on this whole down-low investigation, little sister. But we have to remember that we don't know for sure Divia's death was foul play."

Elise gaped at her brother. "She died of cyanide poisoning, Ross. How can that *not* be foul play?"

"Ah, ah, ah," he said, shaking his finger at her. "We don't know yet how she died, El. We don't even know for certain that cyanide was present. So far, it's all just guesswork."

He put up a hand as she was about to let him have it. "And before you take my head off, yes, it does look like that's what happened. And even though Jax has his suspicions, I will remind you of what he's always so fond of saying. Follow the evidence. Until he gets the confirmation back from Austin, we can't take anything for granted."

Elise heaved a sigh and really wanted to give him a hard shake, but she reminded herself that he was just stating facts and so decided not to hurt him. "True," she finally said with reluctance. "But I want to make sure Gram is in the clear when the reports come back, just in case."

"Hey, I'm with you on that," he replied with a nod. "But even if those reports come back listing cyanide as the cause of death, it still doesn't mean someone actually killed Divia."

"What are you saying?" Elise laughed. "She accidentally poisoned herself with cyanide? That seems a bit much, don't you think?"

"Not accidental. Don't be stupid," he replied with a frown. "I'm saying she could have taken her own life."

Madison spoke up with annoyance then, surprising everyone. "Oh, come on, Ross. Don't *you* be stupid. Divia Larson would never have taken her own life in a million years, and you know it."

"I agree," Elise said. "Not a chance in hell."

"And I would normally agree, as well," Ross nodded. "But there are the text messages and the phone call to Gram to think about."

"What about them?" Madison asked.

"Well, Divia wanted to talk to someone urgently about something she couldn't or wouldn't discuss with Garrett or Toby. Gram told me she sounded pretty upset." He shrugged. "Maybe she'd done something that she couldn't get past, something she saw no way out of."

"And you think she would just give up and commit suicide?" Elise scoffed. "I don't buy it in the least."

"I think she was way too vain and too much in love with herself to do something like that, no matter what she'd done or how bad she thought things would get," Madison added. "Suicide is a desperate way out, and although Divia was many things, she definitely wasn't the desperate type."

"Yeah," Elise chimed in. "Our Divia was no coward. She wouldn't have chosen suicide over manipulating her way around whatever problem she was having."

Ross stood and put up his hands in surrender. "Look, all I'm saying is let's keep our focus on the objective here and not get ahead of the evidence, okay? This was supposed to be just us keeping our eyes and ears open, maybe making some discreet inquiries. Let's not forget the fiasco of Uncle Edmond's murder and how snooping around almost got you killed, El. That's something I don't want to ever live through again."

Elise looked at C.C. She didn't need to hear what her friend was thinking because it was written all over her face. She'd voiced the same basic sentiment earlier.

Reaching over, Elise took Ross's hand. "Trust me when I say that I have no desire to live through anything like that again, either. So your point is well taken. We'll keep our focus on just finding out where everyone on the list was Friday night and leave the rest of it up to Jax, okay?"

He nodded reluctantly. "Okay. So, who else is on your list?"

Elise picked up her pad and read off the names. "Monique, Alain, and Philippe, Toby Raymond, Grace Vanderhouse, and Garrett Larson. Of course, there could be others we don't know about yet, but those are the most obvious suspects."

"Again, I still don't understand why you think Grace should be on that list," C.C. said with a pout. "She is the sweetest thing, and I'm telling you that she doesn't have it in her to kill anyone. Besides, she was in Austin on Friday night, remember? She was supposed to have dinner with us and had to cancel because something came up with the restaurant."

"Then find out for sure that's where she was and we'll take her off the list," Ross said. "Simple enough, right?"

C.C. grumbled a bit, but let it go just as Madison piped up about Toby Raymond.

"And why would you put Toby on the list? Or Garrett, for that matter? Toby was at dinner with us when Gram called. And Garrett was in Austin. Don't you think that lets them off the hook?"

Elise was grateful she didn't have to respond when Ross spoke up and took the heat off of her.

"Maddy, I'm sorry, but Toby came late to the restaurant, remember? He arrived just before Jax got Gram's call. And as for Garrett, we don't know for sure where he was. I'm sure Jax will check out his story and clear him if he can. But again, as we found out with Uncle Edmond's homicide investigation, they always look hard at immediate family first."

Elise's heart went out to her sister. It was obvious Madison was having a hard time with the notion that Toby was still a suspect. And she suddenly became aware that Madison had gotten much closer with him than anyone had understood.

Madison's next comment emphasized that realization. "But you were there at the motel, Elise. You saw how wrecked Toby was—how devastated they both were—when they found out Divia was dead."

Ross put his arm around Madison. "I know this is hard, Maddy, but we have to make sure that Gram's in the clear if this becomes a homicide investigation."

"Ross is right, sweetie," C.C. added. "Finding out where Toby was before he got to the restaurant will put him in the clear, as well."

"I guess." Madison heaved a sigh. "I suppose I can try and find out."

"And I'll see what I can uncover about where Grace was and what she was doing that night," C.C. said. She rolled her eyes at the look Elise shot her before adding, "and if there was a connection between her and the Larsons."

Elise grinned. "Good girl. Ross, since Alain was obviously not with his wife, do you think you can buddy up to him and see if you can get him to spill what he was doing Friday night?"

"I can try."

Elise nodded. "Good. So we have a game plan. Now, let's get it done as quickly as possible."

"Get what done as quickly as possible?"

The group had been so intent on their conversation that nobody noticed Jackson and Deputy Stockton walk up. Elise turned her notepad over as nonchalantly as she could with the hope that Jackson wouldn't notice what she'd written there.

"Hey, Jax," Ross said, gaining Jackson's attention as a distraction. "What are you guys doing out here? I thought you'd have your hands full with Divia Larson's death."

Elise noticed that Jackson gave her and her notepad the eye before turning to Ross.

"That's a fact. We just spoke to Garrett and got his information. We're going to interview the staff at Third Coast's booth to try and put together a timeline of Mrs. Larson's movements. The M.E. will give us an approximate time of death, but right now I'm more interested in what she did leading up to that point."

"How are Garrett and Toby doing?" Madison asked. "They were both in pretty awful shape last night, as you would expect."

Jackson scratched his head and nodded. "Garrett seems to be holding his own—at least, as best he can. Toby is another story. Doc Nagle went out and met with him again this morning. We haven't been able to get much out of him yet."

C.C. gestured toward Third Coast's booth and the long lines still forming across the aisle. "They've been bombarded over there all morning long. It's just gruesome."

"Well, we're going to give them a short reprieve as we interview the staff. So, we better get to it," Jackson said, then looked at Elise. "What time are you done today?"

Leaning against a post, she gave him a smile and wiggled her eyebrows. "What did you have in mind, Officer?"

He laughed and shook his head. "It's going to be probably six-thirty or so when I get a break and can head home. I thought I'd stop by the apartment if you're going to be there."

"Works for me, big guy. I should be home before then. Give me a call when you're on your way. I'll have a cold beer waiting."

"Cold beer?" Madison exclaimed with mock horror. "Sacrilege! You come from wine stock, mister. You're standing in the middle of a wine festival, for God's sake."

Jackson laughed out loud, a rich, warm sound that Elise felt all the way to her toes. "You know, Maddy, I hate to tell you, but sometimes wine just doesn't do the trick."

"I say again, blasphemy. But because I like you so much, I'll let it go. This time," she answered with a twinkle in her eye.

"Whew. I'm glad to hear it. Catch you guys later."

Nobody said a word for a few moments until Jackson and the other officer were out of earshot. Then Ross turned to Elise. "Are you going to tell Jax what we've learned so far?"

Elise narrowed her eyes in thought. "I don't know. I'll see what information I can get out of him first and then make that decision. It may be too soon, and I don't want him to spool up the lecture machine just yet. But at some point I'm gonna have to come clean with him—and hope he doesn't blow a gasket."

# NINE

JACKSON WAS UNDER NO illusion that the four little snoops at River Bend's booth were just innocently hanging out and chewing the fat mid-morning on a Saturday. They were up to something. He could almost smell it on the light autumn breeze.

It wasn't so much their words or actions. But the over-bright chatter and nervous body language that all four exhibited when they realized that he and Jim were standing there had his radar up.

He didn't get a good look at what Elise had written on her notepad, but when she turned it over the minute he arrived at the booth, it was a dead giveaway it had nothing to do with wine. It was so obviously something she didn't want him to see.

Inquisitive little twerp.

Fortunately for them, he had bigger fish to fry at the moment and didn't have time for their nonsense. However, come this evening, he and Elise were going to have the conversation.

Again.

He wondered how many times he would have to remind her to keep her pretty little nose out of his investigations before she finally did as he asked.

Because he was certain that's what she and her playmates had in the works. Almost getting herself killed after meddling in his last investigation had slowed her down for a short time, but it was beginning to look like even that hadn't completely put a stop to her snooping.

"So how do you want to do this?" Deputy Stockton asked, bringing him back to the business at hand. "You want to shut the booth completely down for the interviews? Or just take Third Coast's staff members one at a time?"

"Let's see how it goes. I don't want to disrupt their routine any more than we need to, and I definitely don't want to add to the gossip that's probably already out there."

As it turned out, the Third Coast staff was happy to comply and willing to shut down for as long as it took to complete the interviews. It seemed they were running low on wine after the rush they'd had all morning and needed to restock from their trailer. While Jackson allowed two of the four employees to retrieve the new stock, he and Jim took the remaining two aside to interview separately.

Kayla McGovern had been with Third Coast winery the longest of the four, and Jackson accompanied her to a set of picnic tables in a quiet spot behind the booths.

"This is all so sad and terribly shocking," the short brunette began when they were seated at the table. "I know there were some who had issues with her, but Divia was usually quite pleasant to me. I mean, sure, she could be difficult at times, but I can't believe someone would kill her. Who on earth would do something like this?"

Jackson frowned. "We don't know exactly what happened yet, Kayla. I'm curious as to why you think this is a homicide?"

The woman looked taken aback for a moment. "Oh. Well, you know I don't like to listen to gossip," she murmured with a look that clearly said otherwise. "But that's kind of the scuttle-butt that's been going around this morning. So, are you saying that she wasn't deliberately poisoned? That maybe it was an accident of some kind?"

Jackson pulled out his notepad and pen—and mentally counted to ten. He was rarely surprised by how quickly rumors spread in cases like this—there was always someone listening when you least expected it—but it still chapped his ass. Rumors often had only a passing nod at the truth and became outlandish in nature in a New York minute.

"What I'm saying is that until I hear back from the medical examiner in Austin, I won't speculate on anything." His reply was more abrupt than he'd meant it to be, and with a sigh, he smiled to soften his approach. "What I would like is for you to tell me how the day went yesterday here at the festival. We're trying to put together a timeline of what Mrs. Larson did, where she went, that sort of thing. You worked the booth yesterday?"

Kayla nodded and folded her arms on the table. "Yes. I came in before the doors opened and didn't leave until after closing."

"Was Mrs. Larson here during the day?"

"Off and on." The woman tilted her head and gazed at a point over his left shoulder as if looking back on the previous day. "I seem to remember her coming in sometime around mid-morning, maybe ten-ish. She didn't like the way the booth was organized or how Ricky had stacked the crates at the back. Said it looked cluttered. She gave us some *direction* on reorganizing the booth. Unfortunately, with Divia, direction was always more like ordering folks around. But she was the boss."

"Reorganizing. Uh-huh." Jackson made a few notes without looking up. "And did anything out of the ordinary happen that you can recall?"

"No. Not that I can think of," Kayla replied. "At least nothing like the fireworks of Thursday morning."

Jackson looked up at that. "What do you mean? What fireworks?"

The woman seemed confused for a moment. "Oh, I thought you would have heard. It was quite a display. Divia and that Frenchwoman, Monique Toussaint had a rather explosive row right there in front of the booth. A real catfight."

"Really? Do you know what it was about?" Jackson asked with a frown.

"Well, sure. Everyone heard what they were fighting over. It was loud and proud. Monique told Divia to stay away from her husband or she'd be sorry."

"This fight was over Alain Toussaint?"

Kayla nodded. "It got really ugly, too. Divia told the woman that if she couldn't control her husband it wasn't her problem. That's when Monique asked Divia if Garrett knew about Toby's 'funny business' with the winery's books."

"Wait. The winery's books? What did she mean by that? Is there a problem with the winery's accounting?"

"I don't know, but Divia was visibly shaken by the comment, I can tell you. The next instant they sort of launched at each other. It was crazy—punching, scratching, hair-pulling, the whole bit."

Jackson worked to keep a straight face in light of Kayla's description. "So what happened then? How did this catfight end?"

"Well, Toby showed up about the same time as another man. I think it was Mr. Toussaint's brother. Anyway, they pulled the two women apart and tried to diffuse the situation as quickly as they could."

"And that ended the fight?" Jackson asked, making a few more notes.

"Pretty much," Kayla replied. "But Monique made a very nasty parting shot before the man dragged her away. She said that Divia better watch her step or she just might end up dead."

Jackson's head snapped up at that comment and he narrowed his eyes at her. "She actually used those words?"

Kayla nodded and an almost gleeful look crossed the woman's face. "Yes. She did. And Divia was in such a state when they finally walked away that she yelled at poor Ms. DeVries when she was just trying to help."

"What? Wait a minute. Miss Abby was there during this whole thing?"

"Well, no, not the entire thing. She and the other two girls came running toward the end."

Jackson tilted his head and gave her a quizzical glance. "Other two girls?"

"Yes, Ms. DeVries' granddaughter and her friend. They were working the booth with her."

Here was another thing Elise was going to have to explain when he went by the apartment later. She and C.C. witnessed the incident, and she'd said nothing to him about it.

"Anyway," Kayla continued. "Ms. DeVries was just trying to offer support, but Divia acted horribly toward her. Then everyone went their separate ways, and it was over."

"Okay. Well, thank you for your input. It's been very helpful. Anything else you want to add?"

"No. I think that's it." Kayla started to get up, and then sat back down. "You know, now that I think about it, there was one other thing that I noticed yesterday."

"And what was that?"

"I don't know that it has anything to do with what's happened, but since you're looking at a timeline…"

"Yes?"

"Well, I was on a break out here, and I saw Divia having what looked like a fairly tense conversation with another woman."

"A tense conversation?" Jackson asked, wishing Kayla would just get to the point. "Do you know who this woman was?"

Kayla shook her head. "I didn't know her, but she looked familiar. I think she was from one of the booths over on Restaurant Row. Anyway, I couldn't hear what they were saying, but Divia was pretty animated. She seemed to be trying to convince the other woman of something, but the other woman was not very receptive and looked terribly upset."

Jackson thought back to the incident on Friday at The Plough's booth when he and Elise had run into Toby and Madison. When Grace Vanderhouse's name had been mentioned, Toby's reaction had been extreme, though he'd tried to blame the humidity. Was it possible that Grace was the woman Kayla had seen speaking with Divia? "Kayla, if you saw this other woman again, do you think you would recognize her?"

"Oh, absolutely. I had an unobstructed view of the whole thing." She pointed to an area to the left of where they sat. "It happened right over there."

"All right then," Jackson said. "We'll check out what you've told me and be in touch. Thank you."

As Jackson watched Kayla make her way back to the booth, he turned this new information over in his mind. An interview with Monique Toussaint was definitely in order, and he'd have to speak to Miss Abby, Elise, and C.C. about the events of Thursday as well.

He also needed to positively identify the other woman from yesterday's "tense conversation" and find out what that was all about. With a heavy sigh, he got up and headed back to the booth himself. He definitely had his work cut out for him. And with the festival ending tomorrow afternoon, very little time to sort it all out.

———

It was almost three by the time they'd finished interviewing the Third Coast staff, and Jackson's stomach was grumbling. "Let's go over to Restaurant Row and pick up something. We can compare notes while we eat."

"Sounds good," Jim replied. "I'm starving. We could get lunch at The Plough's booth, maybe check out your theory regarding the Vanderhouse woman."

"That was just what I was thinking," he responded. Jackson had filled Jim in about the meeting between Divia and the mystery woman that Kayla had mentioned. He'd also told him about Toby Raymond's reaction to Grace Vanderhouse's name on Friday and his theory that Grace may have been the woman Divia had met with behind the booths.

"I mean, sure, it could just be an odd coincidence, and we don't know if the Larsons and the Vanderhouse woman even knew each other," Jim said with a wry smile. "But then, I do know how you feel about coincidences."

"Yeah, it might be a stretch to connect the two, but it's always prudent to cover the bases." Jackson shot the other deputy a grin. "I've got an idea, so follow along with whatever I say if Grace is there."

Jim laughed. "Don't I always?"

Though it was mid-afternoon and well past the lunch hour, The Plough had a short line when they arrived. Jackson spotted Grace working furiously on orders at the back of the stall.

"She looks pretty busy," Jim commented.

"Yeah. Let's eat and go over our notes, give her some time to clear the crowd. Then we can come back and have a chat with her afterward."

They gave the woman at the counter their orders, and taking their drinks, headed for the picnic tables out back while they waited for Grace to finish.

Once they sat down, Jackson began by filling Jim in on the cat-fight that Kayla had also described to him.

"Yep," Jim said when he'd finished. "I got pretty much the same story, with some variations, from both of the staff members I interviewed. Man, I gotta say, I would've dearly loved to have seen that!"

"Sounds like it was quite a spectacle," Jackson said with a chuckle. "I'm going to talk to Elise and Miss Abby about it later. But I think we need to interview Monique Toussaint first thing in the morning. Since the festival is over tomorrow afternoon, I asked the M.E. for a rush on the autopsy, so hopefully I'll hear something soon.

Maybe it will give us an indication of whether we're dealing with a homicide or not."

Stockton nodded and took a swig of his soda. "That would be handy to know. If this was murder, we don't want suspects leaving town prematurely."

"Yes. Long-distance investigation is something I don't want to have to do."

"Hello, deputies."

Looking up, Jackson watched Grace Vanderhouse walk up to their table carrying their food. "Hey, Grace. Are you serving orders today as well as cooking?"

She laughed. "Stella said you were here, and we're having a lull, so I thought I'd bring your sandwiches out. We appreciate the business."

"Well, the food here is top notch, I'll give you that." Jackson watched her set the tray down on the table. "And though I can't wait to dig into mine, there is another reason for our visit."

Grace's smile faded, and Jackson thought he saw a quick flash of fear come and go in her eyes. In that moment, he had a gut feeling that his theory was right on the money.

So he went with it.

"Grace, we're investigating Divia Larson's death and putting together a timeline. It's come to our attention that you met with Mrs. Larson yesterday afternoon. I need to ask you about that meeting."

Grace visibly paled, and her eyes widened slightly. "Where did you hear that?" she countered.

It was a delay tactic, and not a particularly successful one. And by the look on her face, she knew it. Jackson could clearly see her alarm rising. Though she was obviously striving to get her emotions under control, she wasn't doing a very good job of that, either.

"We actually have a witness who saw the two of you out behind Third Coast's booth. And from the description, you were quite upset when you left. Want to tell us about it?"

Her façade crumbled at that point. She took a deep breath and blew it out slowly, before looking around to see who was in earshot of their conversation. When she seemed satisfied that nobody was close enough to hear, she sat down next to Jackson at the table. "Okay, yes, I met with Divia yesterday. But it's not what you think. It had nothing to do with her death, I swear."

"I don't think anything yet, Grace. Like I said, we're just putting together a timeline," Jackson said. He pulled out his notepad, and the look he gave her was direct. "Why don't you just tell us what happened and let us determine if it's connected or not."

Grace leaned on the table and put her face in her hands for a moment, before looking up and dropping a bombshell in their laps. "Twenty-two years ago, Divia Larson was married to my father. She was my ex-stepmother."

# TEN

JIM STOCKTON PAUSED WITH his sandwich halfway to his mouth, and then slowly lowered it back to the paper plate. "I beg your pardon. Did you say Divia Larson was your *stepmother*, Grace?"

"*Ex*-stepmother. And it was a very long time ago."

"What happened? Judging by your tone, I take it you didn't keep in touch with her," he said.

She gave a snort and shook her head. "No. I had no idea she and Toby were even in Texas."

Jackson watched a flood of emotions flow across Grace Vanderhouse's face before she quickly recovered and pretended disinterest. It wasn't lost on him that she'd ignored the first part of Jim's question, but they'd get to that later. Right now, he was more interested in her meeting yesterday with Divia.

"Grace, how did you two hook up here at the festival?" he asked. "Did you initiate yesterday's meeting or did she?"

"She did." Grace looked out over the paddocks beyond the fence as if thinking back on the meeting. "She came by the booth yesterday afternoon. I could tell the minute I saw her that she'd figured out who I was. I tried to ignore her, pretend like I didn't know her, but she just waited me out. Divia was good at that."

"So she must have seen you at some point earlier," Jim said. "And recognized you?"

Grace laughed out loud and shot an amused look at the deputy. "Oh, good Lord, no! My dad and I ceased to exist for Divia twenty-two years ago—when she cleaned out the bank accounts, took Toby, and disappeared into the night. I don't know how she knew where to find me, or that I was even here, but if I had to guess I'd say it was probably Toby who told her."

"Toby?" Jackson frowned. "Had you seen him or talked to him?"

Grace blew out a breath. "I don't know how he found me either—I certainly wouldn't have recognized him. He was ten years old the last time I saw him. Anyway, he cornered me on the midway yesterday about midafternoon."

Jackson exchanged looks with Jim. He knew exactly how Toby knew Grace was here at the festival—had been there when he'd found out. He'd known at the time something was up, though he didn't know what. Looking back, Toby's reaction to Grace's name made perfect sense now.

"But until yesterday you had no contact with either of them?" Jackson asked.

"No. None," she replied with a stony look. "I know my dad looked for them for quite awhile after they left, but he never found out where they'd gone. And like I said, I had no idea they were here until I saw her on Thursday."

"Wait. Thursday?" Jim looked perplexed. "You just said that you'd had no contact with her before yesterday?"

"I hadn't," Grace said with a quick shake of her head. "I was at River Bend's booth on Thursday morning talking to C.C. and Elise just before the Larsons arrived. When I listened to the girls talking about her I couldn't help but wonder if it was the same woman. Then here she came, prancing her way up the midway like the queen of the world. She looked almost exactly as I remembered her—just older."

"But you didn't talk to her or make contact at that point?" Jackson asked.

"No. I got out of there before they made it to the booth. I was afraid of what I'd do or say." Grace closed her eyes and paused. She obviously needed a moment to collect herself. When she reopened them and continued, she didn't even try to hide her resentment.

"You have to understand, Deputy. My father loved that woman and was willing to raise Toby as his own. Hell, I was just a child, but I loved them both, too. When she took every penny we had and ran away without a word ... well, it was hard on both of us, but it nearly killed my father. Oh, he tried to give me everything I needed, but he was never the same after that."

"Sounds like you grew up pretty angry," Jim said quietly.

Grace's head snapped in his direction. "Angry? You bet! Have you ever had to watch the self-destruction of a loved one, knowing there was nothing you could do to stop it?" Rage flared in her eyes. "Now, think about that from a child's point of view. I was six years old when she pulled her disappearing act. I watched my father *pine* for that woman until the day he died. She stole from him, broke his heart, and left him—left us both—without a word. Yet, even then he continued to love her until he took his last breath."

She shook her head and made an obvious effort to rein in her emotions where Divia Larson was concerned. "So yes, Deputy, it would be fair to say I grew up furious at Divia. Her actions killed my father just as surely as if she'd put a gun to his head and pulled the trigger."

"But after all those years, did you have enough pent-up rage to retaliate?" Jim asked. "To do her harm?"

Grace scrubbed her hands over her face and sighed. When she finally looked up, her temper had been replaced with something close to regret. "I suppose I would be lying if I said that the thought had never crossed my mind. It's a terrible thing to have to accept that about myself—that there were times when I fantasized about finding her, hurting her the way she'd hurt us. But in the end, what would it have accomplished? My father has been dead for nine years. Nothing can change that, right? Actually, Toby's the one I feel sorry for—having to live with her ridicule."

"Ridicule?" Jim asked. "How so? Did he and his mother not have a good relationship?"

"He was only ten years old when she took him and vanished." Grace folded her arms and leaned down on the table. "I don't know what their relationship became in the years after they left, but back then she used to badger him unmercifully. Anytime he'd screw up even a little, she'd tell him what a loser his biological father was and how if he wasn't careful he'd end up the same way. Even at six years old, I felt bad for him when she'd start in. He was just a kid."

Jim nodded. "So, his real dad wasn't in the picture?"

"Oh no. Divia didn't talk about him at all, except when she was berating Toby. I don't know if the man is still alive, but I don't think Toby's ever met him."

"What was the meeting about yesterday, Grace?" Jackson asked after jotting down a few notes. "She came looking for you. What did she want?"

"She said we needed to clear the air—that she wanted to try to explain what had happened all those years ago—why she felt the need to leave."

"And what was her reasoning?" Jim asked.

"She blathered on about fearing for her life, that she thought Toby's dad had found them and she couldn't risk putting Toby in harm's way, so she'd taken him and ran. She made out like Toby's dad was some kind of maniac and she just did what any good mother would do."

"But you weren't buying her story?" Jackson asked.

"Not a word. She cleaned out the bank accounts and left us with nothing."

Jackson made some notes and then looked up. "Did you ask her about that?"

Grace laughed. "Oh yeah. She didn't have a decent answer, other than to say that I was too young back then to understand her peril. I don't know why she took Toby and left us that way, but it doesn't really matter." Grace made a contemptuous sound. "Her dog and pony show yesterday was nothing but crap. Smoke and mirrors. What she really wanted to do was cover her ... bases."

Jackson gave her a perplexed look. "What are you talking about, Grace? What *bases*?"

The chef's face hardened and she stared at him for a moment before speaking. "Divia disappeared with Toby in the middle of the night twenty-two years ago—just vanished. Well, as it turns out, she never bothered with divorcing my father after they left. She was still married to him when she hitched her traveling circus to Garrett Larson's money train. Since she had no idea Dad had passed away—again, because she didn't give a shit—she was nervous that Garrett would find out."

"So she was worried about polygamy?" Jim asked.

"Yeah. Classy, huh?" Grace chuckled but didn't sound amused. "She didn't even ask about my dad. She just wanted to make sure I didn't squeal on her. Said it wouldn't do anyone any good at this point, that it would just cause trouble and hard feelings. Do you believe that?"

"And did you set her straight?" Jackson asked, glancing up from his notes. "Did you tell her your father was dead?"

When she turned to him, Jackson knew the answer by the sly look that came into her eyes before she spoke. Evidently, Grace had found a way to hurt Divia after all—or at least to give her a nice, hard jab.

"No," she finally said. "I told her I needed to get back to work, that I didn't have time to talk to her. I let her twist in the wind for a few hours. Just for old-times' sake."

"For a few hours?" Jackson asked with a frown. "Did you talk to Divia again after that?"

"Yes." Grace nodded and made a face. "She practically begged me to come to her motel after the festival closed. She said Garrett would be in Austin, and we could talk uninterrupted. That's why I couldn't make dinner with the group last night."

Jackson exchanged glances with Jim, and he knew the other deputy was probably thinking the same thing. "Grace, what time did you go out to the motel?"

"I left here at twenty after six, so it must have been six forty, six forty-five. Why?"

"Well, it makes you possibly the last person to see Mrs. Larson alive," Jim replied.

The color drained from Grace's face, and her eyes went wide. "Oh my God! You can't think that *I* poisoned Divia. Because I left just after seven, and she was alive and well. Okay, maybe she wasn't happy—she didn't care for what I had to say—but she was definitely alive when I left. I swear."

Jackson nodded, thinking that it remained to be seen. "One last question, Grace. Did you bring anything with you when you went to see her at the motel?"

Though he didn't have proof yet of his theory that Divia Larson had been murdered, he suspected someone had brought the wine to the motel with malicious intent. That the same someone had shared that wine with her and then washed out the glass they'd used to cover their tracks. And he had a gut feeling that the wine had been the vehicle used to poison her.

However, Grace shook her head, and at the confused look on her face, his gut also told him that it probably wasn't Grace who had brought the wine. However, his gut had been wrong on occasion, and Grace could be just a really good actress.

"No," she answered with a shake of her head. "I didn't bring anything with me."

"And you didn't have a glass of wine with her while you were there? Maybe from the bottle on the dresser?"

"No. Trust me, I wasn't there long enough to have a glass of vino with her. And there wasn't a bottle on the dresser that I saw. Why do you ask?"

"Just clearing up a few things," he replied vaguely. "Where did you go when you left the motel?"

"Meeting with Divia after all these years, seeing her through adult eyes … well, let's just say that I was in no mood for company," she said. "So I drove to Austin. I got home about eight fifteen, though I don't have anyone to corroborate my story."

Jackson nodded and put away his notepad. "Thanks for your time, Grace. And for being so open with us. The reports haven't come back from the M.E. yet, but I might have more questions for you once they do."

"I understand," she said as she got up from the table. "I'll be around if you need me."

Jackson watched her walk away then turned back to Jim. "What do you think?"

"I don't know," the other deputy said with a shrug. "She's definitely got enough rage underneath the surface to do the deed—given the right opportunity. And there's no way she was ever going to forgive Mrs. Larson for past sins, no matter how the woman would have begged. Plus, I believe pretty much everything she said, but I don't think she's told us the whole story."

"Agreed. I think there's definitely more to it than she was willing to let on. But what's she holding back? That's the question."

———

While they were there at the festival, Jackson decided they could at least snag Elise and C.C. to find out more about the catfight that had taken place on Thursday. Miss Abby wasn't at the venue this afternoon, so they'd have to run out to River Bend later. They'd pretty much gotten the story from the interviews with Third Coast's staff, but he wanted a view from all sides.

There was a small crowd at the counter as he and Jim walked up to the booth, so they waited off to the side until he could catch Elise's eye. When she saw him, she smiled and waved him over.

"Hey-ya, handsome. Did you finish your chats with the Third Coast folks?" she asked as she bagged the last customer's purchase.

"We did. All finished up over there, but I've got some questions for you and C.C."

"For us?" C.C. asked with a look of surprise. "What about?"

Jackson leaned against the counter and folded his arms. "Evidently there were quite the fireworks here on Thursday that y'all failed to mention. Care to tell me about it now?"

Elise frowned. "Fireworks? What are you talking about, Jax?"

"Don't play dumb, pal. I have it on good authority that you two were front and center when Divia and Monique Toussaint went a couple rounds right over there." He hooked a thumb over his shoulder in the general vicinity of Third Coast's booth.

Elise scoffed. "Oh that. It was just your run of the mill catfight. Wasn't really that big of a deal."

"Really? Why don't you tell me about it anyway? Let me decide if it's a big deal or not."

His tone was a bit pissy, and her reaction was likewise. "Like I said, it was just some hair-pulling, scratching, biting fun. I would assume that you heard all about it from the staff over at Third Coast."

"Elise." He tilted his head and narrowed his eyes. "I'm askin' you."

"Okay, okay. Don't get your panties in a wad, Officer. It's not like we were deliberately trying to hide anything from you. Geez, what do you want to know, already?"

Jackson rubbed his eyes—and prayed for patience. "Start at the beginning and tell us your version of what happened."

Obviously unable to contain herself, C.C. jumped right in. "It all started when the scary French chick showed up and called Mrs. Larson out. At least, that's what it looked like from here. Elise had gone on a break and I couldn't really hear exactly what was said, but there was a bit of arguing, and they shoved each other around a little."

"That's about the time I got back," Elise added. "Monique was yammering about Divia staying away from Alain, and Divia was telling her that it wasn't her problem if Monique couldn't control him."

"Yeah, and then French chick says something about Toby and 'financial funny business'. Boy, Mrs. Larson did *not* like that," C.C. said. "That was about the time they got into it. It was quite a rumble."

"Uh-huh," Jackson replied. "And how did you two and Miss Abby get into the middle of it?"

Elise gasped. "What? Who told you that?"

"Never mind. Just answer the question. How did you get involved?"

C.C. came to Elise's aid immediately. "Well, come on, Jax. We had no choice. Miss Abby went charging over there. What did you want us to do? Let her jump in without backup?"

Jackson sighed and pinched the bridge of his nose. "Just tell me the rest."

"To be fair, by the time we got over there Toby and Philippe had already broken them apart," Elise said. "Though Monique wasn't

116

quite ready to let it go. She yelled something about Divia ending up dead if she didn't back off."

Jackson nodded. "Yes, we heard about that. What I want to know is what was said between Divia and Miss Abby."

He watched the two women exchange looks, before Elise heaved a sigh. "Jax, it was nothing. Divia had just been embarrassed in front of a crowd of people. She lashed out at Gram when she was just trying to offer help."

C.C. nodded. "Yeah. Miss Abby only asked if she was okay, and Mrs. Larson lit right into her. Said Miss Abby didn't really care and that she should go back to her own booth and leave them alone. She also made it clear that Mr. Larson was off limits. Like Miss Abby would do something like that. Lame."

"Jax, why are you asking about Gram like this? She didn't do anything but offer support to Divia. And Gram was the one Divia called for help later, remember? The person you really should be talking to is Monique Toussaint. There's something hinky going on with her and Philippe. I'm sure of it."

Jackson stared at her for a moment before answering. "We still have several people to talk to, Elise," he said and then pointed a finger at her. "And just as a heads up, you and I are going to have a little chat later tonight about a very familiar subject. So get ready."

# ELEVEN

ELISE HAD NO DOUBT in her mind what subject Jackson had alluded to earlier. She figured she was going to get the lecture about staying out of his investigations.

Again.

She'd really tried not to interfere this time, but couldn't just stand by and do nothing when her family was involved. To that end, she was still working out how she was going to give Jackson the information she and the others had put together so far without admitting they'd been doing some digging on their own.

*Dicey. Very dicey.*

To keep her mind off the coming retribution, she decided to head out to the vineyard to check on her grandmother before going home. Divia's death had been hard on Abigail, not only because she'd found the body, but also because Garrett Larson had taken his wife's death poorly. Elise knew her Gram still had a soft spot for her former sweetheart and wanted to help him in any way she could.

Unfortunately, her grandmother wasn't thinking about her own predicament. Abigail hadn't told anyone about the texts Divia had sent her—or about the phone call begging her to come to the motel until they'd met her at the scene on Friday night—after Divia's death.

Since Ross, Caroline, and Madison had met Elise and Jackson at the restaurant, and Laura had gone to dinner with Neil Paige, the vineyard foreman; that left no one to corroborate Abigail's story or timeline. Elise figured Jackson would look to verify the phone call and the texts her grandmother had said she'd received. But in the meantime, Elise and her sleuthing team would do everything they could to make sure her grandmother was in the clear when Divia's death was confirmed a homicide.

As Elise was certain it would be very soon.

Jackson had asked the M.E. to put a rush on the autopsy and various reports. She figured he would be hearing something today, or at the very latest, tomorrow. She had a bad feeling about what those reports would hold and stewed over it all the way to the vineyard.

When she arrived at the house, she found her mother in her office going over quarterly reports.

"Hey, Mom. Cookin' the books?" she asked as she plopped down in a chair. "How's it looking? Are we going to stay in business?"

"Actually, considering the whole Lodge Merlot balloon payment debacle of a couple months ago, we're not doing too badly." Laura looked up and smiled. "Your sister did a spectacular job with the Wilkinson wedding, which turned out to be quite lucrative."

Elise nodded. "I know that Mayor Wilkinson was very pleased—as was her daughter—and they were generous with their praise."

"They were generous with their cash as well," Laura replied with a grin. "With the subsequent events we've had since then from the positive word-of-mouth, and a good harvest this season, we'll be able to make the payment on the lodge loan and put a tidy sum away to help keep us fluid when things get lean again. If all goes well, we'll be able to actually pay off the loan in its entirety by the first quarter of next year on schedule."

"That would be awesome."

"Agreed. We won't know for a couple of weeks, but I'm hoping the festival numbers will look good as well. That would give us a nice boost." Laura gave her a sly look. "But you didn't come in here to listen to the financial report. What's up?"

Elise blew out a breath. "I wanted to stop by and see how Gram was holding up. She made out like she was unaffected by the whole mess last night, but I know she's got to be pretty upset by it."

"Well, of course I am," Abigail said from the doorway. "I'm not made of stone, Elise Brianna."

"No, I know that, Gram. That's not what I meant."

Abigail waved her back down when she started to get up. "I know it's not, and I'm sorry. I didn't mean to snap." She sank into the chair next to Elise. "I guess Divia's death has me more disturbed than I realized—that and the fact that Garrett and I have history—however ancient."

Elise nodded. "How's Mr. Larson doing? Have you talked to him?"

"Briefly." Abigail shook her head. "He's a wreck—as you would expect—and trying not to show it. I was there for his interview, and what worries me the most is that he wasn't up front with Jackson."

Elise sat up a little straighter and frowned. "What do you mean, Gram?"

Laura leaned on the desk and gave her mother a frank look. "Do you mean Garrett lied to Jackson, Mom? Because if he did, and you have knowledge of that, you're obligated to tell Jackson."

"Please." Abigail made a face. "I'm obligated to do no such thing. Besides, I don't know that Garrett lied per se, but I've known that man for a lot of years. And though we haven't exactly kept in touch, I can still tell when he's being less than forthcoming with pertinent information."

She gave a tired sigh, and when she continued it was with sadness. "He just lost his wife and he's struggling, Laura. I don't know exactly what he left out of his interview, but I have a bad feeling that Jackson is going to find out what it is, and it will come back to bite Garrett in the butt."

"Do you think Mr. Larson knows something about his wife's death, Gram?"

"I don't see how. And he's taking it pretty hard." Abigail shook her head. "But if he does know something, he's learned some mean acting skills over the years. Anyway, it was when he was talking about where he was last night that my bullshit radar kicked in."

"Mom. For crying out loud." Laura sat back in her chair and rolled her eyes. "Garrett went into Austin for a meeting, right? Or at least, that's what he'd indicated. Are you saying that's not where he actually went?"

"He did say he'd been at a meeting in Austin at the Driskell Hotel from five to nine, but I was watching his body language, and I don't think he was. Or at least, not the entire time." Abigail rubbed her forehead, as if a headache was brewing. "I don't know. I could be wrong, but I have a terrible feeling that Jackson is going to find discrepancies in his story. Discrepancies that will require some fast talking for Garrett to explain."

———

Later that evening, her grandmother's words about being able to read Garrett Larson played over in Elise's mind when she opened her front door to find Jackson on the landing. One look at his face told her that he was not pleased and things were probably going to get heated.

"Well, geez, Jax, don't stand on principle. Come on in," she said as he stormed past her without a word and headed into the living room. Closing the door, she followed him cautiously and watched him pace for a bit before prodding him to talk to her. "Okay, would you just go ahead and get it out before it chews a hole in your gut," she said at length.

He stopped suddenly and turned his angry glare in her direction like a white-hot laser. "You're gonna want to give me a minute here, Elise Brianna," he said with an edgy tone that had Chunk heading for the bedroom to get out of the line of fire. "Because I'm feeling more than a little pissy at the moment."

"Uh-huh. I can see that," she said with a wide-eyed look.

In all the years they'd known each other, she'd seen Jackson in full-on furious mode only a handful of times. This was more than his standard 'stay-out-of-my-investigation' annoyance. Obviously, something else had happened, and he'd get to it in his own sweet time. So, she did the prudent thing—she sat down on the sofa to wait.

When he finally got to that point, he stopped trying to wear a hole in the carpet and jabbed a finger at her. "You just don't learn, do you? You promised me, El. You said you would stay out of this mess. '*No, Jackson, my days of snooping around are over, I promise.*' Isn't that what you told me?"

"Jax—"

"I had the joy of interviewing the Toussaints today," he snapped, cutting her off. "And imagine my surprise when I found out that not only had you and your pal C.C. pumped them for information, but also that Ross evidently questioned Alain Toussaint quite thoroughly about his whereabouts on Friday night."

"Oh."

*Crap.* Leave it to Ross to be as subtle as a sledge hammer.

"Yeah. Nice, Elise. So, what? Instead of poking around on your own, you enlisted not only C.C. this time but Ross as well? Did you get Maddy in on the act, too?"

When she didn't answer right away, she watched an incredulous look light up his face. "Oh-my-*Lord*! You did, didn't you?"

"Okay, if you'll calm down for a minute I'll explain. It's not as bad as you're making it out to be," she said before he could spool up again.

"Not as bad—" He snorted and shook his head. "Really? Because when Monique Toussaint asked me if the Becketts had been put on the sheriff's payroll to help with the investigation, I gotta tell you, if *seemed* pretty bad to me."

Elise blinked up at him. "I beg your pardon?"

His bark of laughter was anything but amused. "You know, those were the exact words that came out of my mouth when she asked me that."

"Ooh, that really gets to me!" Annoyed, she leapt up from the sofa to do some pacing of her own before stopping and pointing a finger at him in the same way he'd done to her moments ago. "She knows we're dating, and that manipulative wench is just trying to deflect the spotlight, that's all. She doesn't have an alibi, and if she told you anything different, she's lying through her teeth." Almost without taking a breath, she rambled on with her rampage. "And let me just say, she's one to talk. She probably didn't tell you that *we* didn't go looking for *them*. She and Alain stopped by the booth first thing this morning— mostly to needle me and pump *me* for information."

When she finally paused to take a breath, Jackson put up a hand. "Hang on a minute. They came by the River Bend booth this morning?"

"That's what I'm trying to tell you," she replied with a note of irritation. "And almost the first damn thing out of her mouth was to ask if we'd heard about Divia's death. Then she made some thinly veiled accusations about Gram and Garrett, which I wasn't about to let her get away with, so C.C. and I turned the tables on her, gave her a few things to think about."

"Of course you did," he said, and pressed his lips together, but not before she saw them twitch with mirth.

Narrowing her eyes at him, she slapped a hand on her hip. "Don't you dare laugh at me, Jackson Landry. That heinous French floozy has more to hide than the rest of us combined. No way does she get to point fingers, and especially not at my grandmother."

"All right, all right. Take it down a notch, champ." He chuckled but then sobered right up. "It may get you off that particular hook, El, but it doesn't explain Ross's behavior, does it? You want to tell me about that?"

She squeezed her eyes shut for a moment, and then squinted up at him. "Okay, that was probably a bit over the line. But I promise you, all we've been doing is keeping our eyes and ears open … mostly."

"Elise."

"Come on, Jax, what does it hurt? It's not like we're nosing around or interrogating suspects. Well, with the exception of Ross's indelicate handling of his chat with Alain Toussaint. He was just supposed to see if he could find out where the man was Friday night, because he wasn't with Monique."

"Oh, for the love of mud. Seriously?" Jackson shook his head.

At the look on his face, Elise caved. "Okay, maybe C.C. was going to talk to Grace Vanderhouse about where she was last night, and Maddy was supposed to find out Toby's location before he got to the restaurant, but that's it. I swear."

While he just continued to stare at her like she was some kind of new organism under a microscope, she threw her hands in the air and went on the defensive. "Look, we talked about it and decided that we just wanted to make sure Gram was in the clear if this became a murder investigation."

"When," he said quietly.

"What?"

"*When* it became a murder investigation—and it has. It's official. I got the call just before five. The M.E. has classified Divia Larson's death as a homicide."

Elise suddenly felt like the air had been sucked from her lungs. She tried to tell herself that it wasn't like she hadn't expected it, but hearing Jackson say it out loud was shocking, nonetheless. She took two steps backward and sank down onto the sofa. "Oh God."

"Indeed," he said with a grave nod. "Shit's about to hit the fan, pal. And after what happened over the summer with your uncle's murder, do you understand now why I don't want you anywhere near this thing? Someone went to great lengths to kill this woman and then clean up after themselves."

"Did she die from cyanide poisoning?"

"Yes. The M.E. said that the head wound, while it happened prior to death and was a pretty good gash, wasn't the cause of death. It was the cyanide that killed her." He came over and sat next to her. "Elise, this was no accident, no crime of passion. This was well thought out and executed."

She turned to him with a frown. "Ross thought she may have committed suicide—which knowing Divia, I can't imagine—but how do you know that's not what happened?"

He shook his head. "There were other indicators. She had several broken fingernails. And I mean, broken into the quick, like she'd grabbed hold of something or someone violently. We found a couple of the tips in the carpet but not all of them. And she had scratches around her throat, as if she'd been unable to breath and had clawed at herself."

"Maybe she took the poison and later had second thoughts, then fell and hit her head in her struggle to get to her cell phone to call for help."

"Her cell was in her purse, which we found holding the door open, remember? No, she fought with someone. She had bruising around her wrists. Plus, there were other suspicious things around the room."

"Like the glass in the bathroom that had been washed?" she asked, and then smiled when his mouth dropped open. "You know there's always somebody listening, Jax. I heard you and Doc Nagle talking about it."

He closed his mouth and sighed. "Okay, yes, there's that. Plus, if she died just outside the bathroom, then how did her purse get to the door?"

"Well, people do that all the time, don't they? Put something in the door jamb to keep the door from locking behind them when they run out to the car or to the ice machine."

"True," he said with a nod. "But how did her glass get back to the dresser next to the bottle when the tainted wine spill was partially *under* her body? Some things just don't add up, and definitely do not point to suicide."

"Maddy and I both tried to tell Ross that she wouldn't have done that." She sighed and slouched back against the sofa. "It's just so sad. I mean, she wasn't the most pleasant person, but what could she have done to deserve this?"

"No accounting for what folks will do," he said then turned to her with a smirk. "So, do you want to tell me what was on the note pad that you tried to hide from me earlier today?"

"I figured you caught that." She couldn't help herself and grinned back at him. "We came up with a suspect list." When he gave her a bland look, she relented. "Okay, I came up with the list."

"Uh-huh. And who's on this infamous list?"

"The three Toussaints, Toby Raymond, Garrett Larson, and Grace Vanderhouse. Of course, that was just for starters."

"Not bad," he said. "It's funny because I've asked all of them except for Grace not to leave town just yet."

She frowned. "Why not Grace?"

"Everyone else lives five or six hours away. Grace is just in Austin," he said with a shrug. "It's not like I can't head into the city if I need to talk to her."

"Good point. But I'd keep an eye out there. C.C. says no, but I'd put money on Grace being linked to Divia in some way."

Jackson nodded. "And you'd be right. Jim and I had a long chat with her earlier today."

"And?" When he clammed up and slid a stubborn look in her direction, she rolled her eyes. "Come on, Jax. It's not like we're talking about State secrets here. How is Grace connected to Divia?"

He scrubbed his hands over his face, then blew out a breath. "Okay. Are you ready for this? Grace used to be related to Divia."

It was Elise's turn to be surprised. "*What?*" she asked with a squeal. "What do you mean she used to be related? How?"

"It seems that twenty-two years ago, Divia was married to Grace's dad."

Jackson related the bare bones of what Grace had told them earlier in the day. Though Elise thought his details were a bit thin, she wasn't about to push it. He was giving her information after scolding her for butting into his investigation. She decided to take what she could get.

Elise stared at him when he'd finished. "That's the craziest thing ever. It really is a small world. I guess Toby's reaction yesterday at the mention of Grace's name makes perfect sense now, huh? So what do you think she's holding back?"

"I don't know," he said, leaning back next to her. "But there was definitely something she wasn't saying."

Turning her head, she smiled up at him.

"What?"

"I was just thinking that if anyone can get a woman to spill her secrets, it's you."

He narrowed his eyes and gave her a dubious look. "You're just trying to butter me up, get on my good side after misbehaving."

"Maybe." She giggled and scooted up close, slipping her legs over his. "How am I doing?"

"I don't know," he replied as his hands began to roam. "The jury's still out."

"Are you hungry?" she murmured as he started to move in for a kiss.

Pulling back, he pursed his lips. "Depends on what we're talking about. Food? Or something else?"

Her laugh was throaty as she ran a finger down the buttons of his shirt. "Maybe both. You could stay over and we could figure it out. Together."

He took her hand and lifted it away from his chest. "I thought you said you wanted to take this slow, El."

"I did, and we have. Don't you want to move forward? Find out where this is going?"

"Of course I do. Unfortunately, your timing sucks. I need to go home because I still have a few things to do before I can call it a night."

"Okay," she said as she pulled him down for that kiss. "But you're gonna hate yourself for it later."

"Don't I know it," he replied as his lips found hers.

# TWELVE

Sales were brisk on Sunday, partially because it was the last day of the food and wine festival, and to some extent, due to the news that Divia's death had turned out to be a homicide. And that little gem of an update had spread at the speed of light.

When Elise briefed Ross and C.C. on her Saturday evening conversation with Jackson, she soon realized how stingy he'd been with details. She brooded on the idea that she'd told him as much or more than he'd actually told her. And the digs she got from C.C. didn't help.

"That's it? That's all you got? Losing your touch, girlfriend," her friend said with a sad shake of her head.

"Hey. There's no reason for insults," Elise replied. "Jax was pretty ticked when he got to the apartment last night. To be honest, I'm lucky he told me anything."

"No offense, C.C., I know Grace is your friend and all," Ross said with a shrug. "But the scoop about her being related to Divia, however briefly, is pretty good intel. It also sounds like she may have had a motive for murder."

"And I'm telling you, Grace wouldn't hurt anyone, no matter what their history was." C.C. huffed. "Anyway, come on, Ross. That's all El got out of Jax? He told her that he'd talked to the Toussaints, but he didn't tell her anything about what was said. We have no idea what they gave him in the way of alibis, or if he found out anything that could point to motive for one or all of them." She shook her head and gestured toward Third Coast's booth. "Did he mention Toby or Mr. Larson? You know he's probably talked to them both, but not a peep about that either?"

"Wow. Really, C.C.?" Elise said after a moment. She couldn't help but feel hurt by her friend's comments. "You're second guessing me now? Or is it perhaps the fact that you may have been wrong about Grace? That maybe your friend was actually involved in Divia's murder? In any case, I invite you to try getting anything of use out of Jackson Landry that he doesn't want you to know."

C.C. put up a hand. "Okay, don't get your panties in a twist. I didn't mean to insinuate that you didn't do your best. And for the record, I don't think I'm wrong about Grace. I'm just sayin'. The only useful information you got out of Jax is a sketchy history between her and Divia."

"Sketchy? *Sketchy?*" Elise gaped at C.C. "How do you figure that? Grace told Jax *in her own words*, I might add, how Divia cleaned them out financially and stole away in the middle of the night. She left Grace and her father bankrupt and struggling, and Grace had to watch her father die a broken man. If that's not motive for revenge, or possibly murder, I don't know what is."

"Hey, time out, you two," Madison said, walking up to the booth. "I could hear you guys arguing halfway to Restaurant Row. You need to dial it back unless you want everyone here to know what we're up to. And if we're going to figure this mess out and make sure Gram is in the clear, now isn't the time to be sniping at each other."

While Elise could admit that Madison was right, it still irked her that C.C. would be so unsupportive of her efforts. She expected her best friend to have her back in all situations, and the fact that C.C. was so adamant about Grace's innocence rubbed her the wrong way. Though it shamed her a bit to think that her feelings may have been borne of jealousy over the friendship C.C. had forged with Grace.

However, in her haste to defend herself against Monique's insinuations, Elise had to admit she'd glossed right over the fact that Jackson had at least preliminarily interviewed both Monique and Alain. And that she had no idea what those interviews had unearthed, if anything. Plus, to add salt to the wound, as C.C. had pointed out, she hadn't even asked about Garrett or Toby when she'd had the perfect chance.

She took a deep breath and let out a long sigh. "You're right, Maddy. We shouldn't be causing a commotion here if we want to keep this on the down-low. I guess I'm feeling a little sensitive because I realize now how distracted I got by Monique's subterfuge. In my haste to point out her lyin' ways, I did fail to get all the details I could have."

"And you may be right about me being defensive when it comes to Grace, El. It's just that I've known her almost since she came to Austin a few years ago," C.C. said with a sheepish look. "I had lunch with her today and wanted to ask her about Divia, but I chickened out. But knowing her the way I do, I can't imagine her being involved in something so terrible."

"I know, sweetie," Elise conceded. "But to be fair, it's really hard to know just what people are capable of, especially those nearest to you. I found that out the hard way, remember?"

"Yes, but to find out that Grace is so closely connected and that she outright lied to us about knowing Divia at all makes me feel foolish and gullible. I'm sorry I took it out on you."

"Are you guys going to hug it out?" Ross asked with a squeamish face. "Because if you are, I might puke."

"Bite me, Beckett," C.C. said and then laughed.

Elise nodded. "Yeah, what she said."

"Hold on," Madison said with a frown. "Go back. What lyin' ways? What subterfuge did Monique employ? I know you've probably already told these two, El, but you want to repeat the story for me?"

By the time Elise finished relating her conversation with Jackson from the night before, Madison was fuming. "That snarky bee-otch! You're right, El. She was just trying to throw the focus somewhere else because she either doesn't have an alibi—at least not one she can put out there—or she's involved in something she doesn't want anyone to know about. Like maybe murder."

"I know. I'm kicking myself that I let Jackson distract me to the point of not getting the full scoop."

Madison nodded. "Yes. That would have been some good info to have. I'm pretty curious to hear where the three Toussaints were and what they were up to. By the way, what did Jax have to say about the little scene I witnessed between Monique and Philippe?"

When Elise cringed and didn't answer right away, Madison's eyes grew round. "Elise! You didn't tell him? What the *hell*?"

"I'm sorry," Elise replied throwing her hands in the air. "So shoot me. I dropped the ball. But again, exactly how was I supposed to tell him what you'd seen without giving up how you'd done it? He was already freaking out about what he thought C.C. and I had done, not to mention Ross's clumsy interrogation of Alain."

"Hey! I was not clumsy," Ross said, and then relented at the bland look she gave him. "Okay, maybe I wasn't as subtle as I could have been, but I will remind you all, I'm no detective and neither are any of you."

"And since you got bumpkus out of Alain on your sad attempt, we shouldn't be so hard on El." C.C. dropped an arm around Elise's shoulder. "Now that she and Jax are dating, it makes it harder."

"What do you mean?" Ross asked.

"Well, before, when they were dating other people, Jax was just one of the family," C.C. began to explain. "There's no need to worry about pissing off someone you consider a brother." She gave Ross a cheeky smile.

"Nice, C.C.," he said in a disgusted tone.

"No, she's right, Ross," Madison added. "When you're dating someone, it's a whole different animal. You tend to be much more cautious about what you say. You don't want to hurt feelings or the relationship, especially if you've been good friends before getting involved. El has to tread a bit more lightly now."

Ross scoffed at the notion. "That's ridiculous. It's just Jackson. She's known him all her life. It should be *easier* to tell him things."

"Oh *really*?" C.C. gave him a skeptical look. "Then let me ask you this. How long have you and Caro been married, Ross?"

"What does that have to do with anything?"

Not to be put off, C.C. just smiled. And Elise figured she knew what was coming next. "Just answer the question. How long?"

He rolled his eyes, but answered. "Ten years come spring. Why?"

C.C.'s smile grew. "You can't tell me you would approach Caro in the same way you would your sisters with something you know would upset or anger her. You'd be much more careful with her than with them."

Ross shook his head and frowned. "That's not true."

"Sure it is," C.C. continued. "With Elise or Maddy, you can argue and bitch without worrying overmuch that you will damage the relationship. They're your sisters. They're blood."

"Bull. Caro and I argue from time to time," he insisted. "It's not all wine and roses, you know."

"No, but with Caro it's a different story. You take care not to upset the balance if you can help it. Face it, sweetie, anytime you throw romantic feelings into the mix it becomes a completely different dynamic."

Ross made a *pfft* sound and shook his head. "Chick logic. You guys just make this crap up to mess with us."

"Please," Madison chimed in with a little disgust of her own. "Don't pretend like you don't know exactly what C.C.'s talking about. I've seen you cave under the Caro stare a thousand times. Pathetic."

Ross laughed out loud, but Elise could tell he was slightly uncomfortable. "I don't have to stand here and be pounded on by a bunch of wimpy girls trying to make themselves feel better. I'm taking a break."

As they watched him walk away, C.C. clucked her tongue. "Poor boy. He wants to pretend he's different—somehow special—but in his heart he knows we speak the truth. It's a hard pill for the male psyche to swallow."

"Yes," Elise agreed. "But you two were a bit hard on him. After all, he's only a boy."

Madison leaned down on the counter and sighed. "Tough love."

Elise laughed at her sister's matter-of-fact attitude. "Tough room."

The rest of the day went smoothly, with customers and sales holding steady until mid-afternoon when the flow of business slowly began to decline. The festival doors were scheduled to close at four o'clock, and by three thirty they decided to start packing up the booth.

Ross and Madison began the arduous task of shuttling boxes of brochures, advertising literature, and unopened cases of wine on dollies to the truck in the vendor parking area. Elise and C.C. took down the River Bend banner and packed all the country decorations into boxes, stacking them neatly in the corner of the booth for transport.

"This was seriously a good time," C.C. said as she taped the last box closed. "I just want to say that I'm in for next year. Of course, hopefully there won't be a repeat of all the death and drama."

"Yes, one can only hope this year's event was an anomaly," Madison replied as she stacked cartons on her dolly for another run to the truck. "I know it sounds callous, but I hope Divia's death doesn't affect next year's numbers. Everyone involved has worked so hard to build up this festival—make it special. It would be such a shame to see it all dissolve because of something out of our control."

"That would be very sad all the way around," C.C. agreed. "We'll just have to keep positive thoughts."

Those words were no sooner out of C.C.'s mouth when several people came running by with one of the EMTs from the festival's medical station hot on their trail.

Madison stepped out into the midway and watched them disappear around the corner toward Restaurant Row. "I wonder what happened."

"I don't know," Elise replied. "I hope it isn't anything too serious. But the way that EMT was moving, I'd say it's probably more than a scraped knee or bloody nose."

Elise was beginning to get a bad feeling as she watched a few more people quickly moving in the direction they'd seen the others go. A quick glance toward the main gate showed Jackson and Deputy Stockton coming up the midway at a fast clip.

*That can't be good.*

As they neared, she called out to him. "What's going on, Jax? Has something happened?"

Jackson shook his head. "I don't know exactly. We got a call about some kind of disturbance. Can't say much more than that right now," he yelled over his shoulder as he and his deputy continued down the aisle and then disappeared around the bend.

"Well, that was cryptic," C.C. commented. "Disturbance. That could mean just about anything. But with all those folks practically running in that direction, including medical staff, I'm suspecting more than just a disturbance, don't you think?"

"Unfortunately, yes," Elise said, continuing to stare toward that end of the midway. And that bad feeling was growing by leaps and bounds. "Yes I do."

By the time the main gate was closed at ten after four, the thoroughfare was fairly deserted with most vendors closing and cleaning up their booths.

Ross took the last load to the truck while Madison did a quick sweep of the area.

Elise couldn't wait any longer. "Come on, C.C. Let's go see what's happening. Since no one has come back this way, I think it may be something major."

"Right behind you, buddy."

They walked down around the corner and headed up Restaurant Row looking for where the others might have gone, but found nothing that seemed to qualify as any kind of disturbance.

"Hey, Christy," Elise called to one of the wait staff from the Toucan's On Main booth. "What was the hubbub all about? Everyone seemed to be running this direction, but I don't see anything down this way to cause such a stir."

The woman shook her head. "I think it was out back by the public bathrooms. I think someone might have been attacked, but that's all I've heard so far. Nobody's come back yet, and I can't leave the booth unmanned."

"Thanks. We'll check it out." She glanced at C.C. as they started back between the booths. "I don't like this one bit. First Divia is murdered out at Lost Pines and now someone is attacked here at the festival. This could really put a damper on things for next year, and that would be bad."

"Let's not get ahead of ourselves, okay?" C.C. replied. "We don't know that anything bad has actually happened. All we've got so far is hearsay and odd behavior."

Elise tried to hold onto that thought, but as they rounded the back of the building, they found a crowd of people huddled near the public restrooms. And Deputy Stockton was taping off the entrance to the women's side of the building.

"Oh my gosh, El," C.C. said with a gasp. "Crime scene tape. Someone really must have been attacked."

As they stood and watched from a distance, Jackson came out of the ladies room with a grim look on his face. And he was wearing gloves.

Another bad sign.

"I'm gonna need all of you folks to go on back to your booths and business, and let us handle this," he told the small crowd. "Go on, now. There's nothing for y'all to do or see here, and you'll just hinder the process. However, if any of you saw something in this area that you think might be of help to the investigation, please see the officers at the south end of the walkway. Thank you."

When the crowd began to disperse, Elise could see that there were more officers and medical people milling around than they'd originally seen coming through the main gate. The extra help must have come in through a rear entrance.

She and C.C. made their way toward the front to where Jackson stood just as two EMTs came out of the building pushing a gurney that held a body bag.

Elise gasped and grabbed Jackson's arm as the EMTs pushed the gurney and its contents around the back of the building toward the rear gate where the ambulance was obviously parked.

"Oh God, Jax. What happened? We heard someone was attacked, but this?"

"El, you and C.C. should go on back to the booth. Pack up and go home. Please."

At the look on his face, a shiver went down her spine. Though she didn't really want to know, she couldn't stop herself from asking. "Who is it, Jax? It's someone we know, isn't it?"

"Elise—"

"Jax, please. Don't make us stew and worry over this. *Is* it someone we know?"

Jackson heaved a sigh and stared off into the distance for a moment before looking back at them with a terrible sadness in his eyes. "It's Grace Vanderhouse, El."

# THIRTEEN

"GRACE?" C.C. STEPPED FORWARD with a confused look on her face. "No. That can't be. There must be some mistake, Jackson. I just saw her, talked to her a couple hours ago. Tell him, Elise. I had lunch with her, for God's sake."

C.C.'s voice was growing more and more frantic by the second, and Jackson could clearly read the disbelief in her eyes. He glanced at Elise and then turned back to C.C. with a sympathetic look. "I'm so sorry, C.C. I know she was a friend, but there's no mistake," he said gently. "It's definitely Grace Vanderhouse."

"*Noooo!*" C.C. wailed.

He had to practically body-check her to keep her from racing after the EMTs. This was the hardest part of his job—breaking the most terrible news to friends and loved ones and then having to watch the impact.

He held onto C.C. in a virtual bear hug as she struggled to free herself and tears began to stream down her cheeks. When she finally stopped fighting him, he held her close while she clung to him, sobbing against his shoulder. Looking over her head, his gaze connected with Elise's and he read the heartbreak in her eyes. She pressed her fingers to her trembling lips as she struggled to hold back her own tears.

"Darlin', I'm so sorry," he murmured again next to C.C.'s ear. "I'm going to find the bastard who did this. I promise."

Madison and Ross walked up at that moment, and both wore concerned looks.

"What's going on?" Ross asked when he saw C.C. crying on Jackson's shoulder. "Good Lord, what's happened now?"

"Grace Vanderhouse was killed," Elise told them in a quiet voice filled with sorrow.

"What?" Madison turned to Jackson, and her shock was clear. "When? How?"

"We haven't gotten many details yet," he said before shaking his head. "It looks like she was strangled in the women's restroom, but we'll have to wait for confirmation. Doc Nagle came in with the ambulance and estimates time of death to be within the last couple of hours, three at the outside. Couldn't have been more than that, since C.C. had lunch with her. But again, we'll have to take statements, put together a timeline."

"What the hell is going on around here, Jax?" Ross asked in anger. "This is crazy. First Divia Larson and now Grace? This is a small community. How does something like this happen in a venue crowded with people? And in broad daylight?"

"I don't know. These are public restrooms, but they're fairly secluded back here behind the restaurant booths." Jackson handed his handkerchief to C.C. to wipe her eyes. "Regardless, someone had to have seen or heard something. We'll follow the evidence from there, see where it takes us."

"Jax, do you think this could have been some sort of coincidence?" Elise asked. "I mean, it just seems odd that Divia and Grace were so closely related in the past, and both have died violently within days of each other."

"I don't know that either, and although I'm not going to speculate, you know how I feel about coincidences. In my limited experience, when it comes to homicide, they're a very rare thing," he replied. "But again, we'll wait and see what the evidence tells us."

C.C. sniffed and seemed to get herself under control. "Jackson, you said you would find the *bastard* who did this. Does that mean you think a man killed her, or is it possible that a woman committed this crime?"

"Well, Grace was a fairly small woman," he answered with a shrug. "I suppose someone larger—man or woman—could have done the deed, but they would've had to have been pretty strong. Why do you ask, C.C.? Do you know something I don't?"

He narrowed his eyes as he watched her shift a glance to Elise before answering. There was obviously something going on there—something he was pretty certain he wasn't going to like.

She shook her head after a brief pause. "I was just wondering, that's all."

Elise gave him a resigned look when he raised his eyebrows at her. "You know we're having the usual Sunday dinner way late tonight because it's the last day of the festival and closing wasn't until four o'clock. Gram wants to sit down at the table about eight. Are you coming by? There are a few things we should probably talk about."

*More like a few things you feel the need to confess?*

He stared at her a moment longer as he worked through his annoyance before nodding. "I'm hoping to make dinner. We'll see how it goes, but for now, I need y'all to clear out. Go home. Please. The less people milling around, the faster we can wrap up here at the scene."

He turned and put a hand on C.C.'s shoulder. "I don't know exactly what your relationship was or how close you were with Grace, but I won't rest until I find the person responsible for her death."

"Thanks, Jax." She dabbed at a fresh round of tears with his hankie before continuing. "I'd known her a few years and considered her a good friend." When she looked up at him, her drenched eyes nearly broke his heart. "I trust you to bring the person who did this terrible thing to justice."

——————

By the time Jackson and Deputy Stockton had wrapped their investigation out at the fairgrounds and left the crime scene crew to do their thing, most of the vendors had closed up shop and headed home or gone back to their motels.

With the family dinner postponed until early evening, he thought he could actually attend if no other calamities materialized before then. He could use one of Miss Abby's home-cooked meals, and the possibility of dragging a bit more information out of Elise was enticing. From the look on her face earlier, he had a sneaking suspicion that she'd left out several crucial details during their previous chat.

Shaking his head, a ghost of a smile touched his lips. The woman drove him to distraction on most days. He may have known her for a large chunk of his life, but now that they were dating, the dynamics of their relationship had changed in subtle ways. And he was more than ready to take it to the next level.

However, the latest report had just come back from the crime lab, and it wasn't good news. He worried about how it was going to affect not just his relationship with Elise, but with the entire Beckett family.

Jackson and Jim drove back to the department in silence, each with their own thoughts. When they walked into Jackson's office twenty minutes later, the deputy spoke up as if clearly reading the troubling thoughts swirling around in Jackson's head.

"So, are you going out to River Bend tonight?"

Jackson sighed. "Looks that way, unless something else comes up in the next hour or so."

"What are you going to tell the Becketts? About the report findings, I mean?"

"I'm going to tell them the truth, though I know it won't be taken well. Finding Miss Abby's fingerprints on the wine bottle isn't a smoking gun, but—"

"It makes the situation sticky," Jim finished for him.

Jackson nodded and opened the report on his desk. "Yes, it does. It helps that we could verify the phone call and the texts that Miss Abby said she received from Mrs. Larson that night. But the Becketts are very tight-knit, so they won't like the rest of what I have to tell them."

Jim leaned back in the chair on the other side of the desk and stretched out his legs in front of him. "They have to know that you've got to follow all the leads, right?"

"Laura and Miss Abby understand that, but I'm sure that at least one of them will see it as an attack on the family the minute that I bring it up."

"Even coming from you?"

"Especially coming from me," Jackson replied with a laugh. "Trust me, that'll be Ross's slant."

"But for all intents and purposes, you're part of the family, right? I thought he was supposed to be your best friend—like a brother."

"Yes. He is." Jackson paused and rubbed his eyes, thinking he really needed a solid eight hours of sleep sometime soon.

"Then what's his problem?"

"Come on, Jim. We went through this dance back during Edmond Beckett's murder investigation. Remember? Ross accused me of being disloyal, of not protecting the family."

"Oh yeah. Wow. That's harsh. But then, you and I both know that there's no way Abigail DeVries killed anyone."

"No, I don't think she killed Divia Larson, if that's what you mean." He grinned at the other deputy. "But that's not to say that I don't think Miss Abby is perfectly capable of committing the crime. Because I spent a lot of time at River Bend growing up, I know that woman would take someone out in a New York minute if she thought her family was being threatened. However, she wouldn't use poison, I can tell you that."

Jim chuckled. "No. I don't imagine she would. I expect she'd use something with a little more muscle behind it—like a shotgun."

"Yeah. And she'd proudly take ownership of the act." Pursing his lips, he perused the report again briefly. "Most of these findings are circumstantial, anyway. Miss Abby manned the festival booth all day Thursday, and then worked out at the Wine Barrel on Friday. She could have sold the killer that bottle of wine at either place, anytime, on one day or the other."

"Which would account for her fingerprints being the only prints on the bottle," Jim added. "She puts the wine in a paper bag when she sells it and hands it to the perp. He or she, being careful not to add their own prints to the bottle, then leaves it in the room after the Larson woman is dead."

"Yeah, that fits." Jackson nodded. "Unfortunately, it doesn't look great that Miss Abby was the one to find the body, or that she has access to cyanide out at the vineyard where they use it for rodent control and the like. She has a romantic past with Garrett Larson and a contentious history with the dead woman. And, to make matters worse, she and Divia had words on Thursday afternoon in front of witnesses."

"You're right. It doesn't look great. And it doesn't sound all that good when you say it out loud, either. But, like you said, it's still entirely circumstantial, and it does help that the poison was only found in the Larson woman's glass and not the bottle itself."

"I guess. I just wish there weren't as many issues to clear up there—circumstantial or not."

Jim frowned and scratched his head. "There are other suspects. What about the Toussaints? You gonna cut 'em loose?"

Jackson leaned back in his own chair and stared at the ceiling in contemplation. "I'd planned to earlier, but nearly everything about their interviews just rubs me wrong."

"You mean, the way they all alibied each other?" Jim shook his head. "I wasn't buying what they were selling, either. No two people tell exactly the same story, even if they're together the whole time and witness the same things. All three of the Toussaints told an identical tale—almost word for word. In my opinion, it had bullshit written all over it."

"Plus Monique Toussaint smoothly glossed over the whole cat-fight deal with the vic, but from all other accounts, the squabble was about what Monique suspected was going on between her husband and Divia Larson."

"So if Alain Toussaint and Mrs. Larson were heatin' up the sheets—and Monique Toussaint found out—do you think she let Mr. Larson in on the fun?"

"Or did he already know?" Jackson asked as he pulled up his email on the computer screen. "And that part about Toby Raymond's 'funny business with the books'? I want to know exactly what she meant by that."

"Yeah, if Toby was cookin' the books out at Larson's vineyard, how did Monique find out, and who else knew about it?"

Jim stared at the wall for a moment, and Jackson could almost see the wheels turning in the man's head. "What are you thinking?" he asked.

"Well, the other thing that bothered me about the Toussaint interviews was Philippe Toussaint's attitude toward his sister-in-law. Did you pick up on that? The way he kept watching her, casually touching her from time to time." Jim shook his head and wrinkled his nose. "Gave me the creeps, but his brother didn't seem to even notice. I couldn't help wondering if there was something going on there as well."

"I know what you mean." Jackson heaved a sigh. The entire sordid affair was beginning to give him a headache. "Anyway, it looks like this thing has a whole lot more goin' on underneath, but the question is how to get to the bottom of it in a short amount of time."

"Definitely a quandary, that's for sure. We can't keep them in town forever, so we need to find out where they were and what they were really up to, PDQ."

"Mmm-hmm. And here's another problem," Jackson said pointing at the monitor. "I just got an email back from the sponsor of the conference Garrett Larson said he was attending in Austin."

"And?"

"They say he was registered, but never checked in or picked up his conference packet."

Jim's eyebrows shot up. "Uh-oh. That's not good. Now where would Mr. Larson have gone if he didn't go to his conference, and he wasn't with his wife?"

"Good question. And why would he feel the need to lie about it to the police when he came back to the motel late Friday night only to find his wife dead, possibly murdered?"

"Think he's having an affair?"

"Oh, man." Jackson made a face. "The dude's, what? Like, mid-seventies?"

"Doesn't mean the drive's not there or the equipment's stopped working."

"Yeah, but that's not something I wanted in my head. Thanks for putting it there."

"You're welcome." The other deputy snickered. "Besides, the late Mrs. Larson was twenty years his junior, right?"

"True." Jackson opened his notebook and jotted down a few reminders. "So, we've got the three Toussaints, Toby Raymond, and Garrett Larson to re-interview."

"Yeah, and to figure out how these two murders are related. Because you and I both know they're connected in some way."

"Have to be." Shutting down his computer, Jackson grimaced. "Looks like we've got our work cut out for us tomorrow. In the meantime, I guess I'd better stop procrastinating and head out to River Bend. Though I think I'd rather have a root canal at this point."

Jim gave him a commiserative look, but his response was anything but sympathetic. "Better you than me, pal. Better you than me."

# FOURTEEN

AFTER PROCRASTINATING AS LONG as he could, Jackson ended up cutting it pretty damn close. It was going on seven forty-five when he turned through the gates at River Bend. And by stewing about how he was going to approach the family with his latest news, he'd managed to add fuel to the headache that was already brewing on the twenty-minute drive from town.

What he'd told Jim about Laura and Miss Abby understanding that he had a job to do was true—at least, he hoped it was. The Becketts were as close to a second family as he would ever get, and while he didn't want to let them down, he had to be as transparent as possible where the investigation was concerned. It was his only way to protect them. Any whiff of partiality or impropriety could get him bounced off the case, and then where would they all be? Nobody in the department knew or understood the lot of them like he did.

He pulled his cruiser in next to C.C.'s pickup and shut down the engine. Lights from inside the main residence spilled from the windows in the gathering twilight, giving off a warm, inviting glow.

Being the only child of a pair of archeologists who sometimes forgot they even had a son, he'd often spent more time in this house than he had in his own. And Abigail DeVries had always treated him no differently than any of her other grandchildren, which made this whole deal that much harder for him.

Just as he climbed out of the vehicle, the front door opened and Elise stepped out onto the porch. She strolled over to the top of the steps and slapped a hand on her hip.

"It's about time you got here, pal," she said with a smirk. "You know, Gram would have skinned you alive if you'd have walked in after she'd said grace."

He nodded as he went up the steps to meet her. "I got hung up at the office. Grace's murder dovetails with Divia's in a very disturbing way, and I don't have a good feeling about where it's going."

"Aw, poor baby." She gave him a welcoming kiss before slipping her arm through his. "You'd better come on in. Dinner is about to be served. We can eat and later you can tell me all about it."

He raised an eyebrow as he opened the door for her. "Yeah? Well, somebody's gonna be talking, but we'll see who tells who what."

"Very funny." She gave him a cheesy smile when she preceded him into the foyer. "You know I love it when you go all macho cop on me. But we'll save that for later as well. Everyone's already at the table."

Following her down the hall toward the dining room, he tried to put the investigation out of his mind for the time being. He'd delayed the inevitable this long, another hour or so wasn't gonna hurt anything.

"Have a seat, you two," Abigail said when they entered the room. She pointed toward the empty chairs on the far side of the table.

"We weren't sure you'd be able to make it with all the recent hub-bub and such, Jackson. But I made sure your place was set just the same."

"Thanks, Miss Abby. You're the best."

She gave him a brilliant grin then turned to snap at Ross. "Quit hogging those mashed potatoes, boy. Pass them around to Jackson."

Ross's mouth dropped open. "Geez, Gram. I just got 'em. Give me a minute to get some on my own plate. Besides, he hasn't even sat down yet." Ross threw Jackson a dirty look. "Gram's favorite," he muttered.

Jackson laughed and shook his head. "It's not so much that I'm her favorite, buddy. It's just that she doesn't like you at all."

"Bite me, Jax."

"Ross Alexander … manners? What have I told you about your language at my table," Laura said as she entered the room and sat down at the end with him to her left and Jackson to her right.

"Yes, ma'am," he muttered.

If Jackson thought he was off the hook, he was mistaken. When she turned to him, it was with a stern look. "And no baiting at the table, either, Jackson Christopher."

"Sorry, ma'am."

She smiled and patted his hand. "Besides, Mom loves all her little darlins equally—right, Mom?"

Abigail set a steaming bowl of mixed vegetables down next to the brisket and took her seat at the other end of the spread. "Nope," she said with a straight face as she passed the basket of dinner rolls to Madison. "They're both right. Jackson's my favorite, and I really don't like Ross."

After a beat, the entire table erupted into a cacophony of laughter, and even Ross cracked a reluctant smile. "Thanks, Gram," he said with a chuckle. "That's just what I needed to hear to give my ego a boost."

Abigail cackled then and sent him a mischievous look. "Oh, you know I'm just having some fun with you. Y'all *are* my little darlins—each and every one of you."

They made it through dinner and were well into Miss Abigail's delicious pecan pie when Ross's wife, Caroline, finally came in.

"Sorry I'm so late. Caleb isn't feeling well. I think he may have picked up a bug," she said, referring to their six-year-old son. She sat down next to Ross. "I wanted to make sure he was asleep before heading this way. Ethan gave me some grief over the whole thing, too. He was pretty miffed that this family dinner was too late for them to attend. Plus, he didn't think he should have to go to bed half an hour early just because Caleb did. After all, he *is* two years older."

"That's my boy," Ross added with a laugh.

She shook her head. "I think they were both asleep before their little heads hit their pillows. I had Sancia come over and sit with them so I could come over here for a bit."

"It must be convenient having your babysitter living just up the road on the property," C.C. said.

"Yes. Having Sancia and Carlos so close is great. That the Maderas live and work here at the vineyard has been a huge plus," Caroline replied, "especially now that I'm helping out at the Wine Barrel several days a week."

"Are you hungry, honey?" Miss Abby asked. "I can heat you up a plate. There's plenty."

"Oh, no. Gosh, don't trouble yourself, Gram. I ate with the boys earlier. But I wouldn't mind a slice of that yummy pecan pie of yours."

"You got it," Miss Abby said before rising to fetch Caroline a plate.

It seemed like such a normal family dinner that Jackson almost put the investigation out of his mind. But it wasn't long before it reared its ugly head. And of course, Ross had to be the one to bring it up.

"So Jax, any news about Grace's or Divia's murders?"

*So much for a normal evening with family.*

Jackson slowly lowered his fork to his plate. Leave it to Ross to put it so bluntly with Grace not even cold and C.C. sitting right there.

"Ross! For crying out loud," Elise said with a frown.

"What?" he asked leaning back in his chair.

She heaved a sigh and shook her head. "Can't we go a measly few hours and at least get through dinner without talking about homicide?"

"Well, geez, El," Ross complained. "Weren't you the one who started this whole 'let's keep our eyes and ears open' thing? I thought you'd want to know the latest news."

"And I thought you'd be more subtle and compassionate." She made a face. "And thanks, way to throw me under the bus ... yet again."

"That's enough, you two," Miss Abby said. "Ignore them and their foolishness, Jackson. They're just bein' nosy. I know you have to be careful what you say about your cases."

Wiping his mouth with his napkin, Jackson figured he'd better get on with it. He'd waited long enough. "Well, now that he's brought it up, there are a few things we need to talk about, Miss Abby."

"Ah-ha!" Ross said, pointing a finger in Jackson's direction. "I knew it."

"Hush, Ross." Abigail slowly sank into her chair. "Should we go into Laura's office for privacy?"

"Oh, hell no!" Ross blurted. "You're not talking to the police alone. No way, no how. Y'all can have any conversation you like right here within earshot of the family."

"Oh, for crying out loud, boy" Abigail exclaimed. "It's only Jackson. He's part of this family, and don't you forget it."

Ross nodded but was undeterred. "You're absolutely right, Gram. Jax *is* part of this family. However, he's also a sheriff's deputy and the officer in charge of two recent murder inquiries," he reminded her. "Remember Uncle Edmond's homicide investigation? Jax has to stay objective or risk being removed from both cases. And, as he's so fond of saying, he has to follow the evidence. Isn't that right, Jax?"

For a moment Jackson was too stunned to respond. This calm, insightful analysis coming from the normally hot-headed and accusatory Ross left him speechless. "Who are you and what have you done with my best friend?" was the question on the tip of his tongue.

"Uh … actually, Ross is right, Miss Abby," he said when he finally found his voice. "Until this investigation is complete, it wouldn't hurt to have someone else present during any conversations regarding

Mrs. Larson's death. And the family should hear what I have to say, anyway."

Abigail frowned, but after a moment, nodded. "All right. You know I trust you, Jackson, and if you think that would be best, then that's what we'll do."

"Okay, the way you're talking it's starting to sound like Gram really is a suspect," Madison spoke up with a worried look.

Abigail laid her hand over Madison's and squeezed. "Of course I'm a suspect, sweetheart. I don't have an alibi. Plus, I was the one to find the body." She glanced over at Jackson, and the look in her eyes was shrewd. "And if I'm not mistaken, there's more to it now. Am I wrong?"

Jackson sighed. "No, ma'am, you're not wrong. So far, we've confirmed the call you received from Mrs. Larson, as well as the texts. However, we've also got several reports back from the lab. Mrs. Larson's were the only fingerprints on the glass found on the dresser next to the wine bottle." He paused before diving into the deep end. "And the only prints on the wine bottle itself were yours."

Again the room erupted, only this time it wasn't into laughter.

"What the hell are you saying, Jax?" Ross yelled. "I don't like your implications."

*There's the Ross we all know and love*, Jackson thought.

Caroline crossed her arms and glared at him. "That doesn't mean a thing, and you know it!"

"Yeah, Miss Abby worked the booth with us on Thursday," C.C. put in. "She could have sold that bottle to the killer. Heck, any one of us could have sold it and just had her bag it."

Elise nodded. "And she worked at the Wine Barrel on Friday, so there was ample opportunity for her to touch the bottle in question."

157

"Whoa! Calm down, y'all." Jackson put up his hands in surrender. "You're all absolutely right. We've taken all of that into consideration already. And it's only circumstantial at this point, anyway. Plus, the good news is that there was no poison in the wine bottle. Only the glass with Mrs. Larson's prints had traces of the cyanide."

When the room quieted down, Abigail's voice broke the momentary silence, and her gaze connected with his. "But it all adds up, doesn't it? That's what you're *not* saying, right?"

"What do you mean, Gram?" Madison asked.

"Maddy—"

"No, Jackson," Abigail interrupted. "Let me."

She looked around the table at each member of the family before continuing. "What Jackson is having difficulty with is that all the circumstantial evidence points in my direction."

"That's just ridiculous, and he knows it," Ross shouted.

She put up a hand to quell the rest of the outbursts of denial that threatened. "No, he's most certainly correct. And if you look at each piece of the puzzle, you'll see what I mean."

When she had everyone's undivided attention, she continued. "Number one—I have a romantic history with the victim's husband, and I've had a prickly history with the victim herself. It's no secret Divia and I had no use for each other. Number two—I have no alibi. I was home alone on Friday night, and I was the one to find her body very close to the time of her death." She ticked off each point with a finger as she went through the evidence. "Number three—the lab report has now confirmed that my fingerprints are the only prints on the wine bottle found in her room. And though there was no trace of poison in the wine bottle, we all know that cyanide is used quite frequently here at the vineyard and readily available."

Though she'd hit every point, it tore Jackson up to sit there and listen to her rattle off the evidence he and Jim had gone over earlier.

"Taken individually, I guess it's not so bad. But when you add it all up, circumstantial as it may be, it doesn't look good." She glanced around the silent room until her eyes met his again. "Did that about cover it?"

"Yes, ma'am. That's it in a nutshell."

"Come on, Jax," Ross spoke up after a moment. "You know damn well Gram didn't kill Divia Larson. I mean, there are other folks around with better motives."

"And we're looking at them, but you guys have to trust me to do my job. As you pointed out at the start of this conversation, I'm walking a really thin line here. And I have to follow the evidence— wherever it leads me."

"And if it leads you back to one of the family?" Ross pushed the envelope with a mutinous look on his face. "If it leads back to Gram? What then?"

"Ross—" Laura began but Ross cut her off.

"No, Mom, I want to know exactly where his loyalties are."

For Jackson, the comment was more than he could stomach, and he shoved back from the table. "You know, buddy, it always seems to come down to this, doesn't it? We went through this same damn bullshit during Edmond's murder investigation. I guess saying that I'm part of the family is easy lip-service, but when push comes to shove, that's all it is."

"Jax, you know he doesn't mean that," Elise said, but he ignored her. Ross's barbs had hit a sore spot and this time he couldn't let it go.

His stare bored into Ross, who'd gone noticeably silent and red in the face. "You say you understand that I have a job to do, that I have to be careful of perceptions, follow the evidence. Then you turn right around and question my loyalty, when the people around this table are closer to me than my own blood relatives."

Jackson stood up and laid his napkin across his plate. "Well, maybe you're right, Ross," he said in a quiet voice. "Maybe I'm not part of this family after all." With that, he pulled out his keys and turned to the woman who'd practically raised him. "I'm sorry for the trouble, Miss Abby. I'll let you know if anything else comes up."

"Jackson, sweetheart, please don't leave like this," she pleaded.

He came around the end of the table and placed a kiss on her leathery cheek. It was nearly his undoing when he saw the tears well in her eyes, and he murmured into her ear. "Don't you dare cry, darlin'. You'll break my heart. I'll be back. I just need some space."

With a brief glance at Elise, he walked out of the room and down the hall. Stepping outside, he hoped the cool night air would clear his head and exorcize all his demons. He'd always considered himself part of this family, had been treated as such as long as he could remember. But he now realized, as much as he'd like it to be, that it just wasn't true. Ross had made that perfectly clear.

# FIFTEEN

SILENCE REIGNED FOR SEVERAL moments after Jackson's abrupt departure from the room, with nobody at the table wanting to make eye contact. To Elise, the sound of the front door slamming shut seemed as loud as a gunshot.

Feeling a bit of her own guilt over the fact that she hadn't done more to support Jackson, she lashed out at her brother. "Well, nice job, Ross," she said in disgust. "What the hell is *wrong* with you?"

"I'm sorry, okay? I didn't mean to make Jax feel bad or suggest that he's not part of the family."

"But that's exactly what you did by questioning his loyalty." Madison gave him a sad look. "You know he would never let anything happen to any of us if he could help it."

"I know, I know." Ross ran a hand through his hair and looked up with regret in his eyes. "This is all just so frustrating, but you're right. I shouldn't take out my concerns on Jax. I just want to make sure that Gram is protected."

"You don't need to worry about me. I've got nothin' to hide, so I'll be fine." Abigail stood up and began to gather the dirty plates from the table. "Jackson's doing the best he can. We all need to be supportive and let him do his job."

"Mom's right." Laura nodded and rose to help Abigail clear the table. "I know this seems all too familiar. We lived through something similar with your Uncle Edmond's death only months ago, but we have to give Jackson as much help and understanding as we can."

"I know," Ross said. "And I'm sorry that I badgered him."

Elise wasn't letting him off the hook so easily. This wasn't the first time Ross had behaved badly toward Jackson in recent months, and she wanted to nip it in the bud. "Yeah, well it doesn't do any good to tell us. You need to talk to him."

"I will."

Jumping up, she grabbed her purse. "I mean it, Ross. You fix this." With that, she started for the door.

"Where are you going, El?" C.C. asked.

"I'm gonna try to catch Jackson. If I can't, I'm going to his house. I don't want this to get out of hand."

She raced down the hall and out the front door, only to be disappointed when she realized his cruiser was gone and that she'd waited too long.

Figuring he only had about a ten-minute start on her Elise got into her car and headed for his house. If he wasn't at home, she'd check his office, but one way or another, she was going to find him tonight.

Jackson lived in a charming little ranch-style house on the other side of Delphine just on the outskirts of town. The twenty-minute drive there seemed to take forever, but Elise was filled with relief when she turned off the highway and found the cruiser parked in his driveway. She pulled her little sports car in behind it and killed the engine.

With not a little trepidation, she climbed out of the car and went up to the porch. She knocked on the front door, and while she waited for him, went over what she intended to say. But her mind went completely blank, and her mouth dry as the Gobi desert when he opened the door. He was barefoot and his shirt was unbuttoned. It hung open just enough to reveal a tantalizing glimpse of his muscular chest.

"El?"

At the sound of her name, she snapped her gaze up to his confused face and did her best to focus on the reason she'd followed him home.

Unfortunately, "hey" was all she managed to squeak out.

"What are you doing here?" he asked.

"Why don't you invite me in and I'll tell you. Or at least try to remember," she added under her breath. Those glimpses of his sexy, bare chest made it hard to concentrate on anything else. Noticing that the top button of his pants was undone didn't help, either.

"Okay. Come on in." He stepped aside, motioning for her to enter.

She moved past him quickly and went into the living room. Tossing her purse into a chair, she steeled herself as she turned around to face him and got right to the point. "First, I want to apologize on behalf of myself and my entire boneheaded family—especially my dumb-ass brother."

"El—"

"Just hold your water and let me finish, would you?" she said, cutting him off. "I know Ross made it sound like you aren't a part of our family, but you know that's not true. You are and always will be. And it shames me to know that we hurt your feelings that way."

Jackson heaved a sigh and walked over to her. "There's no need to feel that way," he said, tucking a strand of hair behind her ear. "People get their feelings hurt all the time. I'll get over it."

"But that's my point." She jabbed a finger in his direction before spinning away from him. "Families shouldn't treat each other that way."

"But they often do, darlin'," he said in a quiet voice. "So let it go."

She turned back to him with an exasperated look. "Well, I can't, and I don't understand how you can just accept it."

"What's the point of railing against it, El? It is what it is."

"Ooh, that really gets to me," she said with a growl. "Sometimes you can be so annoyingly bullheaded."

With his hands fisted on his hips, he stepped right into her bubble and growled back. "And you can be infuriatingly nosy and hard of hearing. But that doesn't mean that I don't love you, in spite of it."

"Yeah? Well, let me tell you something—wait. What did you just say?"

"You heard me."

She crossed her arms and cocked a hip. "I think you need to say it again, just so we're clear."

"Nuh-uh," he replied and mirrored her stance. "Not until you spill whatever it is that you failed to tell me about the case before. And don't say there isn't anything, because we both know you'd be fibbin'."

She tried to stare him down, but in the end, threw up her hands in surrender. "Okay. I give. I should've told you the other day when we talked about that lyin' Monique saying that we'd questioned her."

He raised an eyebrow. "I'm listening."

"Well, in reference to keeping our eyes and ears open, Maddy overheard a conversation between Monique and Philippe Toussaint that I think you'll find interesting. You might want to clear it up before you let them leave town."

He narrowed his eyes. "Go on."

Knowing she would probably regret it, she related everything Madison had told them about what she'd witnessed between the two that day behind Restaurant Row. When she was finished, he simply shook his head.

"What?" she asked, when he continued to stare at her without speaking.

"You guys just never learn, do you?" He paced away and then back. "Do you have any idea how dangerous that could have been for Maddy if it turns out that Monique or Philippe are responsible for Divia's death? What if they'd caught her listening?"

"I told her the same thing."

"Oh, please. You did no such thing."

"Okay, maybe not in so many words," she remarked. *Good Lord, I'm a horrible liar.*

He smirked at her. "I imagine you and the rest of the gang congratulated her on her sleuthing skills."

Feeling the color rise in her face, she thought back on how they'd done just exactly that. "Well, regardless, trust me when I say that she won't be doing anything like that again."

"Yeah, I'm pretty sure I've heard that before, too. I'd suggest you don't make promises you can't keep." When she made a show of pouting, he rolled his eyes. "Wow. Pathetic much? I'm not buying the 'poor pitiful me' act, either."

"All right, but you're going to re-interview all three of the Toussaints, right?"

He stopped and stared at her with an incredulous look, letting out a long-suffering sigh before pinching the bridge of his nose in obvious frustration. "Yes, El. We'd already planned to re-interview them as well as Toby Raymond regarding the suggestion of impropriety with Third Coast's books. We're also going to talk to Garrett Larson about his nonexistent alibi."

"What? Garrett's alibi fell through?" Jackson's grimace suggested that he regretted telling her so much, so she hurried on. "Gram thought he might have fudged on where he was on Friday night."

He blinked at that and raised his eyebrows. "She did?"

"Yeah. She said she'd always been able to tell when he was being less than forthcoming with information, and when you spoke with him that first time, she'd noticed it right off."

"When did she tell you that?"

Elise walked over and plopped down on the sofa. "I stopped by the vineyard on Saturday after closing to talk to my mom, and she told us then."

"So, let me get this straight," he began with a frown. "When I came over to your place on Saturday evening, you already knew this?"

"Yeah," she answered slowly, feeling like there was a trap somewhere ahead that she wasn't quite seeing yet. "Like I said, I stopped by there on my way home."

"For crying out loud, El. Why the hell didn't you tell me this that night?"

She sat forward and stared at him with her mouth hanging open. "Seriously?" she sputtered when she found her voice. "In the first place, as I recall, I was busy trying to defend myself against Monique's unfounded accusations which you were spouting like gospel. So you'll excuse me if an earlier conversation with Gram slipped my mind."

"Yeah, but—" he began before she cut him off.

"And secondly, every time I've come to you with any information that I've collected, I've been chewed out for poking my nose into your precious investigations. Can you really blame me for not being as quick to share information as you'd like me to be?"

She took a breath and mentally counted to ten in an effort to defuse her frustration. "Look, I'm sorry, but you can't have it both ways, Jax. Make up your mind, already."

After a moment, he came over to sit beside her on the sofa. "Okay. You have a point, and I'm sorry. It's not that I don't appreciate the information, El. Or the help, for that matter. I do." He took her hand and linked their fingers. "It's just that I worry about you guys. And when you take risks like Maddy did to listen in on a conversation like that, it makes me crazy. I think about all the things that could go wrong."

"I know, I know. And I promise to do my best not to cause you any more worry than necessary," she said, with a mischievous smile.

"Gee, thanks. That makes me feel *so* much better."

"At least Gram will be happy to know that she can still read Garrett Larson like a book, even after all these years."

"Evidently. I just wish she would have said something the day I interviewed him."

"I think Gram's in a bit of denial because of their history. It's like she refuses to believe that Garrett could have anything to do with something as heinous as murder. I figure she didn't want to get him into hot water."

"Yeah, well, people change. And sometimes they disappoint you when you least expect it."

She got the feeling he was no longer talking about Garrett Larson, but perhaps about those a little closer to home. Still, she let it go. That was a sore subject at the moment and would probably open up another heated debate when she felt they'd just gotten back onto an even footing.

"So, how did you find out that Garrett's alibi was bogus? Wasn't he supposed to be at some conference in Austin on Friday?"

She thought Jackson might not answer at first, but then he nodded. "Yes. He gave me very detailed information about the Central Texas Mead-Makers conference he was supposedly attending on Friday night. And that surprises me, because he strikes me as a very shrewd man. He had to know we would check out his story. If he was going to lie about his movements, you'd think he would have made sure his tracks were covered."

"How did you confirm that he wasn't at the conference? There's a growing interest in honey wines here in Central Texas, so I'm guessing there was a big crowd."

Jackson pursed his lips in thought before speaking. "Well, I can't really prove he wasn't there because he was registered and had paid his fee. It's just that he never checked in and—"

"If he was there, why didn't he sign in and pick up his packet?" she asked, finishing his thought.

"Exactly. That's what I intend to ask the man tomorrow when I talk to him again." When he turned to her, she recognized the determination in his eyes. "And this time, we're going to have our conversation in an interview room at the station."

"Wow. Sometimes you can be a very scary man, Deputy Landry." Her comment elicited a smile, which is what it had been intended to do. "Are you going to talk to Toby at the station, too?"

"Yes. I'm through playin' around with these people. Somebody killed both Divia Larson and Grace Vanderhouse on my turf. And I'm gonna get some straight answers, because I think there's a whole lot more going on under the surface here."

"You think Toby was cooking the books at Third Coast?"

He shook his head. "I don't know, but so far, that's the impression I've gotten from a few folks I've interviewed. We'll see what he has to say about it. I also want to ask him about Grace. She said on Saturday that he'd come looking for her when he found out she was here. She thought it was through Toby that Divia learned of her presence as well. I want to know what his meeting with her was about, what was said."

"You think both murders are connected, don't you?" she asked, knowing the answer she was certain to get.

"My gut says yes. I don't know how exactly … yet. But, yes, I think we're going to find that they're tightly linked. And I think it's the key to solving both cases."

They sat there on the sofa together for a few moments, both in silent thought, before Elise finally stood up. "It's late. I should probably get going and let you get some sleep. Sounds like you have a pretty full day tomorrow."

Before she could walk away, Jackson grabbed her hand and pulled her down onto his lap. "Or you could stay," he murmured as his lips claimed hers in a steamy kiss.

When they finally came up for air, she smiled up at him and slipped her arms around his neck. "I guess I could stay. But then you'd have to explain your earlier comment—the one that included the 'L' word."

"I suppose I could do that. I might even throw in breakfast. I do have some diet soda in the fridge."

Her laugh was low and throaty as she pulled his lips back down to hers. "Done."

# SIXTEEN

Elise was not a morning person by any stretch of the imagination, and it was a rare day when she awoke before eight a.m. without the help of a blaring alarm. So when she surfaced on Monday morning and rolled over, it took her a few moments to realize she was alone in Jackson's bed—and not her own. Glancing over to his night stand, she was surprised to read the time on the clock. So how was it possible that she was wide awake at six forty-five?

Stretching like a lazy cat, she couldn't help the satisfied smile that spread across her face. When she buried her nose in his pillow and breathed in his scent, a flood of memories from the previous night turned her smile into a full-out grin.

*Mmm, mmm, mmm, that man has the most fabulous hands—and really knows how to use them. And for the love of God, is that bacon I smell?*

Climbing out of bed, she picked up the shirt Jackson had been wearing the night before from the chair and slipped it on. Making a quick pit stop in the bathroom, she glanced into the mirror to make sure her mascara hadn't morphed into raccoon eyes over-night. Then she followed the tantalizing aroma to the kitchen.

And found Jackson putting together a couple of breakfast burritos that looked quite tasty.

"I find a man puttering around the kitchen making me breakfast kinda hot. And you *know* how I feel about bacon," she began, leaning against the door jamb. "But I have to admit, there's a part of me that's just a little bit annoyed that you're fully dressed, making breakfast, and it's not even seven o'clock. Especially after last night's Olympic events."

He turned and grinned, wiping his hands on a towel. And damn if her knees didn't go weak at just the looks of him.

"When you taste my breakfast burritos, you won't be annoyed for long," he replied with a smirk.

Eyeballing the shirt she was wearing—his shirt—that ended well above her knees, he ran his tongue over his teeth. When he raised his eyes and their gazes met, the look he gave her had her pulse picking up speed.

"Nice shirt," he said, strolling toward her. When he reached her, he lifted her chin with a finger and settled his lips on hers. "What do you have on underneath it?" he murmured against her lips as his other hand began to gather the shirt material against her leg.

"Not a thing," she replied, melting into him and returning his kiss when his hand wandered higher to further torment and arouse.

But just when he'd gotten her motor good and running, he pulled back. "Though I'd love to continue this delightful morning ... discussion," he said with a sexy smile, "I have to be at the station in about twenty minutes."

She squinted up at him. "Wow. Are you kidding me with this? Are you trying to torture me by getting me all worked up with no intention of finishing the job? If so ... evil, Deputy Landry. Very evil."

He laughed out loud at that. "Trust me when I say that I'd much rather stay here and *finish the job*, as you so romantically put it. But I told Jim I'd be there by seven thirty. So, I guess you'll have to take a breakfast burrito as a consolation prize."

"Yeah? Well, all I can say is it better be one helluva breakfast burrito, mister."

Snickering, he went over to the fridge and pulled out a diet cola. Handing her a burrito and the can of soda, he grabbed his coffee and car keys off the counter.

"Lock up when you leave, okay?"

"Seriously?" She stared at him as if he'd sprouted another head. "You're really leaving? *Now*?"

"Sorry, darlin'. Some of us do have to work for a living."

"What the hell is that supposed to mean? I work."

He gave her a quick kiss and headed out of the kitchen. "Do me a favor and be a good girl today, okay? Stay out of trouble," he said over his shoulder.

"Oh ... my ... God. Just for *that* smart-ass remark, I'm gonna go out of my way to find the first trouble I can get into the minute I get dressed," she hollered after him. "You big tease," she muttered to herself when she heard the front door close.

———

By the time Elise ran home, showered, and changed clothes, it was half past nine. As she hurried out to the car, a delicious idea of just how she could get into the trouble she'd threatened Jackson with popped into her head.

Since he planned on reinterviewing the Toussaints first this morning, perhaps Toby or Garrett would still be at the motel. Maybe a quick side trip would be just the ticket to innocently ask a few questions. It was sort of on the way to the vineyard … in a round-about way … if you drove in the opposite direction and circled back around. Regardless, if neither of the men were there, it wouldn't be too much of her morning wasted. But if they were …

Before she could change her mind, she started her little red sports car and headed out of town toward Lost Pines Motel.

Fifteen minutes later, she was pulling off the highway and into the motel lot. After parking, she sat in the car for a few minutes to gather her thoughts. Although the idea had sounded like a good one in her head, now that she was here, she had no clue what she would say to either of the men to explain her presence. And just how was she going to get them to talk?

Before she could come up with a plan, the door to Toby's room opened and an older man she'd never seen before exited. He stepped out into the breezeway and then turned back to say a few words to Toby, who'd followed him to the door. After a moment, both men seemed to come to an agreement about something, and then to Elise's surprise, they hugged—in a very affectionate way.

*So, now who is this guy?*

She supposed he could be a family member who'd come to provide support. But to her knowledge, Divia didn't have family anywhere in Central Texas, or Texas in general, for that matter. And if the man was one of Garrett's relatives, then what was he doing in

Toby's room? And why would they be so affectionate with one another?

As she climbed out of the car, she watched the man cross the parking lot and made a mental note of the license plate for later. When Toby saw her, she waved and started toward him. Still having no idea what she was going to say, she held tight to her resolve. It was too late to turn back now.

"Hey, Elise," he greeted her as she neared. "What are you doing out this way?"

"Oh, I just thought I'd check on you and Garrett this morning. See how y'all are holding up, if you needed anything." She knew her answer was pretty lame, but it was all she could come up with on short notice.

"That's very kind of you," he repliedd, though the look on his face said he wasn't quite sure about her explanation either. "It's been really hard, but we'll get through it. Mom would've wanted us to soldier on, you know?"

"I understand. We went through something similar a few months ago. Of course, I wasn't as close to Uncle Edmond as I'm sure you and Divia were." She glanced over her shoulder to where the man she'd seen coming out of Toby's room had been parked. "Was that a relative of yours?"

"Was who a relative?" he asked with an innocent look.

"The gentleman I saw leaving as I arrived."

"Oh … uh … him," Toby stammered, beginning to look a bit uncomfortable.

"I only ask because you two looked close." She smiled, hoping to put him at ease. "You know, the way he hugged you."

"Sam was just offering support."

When he made no further comment, the conversation fell into an awkward silence, and Elise struggled to find a way to ask him the questions hovering in her mind. In the end, she opted for the direct approach—with as much tact as she could muster.

"Actually, there is something I'd like to talk to you about, Toby. Do you think I could come in for a minute? It's kind of sensitive."

He looked a little wary, but nodded. "Okay," he said slowly. "Come on in, but don't mind the mess."

As Elise stepped from the brightness of the breezeway into the room, she had to blink several times to adjust her eyes to the dim light.

Toby went about picking up newspapers, fast food containers, and clothing that seemed to litter every surface. It looked to Elise as if housekeeping hadn't seen the inside of the room in several days. Once he'd removed the debris from a chair at the small table in the corner, he gestured for her to have a seat.

"Now, what was it you wanted to talk to me about?" he asked when he'd joined her there.

Not knowing quite how to approach the subject, she took a breath and plunged ahead. "Well, it's about a rumor that's been going around. I know it's really none of my business, but the wine community is pretty tight-knit. Anyway, I know you and Maddy have gotten … quite a bit closer lately, and I just wanted to make sure you were aware of what was being said."

Toby sighed and leaned back in his chair. "I think I know where this is going. Let me guess. You heard that there was a *discrepancy*, shall we say, with Third Coast's books?"

She gave him a sympathetic look and nodded. "Then you are aware. I'm sorry, Toby."

"It's all right, Elise." He leaned on the table and studied his laced fingers for a moment. "I know just who you heard it from, too. Monique Toussaint is a devious, vindictive bitch with a big mouth."

*Wow, tell me how you really feel.*

He raised his eyes and the wry grin on his face had her smiling back in response, despite her best effort not to.

"But by the look on your face, I'm betting you know that as well."

She thought the best course of action was to sympathize with him, and she made a disgusted face. "I will never understand why people feel the need to make things up, to spread terrible rumors. It's like they have to tear others down to feel good about themselves."

"That's nice of you to say, Elise. But unfortunately, the rumors are true."

"Oh," she said, unsure of how else to respond. This was just what she'd come looking to confirm, but hearing him say it so matter-of-factly had kind of taken the wind out of her sails.

"The fact that it's true doesn't make Monique's gossiping about it any less despicable, but it also doesn't make what I did right, either."

"You must have had a good reason to do what you did."

"Not really." He shrugged and then his shoulders slumped in defeat. "I did it because of my mother."

"Because of Divia? Why?"

"Look, it's not an excuse," he said, putting up a hand. "What I did was wrong, and I take full responsibility for my actions. And I loved my mother. But she wasn't a very nice person and was extremely hard to please. She was always telling me what a failure my father was, warning me not to be like him. Said he was not only a loser, but dangerous to boot, and if he ever found us, there'd be trouble."

Elise nodded with understanding. "Was that why she took you and ran away from Grace and her dad? She thought your biological father had found you?"

"Yeah. At least, that's what she said at the time." His eyes took on a faraway look, and she had the feeling he was seeing it in his mind. "She was scared, Elise. Really scared. Then, a few months later, she told me that Grace and her dad had died in a horrible fire."

"Oh, Toby. That's terrible."

He slowly nodded before turning to her with haunted eyes. "Yes, but the *really* terrible part is that she told me she thought my father was responsible."

Elise gasped. "What? She made up a story about Grace and her father dying, and then blamed it on your biological father? Why would she do that?"

"Because it gave her the opportunity to reiterate how violent he was and how important it was that he never find us. And it did one other thing that was just as important to her ... it stopped me asking when we were going home. With Grace and Walker Vanderhouse dead, there *was* no going back."

"I'm so sorry, Toby."

He shook his head as if clearing his mind of the ugly thoughts and shrugged again. "Of course, that was a long time ago, and the sketchy memories of a ten-year-old boy."

*Probably not as sketchy as you'd like me to believe.*

When she didn't respond, only smiled back at him, he continued. "Anyway, as I was saying, when Mom made Garrett give me the job at Third Coast, I kinda went off the rails for a while trying to show her that I was nothing like my father."

Though his story made her uncomfortable, Elise also felt bad for him. How terrible it must have been for a young boy—growing up continually trying to please a mother who would never be satisfied with anything he did, and would lie to him with such terrifying abandon.

"I was living way beyond my means and it all got away from me," he stated. "I kept thinking I would find a way to pay it back, but I just got deeper and deeper into trouble."

"So how did Monique find out, Toby?"

He hung his head for a moment, and she wasn't sure he would answer. Then he looked up, and the sadness that clouded his eyes was almost painful to watch. "We ran into each other at a party about six months ago, and she came on to me pretty strong. Emotionally, I was in a bad place, and she's so beautiful. I was flattered by the attention, and we ended up having a thing for a few months."

Elise watched his eyes, as the previous sadness was replaced by an anger that transformed his normally soft features into a twisted mask of hatred.

And a chill ran through her.

"See, I thought she was interested in me." His short bark of laughter was harsh and ugly. "But she was just using me, looking for dirt on my mom."

"Your mom? What did Monique have against Divia?"

"Oh, she *hated* my mom and with good reason." He shook his head and made an obvioous effort to rein in his fury. "Anyway, one night when I'd had a little too much to drink, I told her what I'd done. It was just the ammunition she'd been waiting for. I begged her not to say anything, but she just laughed and thanked me for the information. Do you believe that?" he asked in an incredulous tone. "She actually thanked me."

"That's horrible, Toby." Elise felt a twinge of guilt but pressed for more details. "But what was she going to do with the information? Was she hoping to blackmail your mom? Or maybe Garrett?"

Toby burst into laughter at that, and it took him a minute to get himself under control. "Blackmail. That's a good one, Elise."

"Well, if not blackmail, then what, Toby?"

"*Mrs. Toussaint* was looking more for leverage than anything else." He wiped his eyes and heaved a sigh. "Because as we've established, my mother was not the nicest person—and she was cheating on Garrett with Alain Toussaint."

"Oh my." Elise stared at him briefly, trying to process the new development. This was something that she'd suspected, had heard whispers about, but hadn't expected to have substantiated in such a blatant fashion. "So that was what you meant by Monique hating your mother with good reason?"

"Yeah. I don't know how Monique found out about the affair, but like I said, she's incredibly vindictive. She would've done anything to destroy my mom and get back at Alain, make his life miserable." He ran a hand through his hair in a distracted manner. "I'm sure that was also part of the motivation for her fling with me."

"Did she ever tell Garrett about the missing money?"

Toby shook his head. "No, I beat her to it. Of course, I went to Mom with it first, because that's what I'd been programed to do my whole life. She told me to keep my mouth shut, that she would handle it. But in the end, I went with my gut and told Garrett the whole story."

"How did he take it?"

Toby shook his head and gave her a look of astonishment. "He was incredibly kind, considering what I'd done. We worked out a deal, a way for me to eventually pay him back."

Elise smiled and laid a hand on his arm. "I'm glad, Toby."

"Garrett Larson is a good man, Elise. I hate to say it, but my mom didn't deserve him. She used him for what she could get and then cheated on him with a neighbor's husband. And to make matters worse, I had an affair with the wife of the guy she had an affair with. Guess the apple doesn't fall far from the tree, after all, huh?"

Elise didn't know what to say and didn't want to make it worse for him, but he looked so miserable. "Toby, you're not responsible for your mother's bad decisions. You know that, right? You can only control your *own* choices."

"I know, and like I said, I'm not making excuses, but I'm not proud of how I've behaved, I can tell you that."

After a moment, another thought crossed Elise's mind. "Toby, you said you beat Monique to the punch with the news of your embezzlement. Do you know if Garrett was aware of Divia's affair with Alain Toussaint?"

Toby shook his head. "I don't know. If he knew, he never let on. Why?"

"Oh, no reason. Just curious."

Leaving Toby's room, Elise headed for the car, her mind racing with the new information she'd gathered and what it might mean to Jackson's murder investigation. Garrett's alibi had proved to be false, and he knew about Toby's embezzlement. What if he also knew about Divia's infidelity?

That would pretty much cover motive and opportunity for murder.

Reaching her vehicle, she glanced toward the motel office and was struck by another thought. Not much escaped Harriet Wilson's careful watch here at the motel. If Garrett had left the property on Sunday during the time of Grace's murder, she'd probably have seen it.

Changing gears, Elise headed for the motel office. Harriet, with her elaborate helmet of a hairdo and heavy 50s makeup, greeted her the moment she stepped through the door.

"Well, Elise Beckett." The woman looked up from her crossword puzzle and smiled. "Whatcha doin' out at Lost Pines this mornin'?"

*Yeah, like you don't know exactly where I've been for the last thirty minutes.*

"Oh, you know, just checking in on a friend."

"Uh-huh." Harriet popped her ever-present gum and smiled suggestively. "That Mr. Raymond? Poor man. I saw you comin' out of his room," she added when she noticed the look on Elise's face.

*I'll just bet you did.*

"You know," Harriet continued. "I don't know who I feel sorrier for, him or his stepdaddy. Such a shame on both counts."

Elise couldn't have hoped for a better segue. "I know," she replied in commiseration. "Just terrible."

Harriet leaned down on the counter and sighed. "I mean, it's a shame for Mr. Raymond, sure. But Mr. Larson? Having his former sweetheart find his wife dead like that..." She trailed off, chewing her cud and giving Elise a sly look.

It was a close thing, but Elise managed to ignore the woman's remark. "And with the tragic death out at the festival yesterday, it's a blessing that they were both here instead of at the fairgrounds, right?" she replied.

Harriet tsked and shook her head. "Truer words were never spoken. Why, poor Mr. Larson's only left his new room a couple of times since his wife's demise. And you're right, it was so fortunate that he was here all day on Sunday. I can't even imagine how another murder coming so close after his wife's would've affected that man."

"Are you sure he was here all day?" At Harriet's narrow-eyed glance, Elise hurried on. "It's just that I'd hate to think that he was anywhere near the fairgrounds yesterday."

The older woman ruthlessly worked the gum in her mouth and stared at Elise as if considering how to answer, before raising her drawn-in eyebrows and shrugging. "Well, his car was right out there in the parking lot all day long," she finally answered, nodding toward the window. "I highly doubt he walked to the fairgrounds, so yeah, I'd say I'm relatively sure."

"Well, that's a relief. Anyway, I should be getting out to the vineyard. I'm already late as it is. Just wanted to stop in and say hello while I was here." Elise turned and started for the door.

"All righty then," Harriet said. "Now, you tell Miss Abby that we're taking real good care of her former beau."

When Elise turned back at the door, the woman gave her a sickening-sweet smile and added, "Set her mind at ease."

Swallowing a few snide comments of her own, Elise smiled back in kind. "You know I will, Harriet. Have a nice day."

# SEVENTEEN

AFTER HER ILLUMINATING CHAT with Toby, it was nearly eleven by the time Elise got out to River Bend. Ross had called her cell at one point during the visit, but she'd let it go to voicemail. She hadn't wanted to interrupt Toby's narrative or give him time to think about what he was saying.

When she finally got to the vineyard, her brother had already left for Austin on business, which left Maddy the only 'sleuthing gang' member she could tell about the encounter. And with her sister defending Toby so stringently in past days, Elise thought it best to talk to Ross before telling Maddy what Toby had said.

While she waited for Ross to return, she tried to get some work done. She knew she should get out to the south quadrant to check on how her most recent hybrid transplants were coming along, but she couldn't put the earlier conversation out of her mind. Finally, near-to-bursting to tell *someone* what she'd learned, she called C.C. to see if her friend could make a late lunch. It turned out that she could, and they decided to meet at Del's Kitchen for catfish and hush puppies.

"Man, I love the food here," Elise said, when the piping hot fish baskets had been set before them. She took her first heavenly bite of hush puppy and could almost *feel* the calories adhering to her thighs. But they were so good that she didn't really care.

C.C. nodded. "Me too. But that's not why you called. So spill."

Elise washed the hush puppy down with a sip of iced tea and leaned forward. "Okay, I stopped at Lost Pines Motel this morning on the way to the vineyard."

"*On the way?* Right, because it's not like it's completely in the opposite direction or anything," C.C. said with a smirk.

"Don't be a smart-ass. Do you want to hear about my conversation with Toby Raymond or not?"

C.C. sat back with a surprised look. "You talked to Toby? About the case?"

Elise nodded. "I did. And I got confirmation on several rumors."

"Oh my God! You've got some stones, girlfriend. What possessed you to go out there in the first place? And how did you get him to talk?"

Elise swallowed a bite of coleslaw before answering. "Jackson and I had a long talk about the case last night, and then he annoyed me this morning by telling me to stay out of trouble." She rolled her eyes, clearly conveying what she thought of *that* advice. "Anyway, he'd said he was going to reinterview Toby and Garrett today, but that the Toussaints were first up on his list. So I thought I might be able to catch one of the two guys before he called them into the station."

C.C. laid down her fork very deliberately and put up a finger. "Hang on and back it up, sister. Did you just say that Jax annoyed you *this morning*? Did you spend the night with him?"

Wiping her lips with her napkin, Elise cleared her throat. "Maybe," she replied with a wicked grin.

"Way to bury the lead! What is *wrong* with you?"

"Sorry." Elise giggled. "I was so excited about what I learned from Toby that spending the night at Jackson's sort of got lost."

C.C. shook her head and heaved a sigh. "Well, all I can say is that it's about damn time. I was starting to wonder if you two were ever going to get around to the good stuff. So? How did it go?"

Elise laughed out loud. "Girl, that man has some pretty sweet moves ... which he demonstrated for me more than once last night."

"Oooh. Jealous, party of one," C.C. said and fanned herself with her napkin. "But, this is very good news. It's always a sad state of affairs when someone who is as easy on the eyes as Jax fails to ... uh ... meet expectations, shall we say?"

"You may rest assured that is not the case where Jackson Landry is concerned, my friend." Elise tilted her head and considered her relationship with Jackson for a moment. "We've danced around each other for so long, C.C., I was afraid if we ever got to this point it would be weird, you know?"

"Uh-huh. And?"

Elise's smile grew. "So far, it just seems ... right."

"I knew it all along. You two are a perfect match." C.C. crowed and popped a piece of hush puppy into her mouth. "Now, tell me about your encounter with Toby."

Elise blew out a breath. "I had no idea what I was going to say when I decided to go out there, but surprisingly, everything just fell into place." She went on to elaborate on the conversation she'd had with the man.

"Good Lord." C.C. made a face when she'd finished. "Just when you think this thing can't get any more sordid or nasty ... it does."

"I know. With Divia having an affair with Alain Toussaint and Monique seducing Toby in retaliation, it's like something out of a bad soap opera."

"Yeah, and Toby embezzling from Third Coast on top of everything else? Amazing. I'm telling you, you can't make up this kind of crazy stuff."

The conversation lagged as the waitress came over to the table to top off their tea.

"I know it looks bad that Garrett doesn't have an alibi," C.C. continued when the waitress walked away. "Especially since he knew about Toby's embezzlement and possibly about Divia's affair, but do you really think he's capable of murder?"

Elise shook her head. "I don't know. For Gram's sake, I hope not. It would break her heart. But if there's one thing I've learned over the last year, it's that you never really know what someone will do when push comes to shove."

"Well, even if he had motive and opportunity to kill his wife, that doesn't explain Grace's murder. And doesn't Jackson think both deaths are related? I mean, I don't think Grace even knew Garrett Larson. If she did, she never mentioned him. So what would be the connection?"

"That's a good question. You know Harriet Wilson out at Lost Pines keeps an eagle-eye on their motel. And when I talked to her this morning after leaving Toby's room, she indicated that Garrett hadn't left the room he'd been moved to but a handful of times since Divia's death. She also said that his car was in the parking lot all day Sunday." Elise pushed her fish basket away, picking up her glass to sip. "Of course, he could have snuck out to the festival at some point, but I'm thinking someone would have seen him. And yes, Jax thinks the murders are connected somehow, but that doesn't necessarily mean they were carried out by the same person."

"You mean, a couple of people working together?" C.C. jabbed a finger in the air. "My money would be on scary French chick and that brother-in-law of hers. If Philippe Toussaint isn't in love with Monique, he has the weirdest fixation on her that I've ever seen. Creeps me out. He'd probably do anything she asked. And I don't think he'd even think twice about killing or cleaning up any mess she'd created."

"I agree, and that's a nice, neat scenario." Elise nodded but couldn't help the nagging doubt teasing the back of her mind. "But then why would Monique get so bent about Alain having the affair with Divia? And why seduce Toby to try to gather dirt on his mom? If that was the case, you'd think she would've been glad that Divia was occupying Alain's time."

C.C. frowned. "Good point."

"Of course, like Toby said, Monique is a vindictive, manipulative woman. Maybe she just didn't want anyone else playing with her toys—didn't want to share."

"You know, I've never understood that I-can-screw-around-but-don't-you-dare mentality. In my opinion, it's just selfish in the extreme, but again, we're talking about Monique Toussaint."

As they sat there in silence, each mulling over what they knew, a thought occurred to Elise. "The other thing that bothers me about the Toussaints is Alain's attitude," she said after a moment. "It was pretty clear that he knew nothing about Monique and Divia's little scuffle on Thursday and was pissed off when he heard about it. But I don't think he and Monique were anywhere *near* each other Friday night when Divia was murdered, yet he gave her an alibi."

"Well, she is his wife." C.C. finished her lunch and sat back with her tea. "Alain Toussaint strikes me as a pretty sharp guy. Do you think if Monique's having an affair with Philippe, his own brother, that he's clueless about it? Or just turning a blind eye?"

"Who knows? Hopefully, Jax can get to the bottom of things. Last night he seemed pretty determined to get the truth out of them one way or another."

C.C. leaned forward and narrowed her eyes. "El, I know you got all this intel out of Toby, but what about him? Do you think he could be involved somehow?"

Elise nodded. "I've thought about that. From all accounts, Divia was hard on him growing up, and that didn't change as he got older. I suppose he could've snapped after years of abuse, but poison his mother? I don't know."

She thought back to the morning hours and her conversation with the man. "At one point, when he was talking about Monique's betrayal, he got a really scary look in his eyes, and I thought, yeah, this guy could kill someone. But I would think Monique would have been the one he'd go after, not Divia."

"Yeah. I guess that would make more sense. And he was just a kid when his mom was married to Grace's dad. So, I can't see a motive for him to go after Grace, either."

"Oh, crap!" Elise slapped a hand to her head. "That's the other thing we talked about. Before I left, I asked him why Divia took him and ran away."

189

"And what did he say?" C.C. asked with eager interest.

"He said that Divia told him they were in danger. She said they had to run because his biological father was an evil man and he'd found them. And that she was really scared."

Elise paused as the waitress brought them their checks. Searching her purse for her wallet, she continued when the woman walked away. "Then a few months later, Divia told him she'd heard that Grace and her father had been killed in a mysterious fire. He said Divia suggested his real dad might be responsible, and that they'd been lucky to have gotten away when they did."

"Wow, that's cold," C.C. commented with big eyes. "I imagine he was shocked when he found out Grace was alive."

"You can say that again. Jax and I were standing in line with him at The Plough's booth when he got the news. He paled so fast we all thought he'd suddenly taken ill. Then we heard him and Divia arguing about it in the parking lot later. She tried to tell him it was a coincidence, but he wasn't having it. He was royally torqued—told her she was a *piece of work*."

"Well, that could have been the last straw, so to speak—the thing that made him snap," C.C. commented as she slid from the booth. "But it still doesn't explain a motive for killing Grace. You would think he would have been happy finding out she was alive."

"Yeah, but that's the thing, C.C.," Elise said as she stood to gather her belongings. "When he finally went to see Grace, he said she was angry—almost hostile—and didn't want anything to do with Divia or him. Remember, Grace had to watch her dad die a broken man. And she blamed Divia all those years."

"Okay, but wouldn't that be just another mark against Divia? Why would that be a motive to kill Grace?"

Elise sighed. "You're right. It wouldn't."

As they paid their bills and stepped out into the sunshine, Elise dug out her keys. "I guess the good thing is that even with some of the circumstantial evidence pointing at Gram, there are definitely several other suspects with strong enough motives to kill Divia. However, Grace is another story. And I have a feeling when we find that connection, we'll have our killer."

"Or *killers*," C.C. added.

As Elise drove back to River Bend, she mentally reviewed the evidence that had been uncovered so far and the motives of everyone involved. She wished she could be a fly on the wall when Jackson re-interviewed the three Toussaints. They'd alibied each other for the time of Divia Larson's murder on Friday night, but she knew in her bones they were lying through their teeth.

Unfortunately, Ross still hadn't returned from Austin when Elise got back to the vineyard, so she hopped into a vineyard truck and headed out to the south quadrant. She could at least check on her hybrids while she worked on the murder puzzle in her head.

The longer she thought about it, the idea that there was more than one person involved—and that the murders were connected—seemed not only plausible, but probable. And she had a feeling that the killer—or killers, as C.C. had put it—were right under their noses.

# EIGHTEEN

JACKSON SPENT THE FIRST two hours of his morning with Jim Stockton, going over the evidence and what they knew so far about both murders. He had a sense that a more recent connection between Divia Larson and Grace Vanderhouse was present, but couldn't for the life of him see it.

In the meantime, they'd reinterview the key suspects. And they'd start with the three Toussaints, because he had questions, and he wanted more satisfying answers than he'd gotten from them so far.

The first time he'd spoken with the French vintners had been a very casual affair—and with them all together—out at the festival. This time would be different. He and Jim were interviewing them separately at the station—starting with Alain, who was waiting in Room One. Jackson felt that the older Toussaint brother was the weak link in the chain.

A chain Jackson intended to break.

"Thank you for coming in on such short notice, Mr. Toussaint," Jackson said as he entered the interrogation room and sat down at the table facing the man.

"Since you've forbade us to return home, we didn't have much of a choice, *n'est-ce-pas?*"

Jackson studied the man's demeanor—his abrupt attitude and defiant posture. It was obvious the Frenchman thought he and his family were in the clear.

*We'll just see how that goes for y'all, pal.*

"I guess that's true," Jackson replied. "But then we are smack-dab in the middle of a couple of murder investigations."

Alain shrugged. "I don't see what that has to do with me. I knew Mrs. Larson only slightly, and I didn't know the other woman at all."

Jim closed the door, then sat down next to Jackson and leaned forward. "You might want to back that up a bit. Don't want to dig yourself any deeper into a hole by lyin', my friend."

"By lying?" Alain's mouth dropped open and he made a show of his outrage. "I don't think I like your insinuation, Deputy!"

Jackson put up a hand before the confrontation could get them off track. "See, it's just that there are some inconsistencies in what you and the other members of your family told us in our earlier interview. And we need to clear them up."

"What are you talking about? What sort of inconsistencies?" A wary look crossed Alain's face, and Jackson caught the briefest scent of fear in his tone.

"Let's talk about Divia Larson first," Jackson suggested. "You say you barely knew her, but that's not the case, is it? Isn't it true that you were having an affair with the woman?"

"I have no idea what you're talking about?"

"Before you start denying and backpedaling," Jim warned, "You should be advised that we have several statements confirming the affair, one of which is from your own wife."

Alain opened and closed his mouth a few times without speaking, and his confused anger was apparent. "All right, fine!" he said at length, waving a hand in the air. "I had a brief fling with the woman and then ended it. What of it? That's not a crime, is it?"

"No, but murder is," Jim said with a slight smile.

"*Murder?*" Alain replied with raised eyebrows. "How did we go from a concluded affair to murder?"

"You said you ended it with Mrs. Larson, but that isn't quite factual, now is it?" The deputy shrugged. "And weren't you having a hard time getting out of the affair? Well, that's a pretty good starting point for motive. Add in opportunity, and how do you say it? Oh yeah, *voilà!*"

Alain made a face. "You're quite amusing, Deputy. And your French pronunciation is atrocious."

"Maybe. But the fact remains that Divia Larson wasn't letting you go as easily as you'd like us to believe, correct?"

"Ach! Very well. If you must know, it's true that Divia was being… difficult. She wasn't as ready to end it as I was, but it's hardly a reason to kill her. It made absolutely no difference."

Jackson looked up from the file folder he'd been perusing. "Not even when she threatened to go to your wife with it if you didn't fall into line?"

"Who told you that?" Alain asked and the stricken look that crossed his face was almost comical.

"But what you didn't know at that time was that Monique already knew and was just biding her time with the information," Jim continued, ignoring the man's panicked question.

Jackson watched the emotions flood the man's face one after the other and knew that he and Jim were on the right path. "You might as well come clean with it all, Alain. When did you find out that your wife knew about the affair?"

Toussaint heaved a sigh and rubbed his forehead as if a headache might be brewing there. "I found out shortly before coming here for the festival—when Monique threw it in my face, along with the fact that she was having an affair of her own ... with Divia's son."

"Seriously?" Jim's surprise was evident, though he tried to hide it. "Your wife was having an affair with Toby Raymond? Why?"

"*Oui*, I assure you, as distasteful as it may sound, I am most serious." A look of disdain passed over the Frenchman's face. "And as to why? I would think that was obvious. She did it to get back at me, of course. That, and to try to find something she could use to destroy Divia's life."

"But why was she so bent on destroying Divia's life? Why not just tell Garrett about the affair?" Jackson asked. "Why go to such lengths to dig up more dirt?"

Toussaint brushed at his jacket sleeve and sat back in his chair with a smirk on his face. "Because my wife is a vindictive, hateful bitch, Deputy Landry. And because Garrett Larson already knew about the affair."

"What?" Jim asked, and this time he didn't bother to hide his surprise. "How do you know that?"

"Monique told him, didn't she?" Jackson asked and was baffled when the man laughed out loud.

"Yes, she went to him with the information, thinking he would be outraged."

"And that's funny?" Jim asked.

"*Absolument!*" he said and continued to chuckle. "It was her first volley, you see, but it missed the mark because somehow Garrett had found out beforehand. He told her he was sorry if the circumstances caused her pain, but to be patient. He said the affair would blow over soon enough, but obviously that wasn't as accurate as he'd hoped. Monique was furious."

"And you don't know how he found out?" Jim asked. "Do you think Mrs. Larson told him?"

"Doubtful. But I don't think Divia would've cared one way or another. She was only using Garrett Larson for his money and the prestige of being a vineyard owner's wife. In any case, she was as selfish and vain as my wife is vindictive and manipulative."

Jackson nodded and then pinned the man with a steely gaze. "If you have such contempt for your wife, then why give her an alibi?" He tilted his head and regarded Toussaint as another thought dawned on him. "Or was the alibi for you? Because we both know you weren't together on Friday night when Divia Larson was murdered. And before you dispute that fact, know that we have a witness that saw Monique and your brother just before the time of Divia's death … but not you."

It was a bluff, but to Jackson's surprise, the man didn't even blink. "No, you're correct. We weren't together Friday night, but we thought it would be best—less awkward for everyone involved—if we said that we were."

196

"Less awkward. Uh-huh. Well, since we've established that you had motive, I'm going to need to know where you were and if there's anyone to corroborate your story," Jackson replied. "Because I gotta tell ya, it sounds like you might've had ample opportunity as well."

Toussaint frowned and waved a hand in the air again, as if swatting away an annoying insect. "I was with a dancer friend of mine in Austin all afternoon and into the evening. I didn't get back to the motel until the early hours of the morning." Pulling out a business card, he took Jim's pen from him and scribbled on the back before handing it to Jackson. "Here is my friend's name and number. Claudette will corroborate my story, I assure you. Now, am I free to go?"

"Sure … for now," Jackson said, but thought of something else before the man got to the door. "One more question, Alain. Where were you on Sunday afternoon between two and three o'clock?"

Toussaint shrugged. "Monique and I were both helping to pack up the booth. There are several employees who will confirm that for you."

Jackson waited until the man had left the room and closed the door behind him before turning to Jim with a questioning look. "So? What do you think?"

Jim shook his head and looked as if he'd just smelled a rotten odor. "I think that's pretty messed up all the way around. You got him doing the neighbor's wife, his wife doing the neighbor's wife's son. And I don't think I even want to know what's going on between his wife and his brother."

"Yeah, I'm right there with you, buddy." He held up the business card that Alain had given him. "And if this pans out, it means we can take at least one of the Toussaints out of the suspect pool. Now, let's go see about the other two."

Over in Interview Two, Alain's brother, Philippe, proved to be a tougher nut to crack. He was surly, arrogant, and tight-lipped. About the only thing they got out of him at first was that he thought Alain was an idiot, that he was in love with Monique, and that he was in Austin playing golf with clients on Sunday afternoon.

He did say one thing of interest at the end of the interview, though. He told them he and Monique had been dining at a friend's house in Smithville on Friday night. And though he didn't give much detail, he did let it slip that said friend just happened to be a lawyer. Jackson wasn't sure if he'd mentioned the lawyer on purpose thinking they would tread more carefully, or if he'd done it by accident. But he was leaning toward accidental, because Philippe Toussaint didn't strike him as the brightest bulb in the lighting array.

When questioned further about the specifics of their dining extravaganza, the Frenchman clammed up and refused to say another word. However, it gave Jackson an idea to run with when they went into Interview Room Three to speak with Monique, whom they'd intentionally saved for last.

"It's about damn time," she said with a huff before they could even sit down. "Do you know how long I've been waiting in this horrible little room?"

"Sorry for the inconvenience, Mrs. Toussaint," Jim said smoothly. "We got hung up chatting with your husband and your brother-in-law. They had a few very interesting things to say."

"Really?" she asked in a doubtful tone. "Like what?"

Jackson leaned forward and laced his fingers on the table in front of him. "Well, for one thing, that y'all lied about your alibi, Monique, which we already knew. And for another, that you had motive and opportunity to poison Divia Larson."

That statement set off a barrage of heated French and fist pounding from the woman that was amusing and at the same time a little scary. It had both Jax and Jim backing away slightly, just in case.

When it didn't seem like she was going to finish up anytime soon, Jackson put a hand up and spoke over the top of her yammering. "Look, you can continue to yell at us in French—which will get you nowhere—or you can simply tell us where you were on Friday night between six-forty-five and seven-fifteen."

Jackson watched her closely, and thought that, as angry as she was, her head might explode. Whether he wanted it or not, he had a very clear picture in his mind of what that might look like. Her face was flushed and her eyes were shooting daggers at him, but at least she'd stopped shouting. After a moment she finally took a deep breath and let it out slowly.

"I did not kill that terrible woman, though I am not at all sad that she is dead."

"You realize your statement doesn't instill a whole lot of confidence, right?" Jim asked, tongue-in-cheek.

Monique glared at him.

"Come on, Monique," Jackson said, drawing her attention away from poor Jim, who was looking more uncomfortable by the second. "Alain already told us that you were having an affair with Toby Raymond, and that you were looking for a way to destroy Divia. He also said that the alibi y'all gave was a load of manure. Care to give us your side of the story?"

Monique studied her manicure for a few moments and just when Jackson thought she'd clam up as well, she spoke. "It's true. I was having an affair with that imbecile, Toby Raymond. But only to get back at my husband."

"And to dig up dirt to use against Divia?" Jim asked, and was rewarded with another glare.

"I thought telling Garrett Larson of his wife's infidelity would do the trick, but he already knew. He told me to be patient." She gave Jackson a wicked smile. "I am not the most patient of women. So I seduced Toby to torment my husband, yes, but also in hopes of finding something with which to ruin her selfish little world."

"And you found something you thought would be perfect, didn't you?" Jackson asked on a hunch.

Her wicked smile grew to a grin. "Toby gets very talkative when he's had too much to drink. That stupid, stupid man was stealing from the vineyard, and he ... how do you say ... spilled the beans?"

"Toby was embezzling from Third Coast and fixing the books? Is that what you're saying?" Jim asked for clarification.

"*Oui*. He begged me not to tell, but I told him that I would as soon as I felt the time was right. He was very unhappy with me. I planned to tell Garrett what his step-son was doing, but I wanted to torment Divia with the news first."

Jackson nodded. "Which you did on Thursday during your little scuffle, but did you get around to telling Garrett?"

"No. I never got the chance."

"You understand this all gives you a stellar motive for killing the woman, right?" Jackson asked. "Can you give me a decent ... *confirmable* ... alibi, Monique? Or do I add opportunity to your résumé?"

She gave him a very pretty pout, but he continued to glower at her. Finally she relented. "Oh, all right. Philippe and I went to dinner at a friend's home in Smithville Friday night. We were there from six-thirty until almost eleven."

"Yes. Philippe mentioned that you had a dinner meeting with your lawyer." It wasn't exactly what the man had said, but Jackson thought he'd do a little more bluffing and see what popped up. And by the look on her face, he was doing just fine. "Does Alain have any idea what you and his brother are up to?"

"I-I don't know what you mean."

"Oh, come on, darlin." Jackson folded his arms, leaned down on the table, and gave her a conspiring wink. "Philippe already gave us the bare bones of the plan. Though I have to say, I'm a bit surprised that Alain's own brother would be involved with something like this, aren't you, Jim?"

"Downright shocked. Poor Alain won't know what hit him."

Monique narrowed her eyes and gave the deputy a look that Jackson was sure would wither a lesser man. "Bah! Poor Alain, indeed. He doesn't care about me or the vineyard. All he wants is to go back to France." She turned back to Jackson, a pleading tone in her voice. "Philippe loves me and wants to help me make something of importance here. We can be happy together as soon as I can get a divorce."

"And, of course, steal the vineyard away from Alain," Jim added.

That seemed to be the last straw for Monique, and she gave them both a mutinous stare. "I have nothing more to say. I will have Philippe give you the name and number of my lawyer. You can call him for confirmation."

# NINETEEN

It was after four when Elise finally finished up her day and left the greenhouse for the main residence. She'd heard rather than seen Ross come home a while ago, but since her lunch date with C.C., her burning need to tell Ross about her morning chat with Toby had waned. It could wait until later. Besides, she was more interested in what her grandmother was planning for Monday night dinner.

She hadn't heard from Jackson, but that didn't mean much. He was buried in the two recent homicide cases, and probably up to his eyeballs in work. When she'd tried his cell earlier, she'd gotten his voicemail and left a message. He'd call her back when he came up for air.

*In the meantime, a girl's gotta eat. And if I waited on Jackson Landry, I'd no doubt starve.*

"Hey, Gram," she said as she came through the back door and found Abigail leaning on the counter, writing out what looked to be a grocery list.

Abigail looked up and smiled. "Well, hello, sweet girl. You knocking off for the day?"

"Yes, ma'am." Elise set her purse down on the counter and leaned in from the opposite side. "Got a few more of the hybrids in the ground today. Put them out in the south quadrant where we planted that last batch. I think they're gonna do real well there. The first group has already just about doubled in size."

"That's good news," Abigail replied absently and continued to work on her list.

"Whatcha doin'?"

"I'm out of a few things that I need for dinner, so I thought I'd make out a list and head into the H-E-B." Abigail looked up and speared her with a suspicious glance. "Why?"

Elise laughed. "I was just wondering what you were cookin' up for dinner." She batted her eyelashes innocently. "And if you might be makin' enough for company."

At her grandmother's hopeful look, Elise realized she was thinking about Jackson and what had happened at dinner the previous evening. Elise went on quickly to clarify. "Jax is probably gonna be late, and I didn't really feel like going home and cooking something for just me."

As Abigail's disappointment was evident, Elise reached out and laid a hand on her arm. "Don't worry, Gram. He may have his nose out of joint for the moment, but you know Jax won't stay away for long. After last night's debacle, he just needs some space."

Her grandmother patted her hand and nodded. "Oh, I know, honey-pie. I just hate the way he left, is all. I tell you, I love his parents dearly, I do, but they've never really had much time for that boy. Bein' so caught up in their diggin' for artifacts and the like. He may not be our blood kin, but he's still kin all the same. It just breaks my heart to think that he might be doubting that right now."

"No matter what he says, deep down he knows that," Elise replied, then wiggled her eyebrows to lighten the mood. "Now, about that dinner ..."

Abigail chuckled and shook her head. "Of course you can stay. Madison's eating with friends in town, but you know I usually make plenty, and you're always welcome. But I need to get a move on, get to the store and back."

"I could run into town for you. That way you won't have to wait to get started."

After a moment, Abigail nodded. "Works for me. And there's nothing too complicated on this list, so you shouldn't have any problems."

Elise rolled her eyes and fisted her hands on her hips. "Come on, Gram. I have a master's degree in horticulture. I think I can navigate a grocery list." At Abigail's skeptical look, Elise held out a hand and made a 'gimme' gesture with her fingers. "Hand it over."

With a comical and inflated sigh, her grandmother complied. "Okay, but make it snappy, kiddo. I've got cookin' to do."

"You got it."

Grabbing her purse and keys, Elise headed for the car. Twenty minutes later, she was in the produce section at the H-E-B looking for organic broccoli, of all things. It seemed that her Gram was big on organic fruits and veggies these days.

It took her longer than she'd figured, but she finally found everything on the list, and soon she was checking out and schlepping her purchases out to the parking lot.

As her little sports car came into view, she could see from a distance that there was something tucked under the windshield wiper on the driver's side. The closer she got, the more it looked like a flyer of some kind.

She'd never understand why folks found it helpful to paper an entire parking lot of cars with ads for this or that. As far as she was concerned, it was nothing but an annoyance and just something else to dispose of. Of course, it looked like hers was the only vehicle in her section to get the treatment. But still.

Depositing the groceries in the passenger seat, she went around to the driver's side. Before climbing behind the wheel, she jerked the folded piece of paper loose and tossed it to the floorboard of the car. Planning to throw it out when she got back to the vineyard, she promptly forgot about it.

That is, until she pulled in at the residence and turned off the engine.

Glancing down, something about the flyer caught her interest. For some reason, it didn't look like your average, everyday flyer any more. Reaching down, she picked it up, unfolded it, and froze.

No, this was definitely *not* a flyer or an advertisement. This was something much more disturbing. Large, irregular letters had been cut randomly from magazine pages and glued onto a plain piece of paper. It was like something right out of a movie script. She read its message over twice as the first icy fingers of fear took hold.

POKING AROUND WHERE YOU SHOULDN'T
BACK OFF BEFORE YOU GET HURT OR WORSE

Seriously? What had she done to deserve this? Poking around in what? She'd stopped in to chat with Toby this morning, but that was the only thing she could pinpoint deserving of this kind of threat—and she wasn't even sure *that* qualified.

She and the others had only been asking subtle questions, unless you counted Ross's heavy-handed interrogation of Alain Toussaint over the weekend. But why single her out? And how would they know she'd be at the H-E-B at that specific time?

Unless they'd been following her or staking her out.

Through the nibbling of fear, anger made its way to the surface, and she began to simmer.

*How dare they … whoever they were?*

Her mind went crazy with scenarios before she realized that she was jumping to incredible conclusions she had no way to confirm. The note didn't have her name on it anywhere—nothing to indicate it had anything to do with her at all—or the murder investigations, for that matter. Maybe it was just a prank. It was possible, right?

Climbing out of the car, she scanned the driveway and area surrounding the house before she caught herself. Shaking her head, she stuffed the note into her purse and went around to retrieve the groceries. What exactly was she looking for? Did she think that whoever had left the threatening note would follow her right up to her mother's doorstep?

*I'm such a moron.*

In any case, she wasn't going to worry about it. Maybe she'd run up to Ross's after dinner—kill two birds. She could fill him in on what Toby had to say this morning, and also see what he thought about this stupid note.

As it turned out, Ross and Caroline, along with their two boys were in the kitchen with Abigail and Laura when she walked through the door. Evidently Caleb was feeling better after being ill the night before, as both boys looked to be in high spirits.

"Auntie El!" Caleb and Ethan shouted her name in unison and just about tackled her to the ground when she entered the room.

"*Auntie El, Auntie El,*" Ross mimicked them in a pretty good imitation of the Wicked Witch of the West, and had the boys groaning.

"We just watched that movie again last night," Caroline explained. "Ross continues to insist that the witch is horrible and scary, but the boys aren't impressed."

"Nah." Ethan made a face. "She's not scary at all."

Not to be left out, Caleb chimed in. "Yeah. She's green and *boring.*" He shook his head. "But I don't like the monkeys."

Elise set the groceries on the counter and ruffled Caleb's hair. "I don't like them either, pal. I think they're way scarier than the witch."

"Uh-huh." He looked up at her with huge, cornflower-blue eyes and swallowed hard. "And they gotts wings," he whispered. "And they can fly and chase a guy and stuff."

Elise gave an exaggerated shudder and had him giggling. As she did, the threatening note she thought she'd stuffed deep into her purse dropped out onto the floor, and Caleb bent to pick it up.

"What's this, Auntie El? Did you do art today for work?" he asked. "We do art in kindi-garden."

"Um … no, honey. It's not my art." Grabbing it from him, she folded it up, intending to put it back, but she wasn't fast enough and Ross nipped it from her fingers.

"Exactly what do we have here, Auntie El?" he asked, before unfolding the paper. His eyebrows shot up as he read. Looking up, he trained a hard stare in her direction. "El? What's this all about? Where did you get this?"

Abigail came around the counter and took the note out of his hands. After reading it, she, too, gave Elise a steely look. "Yes, baby girl. Do tell. Where did this come from?"

Elise blinked several times and looked back and forth between them. The thought briefly crossed her mind of trying to pass it off as nothing or make something up, but how in God's name did she do *that*? In the end, she came clean. "I found it underneath the windshield wiper on my car when I came out of the store. I thought it was an advertisement or some kind of flyer at first. I didn't even look at it until I got back here."

Reading the note over Abigail's shoulder, a disgusted look crossed Caroline's face. "Why on earth would someone do that? Leave something so sinister and upsetting for a person to find?"

"And *have* you been poking around in something you shouldn't?" Abigail asked, repeating the note's sentiments. "Maybe something you've been told to stay out of?"

"No," she replied with a straight face, though her tone was colored with guilt. She glanced at Ross, who made a point of looking everywhere but directly at her.

"Come on, boys," Caroline said in the uncomfortable lull. "Let's go into the living room and play some video games for a while before dinner." She wisely herded them out of the kitchen. Elise strongly suspected that her sister-in-law wanted to escape the coming conversation as well.

"Okay, spill it, you two," Laura demanded. "What's going on here? Elise Brianna? What have you done?"

"Me?" Elise squeaked. "Why do you assume I've done something wrong? How is it that I'm always the one who automatically gets the blame for every little thing?" She gestured toward the note still in her grandmother's hand. "Maybe this is just someone's idea of a prank."

"Yeah. All we've been doing is keeping an ear to the ground and an eye out for anything unusual," Ross added, though Elise thought his comment was anything but helpful.

"What do you mean *we*? The two of you? Or have you dragged Madison and C.C. into whatever you've been doing as well?" Laura asked with a frown. "And watching and listening for what?"

"Are you talking about these murder investigations?" Abigail narrowed her eyes and drilled them both with a hard stare. "Have you two been poking around in Jackson's business again?"

"No!" Elise and Ross answered in unison but only ended up sounding more guilty.

"Oh, Elise." Laura shook her head, disappointment etched on her face. "I thought you'd learned your lesson after what happened during the summer. Poking around in your uncle's murder investigation almost got you killed."

"Yes, but—"

"Now, we're all real proud of the way you handled yourself during that frightening experience, baby girl," Abigail said, cutting her off. "You didn't panic. You used your head and saved the day. But if you think there wasn't a healthy amount of dumb luck involved, you're just foolin' yourself. And I know you're not a fool. That fiasco over the summer could've gone the other direction lickety-split. That's why you need to stay out of these investigations Jackson's got goin' on."

"In El's defense," Ross said, holding up a finger to emphasis his point. "She was just trying to make certain that you were in the clear where Divia Larson's death was concerned, Gram."

Elise's mouth dropped open, and she slapped her hands on her hips. "In *my* defense? How about *we* were just trying to clear Gram? You've been neck-deep in that plan from the start, pal."

Abigail turned and pointed at him. "And you should've known better, anyway, Ross Alexander. If it wasn't for your sister here keeping that cool head under fire, you could've been in big trouble during that last showdown with your uncle's killer. She saved your bacon, mister. Besides, I don't need you two nitwits messin' around and tryin' to clear me for anything. Jackson will make sure I'm covered."

"Okay, okay. Calm down, both of you." Ross put up both hands in surrender. "*We* were just trying to clear Gram," he said to Elise, before turning to Abigail. "And you're right, Gram. I should've known better." He gestured to the threatening note. "But we really haven't done anything worthy of this kind of retaliation, so I find the whole thing kind of baffling."

"Elise?" Laura gave her a questioning look. "Anything you can think of that might explain these threats?"

Elise shook her head and blew out a breath. "I stopped by and talked with Toby this morning, just to see how he and Garrett were doing, but that's all I've done. I *swear*," she added when she received skeptical looks all around.

Laura took the note from Abigail and handed it back to Elise. "I want you to take this note to Jackson first thing in the morning and confess your sins. I mean it, Elise." She looked back and forth between her children. "And no more nosing around in Jackson's police business. Do you both hear me?"

Elise felt like a child being scolded for bad behavior and again responded like that naughty child in tandem with her brother. "Yes, ma'am."

As she went about helping her grandmother put away the groceries, Elise couldn't help wondering if someone's feathers had been ruffled with her morning visit to the motel. But why? If the note was a warning regarding the homicide investigations, it could only mean that she'd struck a nerve, maybe gotten close to something the killer didn't want her to know or see. But what on earth could that be?

Even as she'd told her mother she'd let it go, an idea had been brewing in the back of her mind. An idea that involved another trip out to Lost Pines Motel.

# TWENTY

ELISE AWOKE ON TUESDAY morning with the beginning of a head-ache and feeling like she'd been beaten with a stick. After finding the threatening note on her windshield the previous day—and her family's reaction to it—she'd worked hard to avoid the topic all through dinner. But it had certainly been the elephant in the room and never far from her mind. The whole thing had made for an unnerving drive home, wondering if someone was out there in the dark watching, or if she was just being paranoid.

Adding to her anxiety was the lengthy conversation she'd had with her brother after dinner about her morning visit with Toby Raymond.

Ross was of the mind that Toby wasn't being completely honest, though he'd been vague on what he thought the man was withhold-ing. He also felt that Toby couldn't be trusted, though again, had no concrete reasoning why, other than he'd embezzled a goodly amount from Third Coast's coffers. With Ross, that alone was a sin worthy of punishment with extreme prejudice.

Hence, the fodder for the nightmares that had kept her tossing and turning all night long. By the time her alarm blared at seven forty-five, she was exhausted and more than ready to get out of the torture chamber she called a bed.

Chunk, however, was not as willing to rise. Sprawled across the middle section of the bed like a big, furry lump, he was perfectly content to stay right where he was. Somehow he'd managed to relegate her to the very edge of the mattress even with her restless night of bad dreams. With a fatigued sigh, she rolled out of bed, leaving him to enjoy as much space as he desired.

The first order of business was to get some much needed caffeine into her system, so she stumbled into the kitchen on that particular quest. Grabbing a diet soda out of the fridge, she took it with her to the shower in hopes that the caffeine would fire up her brain and the hot water would energize her body. She also prayed it would ease the tenuous pounding behind her eyes before it blossomed into something ugly.

The combination of the two seemed to beat back the worst of the headache, and soon her mind was racing with plans for the day. She still had some tasks to accomplish in the greenhouse—some starts and young vines that needed a bit of attention—but she zeroed in on making the most productive use of her lunch hour.

Jackson had finally surfaced late the previous evening and returned her call. It seemed that he and Jim Stockton had had their hands full with the Toussaints from mid-morning until well into the afternoon. Once he'd finished the paperwork, returned emails, and made some calls, there hadn't been much time left for anything else.

She knew she should tell him about the threatening note but she didn't want to add to his stress. At least that's what she told herself. She'd tell him when he wasn't so buried in suspects and paperwork.

Jackson had yet to requestion Garrett Larson or Toby Raymond. He did mention that those interviews were on the agenda for later today after he finished confirming the new alibis the toxic Toussaint trio had given him. If so, maybe she could catch Garrett on her lunch hour and see what she could get out of him before he headed into the station.

Of course, if not, there was something out at the motel that had been nagging at her, and if Garrett wasn't around, she could check that out instead. She had a mind to get into the room where Divia Larson had died. That is, if she could wrangle the key out of Harriet Wilson.

Officially, the room was still a crime scene, but the CSIs had already scoured the place, so she didn't see it as a big deal. They'd be releasing it any day now, anyway. There probably wasn't anything left to find, but she'd worry about that and how she was going to finagle her way inside once she got there.

However, with the threatening note she'd received still fresh and looming in the back of her mind, she thought it might be prudent to take someone along with her on the trip out to the motel. Keeping the whole thing on the down-low was another priority, because she didn't want yet another lecture on snooping from either her mother or grandmother.

And it wasn't like she was worried or anything. She'd be going out in broad daylight, so what could happen? But it usually paid to think these things through, especially after her ordeal over the summer. She'd gotten herself into a bad spot with no backup. That was something she wasn't about to do again.

An hour and a half later, she was bidding adieu to the fat cat and heading out the door. She went straight to River Bend with the intention of getting as much done as she could before her lunch-hour trip to the motel. She also wanted to talk to both Madison and C.C. to see if either of them could spare the time to accompany her. Having another set of eyes and ears would be helpful.

Hitting the main residence just shy of ten o'clock, she was surprised to see an SUV tagged with Third Coast's logo parked outside. When she entered the dining room, she was even more surprised to find Garrett Larson seated at the table, sipping coffee with her grandmother.

"Sorry. Didn't mean to barge in," she said when they both looked up. Though the couple hadn't chosen a secluded spot to talk, Elise felt the scene seemed somehow private.

Abigail smiled and greeted her. "Mornin', baby girl. No worries. Come on in and get some coffee." She gestured to the sideboard where a pot sat on a warmer. "You feelin' okay? That frown you're sportin' tells me something's up."

Elise deposited her purse in a chair and went over to grab a scone and possibly a cup to go. "I'm fine, Gram, other than a slight tension headache. But I had a couple of things I didn't get to yesterday, and I wanted to take care of them this morning." Sitting down opposite Garrett, she gave him a wan smile. "Good morning, Mr. Larson. Looks like you're up and about early this morning."

He took another sip of his coffee and nodded. "I'm due at the sheriff's office in a little over an hour, but I wanted to come by and clear the air here first."

"Clear the air?" Elise frowned. "What do you mean?"

He sighed and glanced briefly at Abigail before giving her a tired look. Elise thought in that moment he looked every bit of his seventy years, which was unusual for him. The man was normally so full of vitality.

"You'll probably find out in due course, so it really doesn't matter," he replied, but still hesitated a moment as if embarrassed. "I lied to the deputy on Friday night when I got to the motel and found y'all there. Your grandmother already knew that, though." He trained a gentle, affectionate gaze on Abigail and continued with humor. "She always could tell when I was being less than truthful."

Abigail laughed softly. "You never could fib worth a damn."

He turned back to Elise. "Anyway, I wanted to explain myself to her before I go in and tell the police that what I told them about my whereabouts on Friday—while not completely false—wasn't entirely true, either. That's what we were just discussing."

"He didn't kill Divia, Elise," her grandmother clarified. "He couldn't have. But what he told Jackson was more of a smoke screen to protect others."

"I'm not sure I understand. Protect others? What others?" Elise got up to retrieve the coffee pot from the warmer and freshened Garrett's cup. "You told Jax you were in Austin at a conference until late. If you weren't attending the conference, then where were you, if you don't mind me asking, that is?"

"I don't mind. I aim to tell your Deputy Landry everything shortly, anyway." Garrett rubbed his eyes with his thumb and forefinger before answering her questions. "The truth is, I did register for that conference, but never intended to go. You see, I have a daughter in Austin that Divia didn't know about. I'd always meant to tell her but kept putting it off. I didn't think she'd handle it well."

"Why wouldn't she handle it well? She knew you'd been married before for all those years. Why would the fact that you had a daughter make any difference?"

"Carrie-Ann isn't from Garrett's marriage, sweetie." Abigail gave her a meaningful look, and Elise began to get the idea.

"I'm not proud of my actions, Elise, but I cheated on my first wife very early on in our marriage. It was just the one time and a guilty secret that I kept to myself our entire life together." He gave her a sorrowful look. "You see, my Doris couldn't have children, and I was fine with that. Kathryn, Carrie-Ann's mother, was a good friend to us both in those days, and our slip was a thoughtless indiscretion that put a strain on our relationship all the way around from there on out."

Abigail patted his arm. "Water under the bridge."

"Of course, you're right, Abby. It makes no difference now," he said with a nod. "Anyway, Kathryn didn't tell me about Carrie-Ann until several years ago, after Doris had passed. And I didn't tell Divia because I knew she probably wouldn't accept Carrie-Ann, at least not right away. Frankly, I just wasn't prepared for more drama."

"And you figured she wouldn't accept your daughter because of Toby?" Elise asked before she could help herself.

Garrett nodded again. "Divia was always very focused on Toby, on being certain he toed the line and made something of himself. Evidently, his biological father was something of a wastrel and quite violent to boot, or so she said. In any case, she was adamant that the boy avoid the same fate."

Though uncomfortable listening to the man's personal history, Elise couldn't help feeling badly for him. To lose a much-loved wife and then find out about a daughter he didn't even know he had, only to be unable to share that joy with his new partner? It was unfortunate.

Some of her discomfort must have shown on her face, as a pained look crossed his features, and his voice held a note of embarrassment when he spoke. "You must think I'm addled or worse, blurting out all this personal information. You don't even know me that well."

When she started to contradict him, he held up a hand. "It's okay. Maybe I am."

"Oh, what a load of hooey." Abigail made a face. "We have a long-standing history, Garrett Larson, in case you've forgotten. You're no more addled than any of the rest of us. You've just suffered a terrible loss is all." She waved a hand in the air. "I imagine just talking about it with folks who will listen without judgment is a blessing."

He chuckled and squeezed her grandmother's hand. "You always did have a way with words, Abby. And truth be told, it is sort of freeing."

Turning to Elise, he went on with his story. "Anyway, all of that information was to explain about my real alibi. I was visiting my daughter and her lovely family all day Friday and on into the evening. I knew Divia wouldn't expect me back until late, so I lingered. As you would guess, I haven't gotten to spend much time with my grandchildren."

He ran a hand over his face and the sadness in his eyes was terrible to witness. "I stayed in town and enjoyed myself with a family my wife knew nothing about while she was being murdered in our motel room. No matter what Divia had done or what my relationship with her had become, that's something I will have to live with for the rest of my life."

"You couldn't have known, Garrett," Abigail murmured. "There's no use in torturing yourself over it."

While Elise had listened to his story, several scenarios began to pop up in her mind. If what Garrett said was true, then he had an air-tight alibi for the time of his wife's murder. In which case, even if he knew about Divia's affair and was angered by it, he couldn't have killed her.

And as far as she knew, he didn't even know Grace Vanderhouse, so he had no motive in her homicide, either. Thinking that he may have fresh insight into who might've wanted to harm his wife, Elise debated with herself about asking him the questions that were burning in her brain. With her grandmother sitting right there next to him, she was sure to get the stink-eye.

In the end, Elise decided to go ahead and ask ... as prudently as possible. "Mr. Larson, was Divia having trouble with anyone that you knew of?" Seeing the almost imperceptible narrowing of her grandmother's eyes, she hurried on. "I mean, I know that she and Monique Toussaint were at odds. Gram and the rest of us witnessed a bit of a row between the two this last Thursday. But can you think of anyone else who might have wanted to harm your wife?"

"Elise Brianna, what did we just talk about last night?" Abigail asked with a frown.

"It's okay, Abby," Garrett replied. "I'm sure I'm going to have to answer that very question when I speak to Deputy Landry, and I've turned it over in my mind quite a lot over these last few days. Unfortunately, I don't have a satisfactory answer." Turning to Elise, he shook his head. "I'm sorry, Elise, but Divia rubbed a number of people the wrong way—and that includes those closest to her. Even so, up until Friday, I wouldn't have thought anything she did could inspire someone to take her life. Obviously, I was wrong."

In the uncomfortable silence that followed, Elise decided to get while the getting was good—and before her grandmother could give her a chewing. "Well, I guess I'd better get to work. I have quite a few things to do before lunch," she said, finishing the last of her coffee before rising. Taking her purse and her cup, she quickly headed toward the kitchen before she got waylaid.

"I should get going as well. Don't want to be late for my inter-rogation with the sheriff," she heard Garrett say as she let the con-necting door swish shut behind her.

Hurrying to rinse her cup, Elise slipped out the back door in hopes of getting out to the greenhouse before Garrett left and Abi-gail could turn her focus on her. Plus, she wanted to put in calls to C.C. and Madison. If Garrett was at the sheriff's office during the noon hour, it meant there would be one less person at the motel to question her request to get into the crime scene.

Once in the safety of her work area, Elise set about planning her afternoon. She tagged C.C., and then called down to the Wine Bar-rel where Madison had the morning shift.

"El, I thought Mom told you to stay out of Jackson's investiga-tion," Madison whined when she got her on the phone. "What am I going to tell Gram when she comes down here to relieve me? You know she'll ask where I'm going."

"Oh, for crying out loud, Maddy. Don't be such a baby." Elise paced back and forth in agitation. "Tell her we're going to lunch in town. That will satisfy her."

"I just don't see why you want to get into that room in the first place. I mean, keeping our eyes and ears open for clues was one thing—we were trying to keep Gram off the suspect list, but asking questions, poking around at the crime scene, that's another story. I don't understand why you would even want to go out there. I don't like it, and I *know* Jackson wouldn't like it."

"Maddy, come on," Elise begged. "C.C.'s going to meet me there, but she's buried in work right now after taking so much time off to help us with the festival, and she said she might be late. I promise we won't stay long. I just want someone else with me. *Please.*"

After a long moment of silence on the other end of the line, Madison finally gave in. "All right, fine! But just so you know, if we get into trouble for this, I will have no qualms about tossing you right under the bus. And I'm driving, too. I refuse to be held hostage when you find something else you want to stick your nose into."

Elise laughed out loud. "Thanks, sis. See you after awhile."

Hanging up the phone, she thought about what Madison had said. She didn't really know *why* she wanted to go out to the murder scene. It certainly wasn't something she was looking forward to, and she didn't expect to find anything new. It was just an intangible feeling she'd had since visiting with Toby yesterday morning. There was something nagging at her, something she had seen or heard that she couldn't quite put her finger on but felt might be important.

Hopefully, their trip out to Lost Pines would satisfy her curiosity and put these vague feelings to rest.

# TWENTY-ONE

By mid-morning, Jackson was certain he'd already guzzled enough coffee to power a small city and decided it was time to switch to bottled water. He'd asked both Garrett Larson and Toby Raymond to come into the station to have another chat, and being hopped up on caffeine wasn't going to do anyone any good.

He and Jim had blown the lion's share of their Monday on the Toussaint family circus, only to find out that, crazy as they may be, they each had a solid alibi for the time of both murders.

*Why the hell hadn't they just said so in the first place?*

It was a complete mystery to him. Telling him the truth up front would have been so much easier than dragging them down to the station and having to pry it out of them one by one. The whole thing had been exasperating and a major waste of time.

And Jim was still holding a mean grudge, wanting to charge the three of them with obstruction or *something*. But in the end, as much as it pained them both, Jackson had cut them loose. The sooner they left his county and headed back to their own version of crazy town, the better.

But this was a brand-new day, Jackson reminded himself. With new challenges and new hurdles. To prepare for the next round of interviews, he'd gone over both Larson's and Raymond's previous statements with a fine-toothed comb.

Garrett Larson was first up at eleven. Jackson knew now that what the older man had told him the night of his wife's death was bogus. He'd signed up for a conference in Austin that he hadn't attended, but where the man had actually gone and what he'd done were questions Jackson wanted answered.

Toby Raymond's interview was scheduled for twelve-thirty. The man had met Jackson's group for dinner that night but had arrived late, just moments before Miss Abby's call about his mother's death. He'd never really been able to come up with a satisfactory answer for Jackson about where he'd been before arriving at the restaurant. It was conceivable that he could've gone to his mother's room, killed her, and then met up with the rest of them at Toucan's On Main in an effort to garner an alibi for himself.

And he didn't even want to think about Miss Abby's alibi, or lack thereof. He knew in his heart she had nothing to do with Divia Larson's murder, but she had to stay on the list until he could figure out just what had happened in that motel room the night of the woman's murder.

The pisser was that he was rapidly running out of suspects. If he didn't get a break in either case soon, he'd have to go back to square one on both. And he was well aware that the more time that passed, the less likely it was that he'd find the killer … or *killers*.

As these disturbing thoughts swirled around in his head, a knock from the doorway snagged his attention. He looked up just as Jim Stockton sauntered into the office and plopped down in the visitor's chair.

"Garrett Larson is here for his interview, right on time, I might add. I put him in Interview One when you're ready for him." Jim tilted his head and gave Jackson a questioning look. "I know that frown, son. Something's got you worried. Spit it out."

Jackson nodded toward the board he'd put together for the homicides of both Divia Larson and Grace Vanderhouse. Of the six clear suspects he'd had in the Larson case as recently as yesterday, only three names remained on the board.

"I was just pondering the fact that we're running out of suspects for Divia Larson's murder at the speed of light." He shook his head. "We're down by fifty percent in just twenty-four hours. And the same goes for Grace Vanderhouse."

"Maybe that's a good thing." Jim glanced at the board and pursed his lips. "We both know that Abigail DeVries didn't kill the Larson woman, no matter what the circumstantial evidence says."

"I agree. And Divia Larson didn't go to her death without a struggle. She fought mightily with someone before succumbing to the poison she'd ingested, and that struggle would've left signs. Hell, she grabbed someone or something so hard it snapped off several of her fake nails right to the quick. And the bruising around her wrists, the scratches around her neck?" Jackson shook his head. "Miss Abby was neat as a pin when we got there. And her fingerprints weren't found anywhere else in the room with the exception of the wine bottle and the door knob."

"Yep, and the wine bottle had no trace of the poison," Jim commented with a thoughtful nod. "Of course, she could've cleaned up after herself, washed the other glass, and then carefully set Mrs. Larson's tainted glass on the dresser next to the bottle. But why bother with all of that only to leave fingerprints on the bottle itself?"

"That was my thought exactly. If you're going to clean up, be thorough. And Miss Abby is nothing if not thorough." Jackson chuckled. "If she'd killed Divia and wanted to get away with it, we wouldn't have found one single trace to link her to the crime—she'd have made sure of that. Plus, she was at River Bend at the time of the Vanderhouse murder."

"You and I are both of the mind that the two murders are connected." Jim shrugged. "So, that leaves Toby Raymond or Garrett Larson."

"Yeah. Or someone we haven't considered yet—or even know about." Jackson squinted at the board. "And that's what's got me worried. I have this gut feeling that we're missing something. Some piece of the puzzle that we haven't stumbled across yet."

"Yeah, I know what you mean. I have that same feeling." Jim got up and stepped closer to study the board. After a moment, he tapped Grace's photograph with a fingertip. "Here's another thing I don't get. I can see either Raymond or Larson committing the first murder, but Vanderhouse? Supposedly, until Friday, Raymond hadn't even seen her since he was a boy. And as far as we know, Larson didn't even know her nor did he have any idea of her history with his new wife and stepson. So even with opportunity, where's the motive?"

"That's a great question." Jackson got up and gathered his files. "How about we go get some answers, starting with Garrett Larson?"

Down the hall in Interview One, Larson looked up from the small notebook in his hand as Jackson and Jim entered the room.

"Thanks for coming in on short notice, Mr. Larson," Jackson said. Pulling out a chair, he sat down opposite the man and laid his files on the table between them.

Jim took the chair to Jackson's left and turned on the recorder, stating the date, time of interview, and those in the room.

"Sir, do you understand why we've asked you to come in today?" Jackson asked, opening one of the files and making a show of looking through the pages before training a serious gaze on the man.

Larson nodded and looked Jackson directly in the eye. "I'm assuming it's because you've checked out the statement I gave you on Friday night and now realize I was less than truthful with you."

"That's exactly right. Would you like to amend your statement now for the record? Because we both know you didn't attend that conference in Austin like you said you did. I'm going to need to know where you actually were on Friday between seven and seven-thirty when your wife was murdered."

The man closed the little notebook and fumbled around with his pen as if he was uncertain where to begin. But when he finally launched into his story—a tale of infidelity and illegitimate children—Jackson was taken by surprise. This was definitely not what he'd been expecting, an affair perhaps, but not a long-lost daughter from an indiscretion years before.

"So, to clarify for the record," Jim said. "You were with your daughter and her family all day Friday until arriving at the Lost Pines Motel at just after eleven p.m. Is that correct?"

Larson sighed and ran a hand through his gray hair. "Yes, Deputy, that is correct."

Jim nodded. "I'm sorry, but we're going to need your daughter's contact information to substantiate this new statement."

"Understood," the man said and gave Jim his daughter's name and number. "I called Carrie-Ann on Sunday and explained everything. She's awaiting your call."

"Why didn't you just tell me this on Friday night, Mr. Larson?" Jackson asked. "You could have simply mentioned that you were with your daughter and her family and wouldn't have had to drag out all the rest. I understand that your wife didn't know, but at that point it didn't really matter anymore, did it? Why give me an alibi that you knew I'd check out and disprove?"

Larson put up a hand, a hang-dog look on his face. "I know, I know, it was stupid. But in my defense, I was in shock. You'd just told me that my wife had not only died but that she'd been murdered. It was naïve to think you wouldn't corroborate my statement, and that it wouldn't lead straight to my daughter and her family, anyway. I'm truly sorry if I caused you any extra work or muddled the situation in any way."

"One other question," Jim said. "Where were you on Sunday between three and four o'clock in the afternoon? Were you out at the festival at all that day?"

Larson shook his head. "No. In the morning I went for breakfast in town, but when I got back I didn't leave the motel again all day. Actually, I think I was talking to my daughter on my cell in the breezeway about that time. I saw Mrs. Wilson with her laundry cart and waved. She could probably tell you what time that was for sure."

"Thanks for clearing that up as well," Jackson said. "The medical examiner is ready to release your wife's remains. As soon as we've verified your revised statement, you can make arrangements for committal services." He made a couple notes of his own and then closed the folder in front of him. Pulling out a business card, he handed it across the table. "If you think of anything that might have a bearing on your wife's death or may help in any way, no matter how trivial it seems, please give me a call. I promise you, we'll do everything we can to bring the person responsible for her death to justice."

The older man's eyes watered up and he cleared his throat, obviously working to get his emotions under control. "Thank you, Deputy Landry. I appreciate all your hard work on Divia's behalf, and I know you'll do your best."

"This concludes the interview with Garrett Larson," Jim stated for the record at Jackson's nod, and then turned off the recorder.

"And then there was one," Jackson said the minute Larson had left the room. "At this rate, Toby Raymond is going to have to walk in here and confess, or we're out of suspects and totally screwed."

Jim moved to the other side of the table and sat in the chair vacated by Larson. "Now don't panic, boss. It could happen," he said with a grin. "He might be so wracked with guilt that he comes in here and confesses to both homicides. Case closed … or *cases* closed."

Jackson shot the other deputy a wry smile. "You're so funny. You're killing me here." He rubbed his eyes and then stretched trying to work out a kink. "Seriously, though. If Raymond has a solid alibi, too, I don't know where we go from here."

Jim shook his head. "We'll just have to cross that bridge when we get to it." He looked at his watch. "Twelve-thirty on the nose. Raymond should be here any minute."

As if conjuring him up by words alone, Deputy Yancy stepped in at that moment to tell them that Toby Raymond had arrived.

228

"Well, let's go see what he has to say," Jim said. "We'll keep our fingers crossed about the confessing deal."

Jackson gathered his files, and they moved down the hall to Interview Two where Yancy had left Raymond to wait. As they entered the room and got a good look at the man, Jackson thought that perhaps Jim's tongue-in-cheek comments about the confession might not be too far off the mark.

Raymond looked terrible. Disheveled and haggard, with dark circles under his eyes, he looked as if he'd been up all night or perhaps recovering from a binge. And the man was nervous. You could almost feel the tension in the air around him.

"Hey, Toby," Jackson said as he sat down across from him at the table. "You okay? You don't look so good."

Raymond scrubbed his hands over his face and then turned his red-rimmed eyes on Jackson. "I've been better. I didn't sleep very well last night."

"Well, hopefully, this won't take long." Jim repeated the process with the recorder stating date, time, and participants, signifying the commencement of the interview.

"Is that really necessary?" Toby asked, eyeing the recorder.

"Yes. I'm afraid so, Toby. We need you to clear some things up for us," Jackson responded, "for the record."

Toby frowned and looked as though he didn't quite know what to do with his hands. "Things?" he repeated. "What things?"

"For starters, where you were Friday night," Jim asked him.

The man looked from Jackson to Jim and back to Jackson again. "I was with you at the restaurant on Friday when Ms. DeVries called about my mother. Remember?"

Jackson nodded, but gave Toby a narrowed look. "Yeah, but, Toby, you arrived late. You never clarified where you were beforehand when I asked you earlier. Now we need to know."

Raymond's anxiety seemed to jump a notch, and he hemmed and hawed. "I-I went back to the room to change my clothes and then drove straight to the restaurant."

"And what would you say if I told you that someone had seen you coming out of your mother's room right around the time of her death?" Jackson asked.

It was yet another ruse, but bluffing had worked pretty well for him through the last few interviews. And it looked like it was going to work for him again.

Raymond's shoulders slumped, and he leaned on the table with his face in his hands. After a moment, he took a deep breath and nodded. "Okay, I should have told you straight out the minute you asked, but I was distraught, and I knew how it would look."

"Should have told me what, Toby? Were you in your mom's room at that time?"

Wringing his hands, the man swallowed hard and nodded. "Yes. And we argued."

"Argued about what?" Jim asked.

"About Grace."

Jackson didn't think it was possible, but the man's condition seemed to deteriorate even further, and his eyes took on a distant look.

"I was ten years old when we left Georgia in the middle of the night. Mom said we had to leave because my biological father had found us, and that he was a loser with a violent nature. She was afraid of him. At least, that's what she always said."

He took another deep breath before continuing. "Anyway, a few months later Mom told me that both Grace and Walker Vanderhouse had been killed in a terrible accident. And she alluded to the fact that she thought my biological father might have had something to do with their deaths, that maybe it hadn't been an accident at all."

"But Grace wasn't dead, was she, Toby?" Jim asked. "And you found that out at the festival. Is that what you argued with your mother about?"

Raymond nodded. "I'd heard Elise mention Grace's name and knew there was no way it was a coincidence. I confronted Mom about it in the parking lot on Friday afternoon, but she said I must've misunderstood. She wouldn't even discuss it."

Jackson remembered witnessing that argument from a distance, remembered Elise commenting on it before they'd headed out on the bike.

"And between that confrontation and going to her room right before her death, you tracked Grace down, right?" Jackson asked. "Because Grace told us Divia came to see her, wanted to talk to her. Your mother asked Grace to come to her motel room later that evening, and though she didn't want to, Grace complied."

Toby nodded. "I know. But Grace wasn't there long, and when I saw her leave, I went down to Mom's room to have it out with her."

The man paused and rubbed his eyes as if trying to rub away the exhaustion residing there. When he looked up at Jackson, it was with incredible sadness for what had been lost. "Walker Vanderhouse was the only father I'd ever known, Jackson. My mother cleaned out the man's bank accounts and spirited me away in the middle of the night, for God's sake. Grace told me what happened

231

to her dad after we left Georgia, how Walker had just given up. I wanted to know how my mother could've done such terrible things. She left Grace and her father without a penny, took me away from the only real family I'd ever had. I mean, what mother *does* that?"

"Toby, did you kill your mother?" Jackson asked flat out in a quiet tone. "Did the argument get out of hand? Is that what happened? Did you poison her?"

"*No!*" Toby shouted, a horrified look crossing his gaunt face. "We argued and when I went to leave, she grabbed the front of my jacket. I shoved her away from me and stormed out. That must be when I lost the button on my jacket, but I swear she was angry and shouting nasty things at me from the doorway but very much alive when I left the room."

Jim got up and poured a cup of water from the dispenser in the corner. When he walked back to the table with it, Toby literally grabbed it from his hand before he could set it on the table and guzzled it down like a man dying of thirst.

"Look, Jackson," he said at length. "My mother was a piece of work, granted, but she didn't deserve to die that way. Nobody does. I didn't kill her, or Grace, for that matter, but I'm pretty sure I know who did."

# TWENTY-TWO

ELISE MADE HER WAY down to the Wine Barrel just before the noon hour and then had to wait while Madison concluded a sale for a couple of tourists. It seemed to take her forever, and Elise was chomping at the bit by the time she'd finished.

"So, where're you girls off to for lunch?" Abigail asked when Madison pulled her purse out from under the counter and searched for her car keys.

Elise shrugged and was noncommittal. "Haven't decided just yet, Gram. We're going to head into town and stop whenever the urge strikes."

"But don't worry, Gram," Madison began as Elise took her arm and herded her toward the door. "We won't be too long. I'll make certain of that," she said over her shoulder.

"Yeah, yeah," Elise whispered into her sister's ear. "Keep it moving. We haven't got all day."

Madison jerked her arm out of Elise's grasp the minute they were outside. "Oh my *God!* What's the matter with you? I don't need you tugging on me like I was some kind of wayward child, you know."

Elise rolled her eyes as she climbed into the passenger side of Madison's economical hybrid compact. "I thought you wanted to get out there and back with no dallying. You were the one bitching about it earlier."

"No, I wasn't." Madison started the car and backed out of her space. "I was merely pointing out—quite correctly I might add—that you have no business snooping around another one of Jackson's crime scenes."

"Uh, since you've agreed to go with me, don't you mean *we* have no business snooping around? Besides, this is different," Elise argued, rubbing her forehead where her headache was beginning to return. "Lost Pines is a very public place, so what trouble can we possibly get into? Plus, it won't be long before Jax releases the room, anyway. Then the Wilsons will have it cleaned and rented again in the blink of an eye. I just want a quick peak before they do."

"But *why* do you want to go in there?" Madison asked with a tiny shudder. "I think it's just plain creepy."

Elise shook her head and glanced out the side window at the acres of grapevine rows they were passing. Hadn't she asked herself that very question several times over the last day or so? She still didn't have a decent answer. She only knew she needed to see it for some intangible reason that she couldn't seem to shake.

"I don't know, Maddy," she said after a moment. "Something has been nagging at me for the last few days, and I can't put my finger on it."

"Well, this trip had better take care of that nagging, big sister, because I'm only doing this once."

They pulled into the parking lot at Lost Pines Motel twenty minutes later, and Madison parked directly in front of the room where Divia had been poisoned.

Elise turned to her sister before opening the car door. "Now listen, we need to get the key from Harriet, so let me do the talking. It'll have to be handled very carefully."

"Whatever, Secret Agent Girl," Madison muttered as they both climbed from the vehicle and headed over to the motel office.

The little bell over the lobby door jingled cheerfully as they entered the building, signaling the arrival of potential customers. Harriet Wilson had been in the back room but hurried out to the front desk as soon as she heard the bell.

"Hey, Elise, Maddy," she said and punctuated her greeting with a snap of her gum. "What brings you girls out this way in the middle of a Tuesday? Elise, this might be a record. Two days in a row?"

"Ha! That's funny, Harriet. We're actually on a mission and hoping you can help."

Harriet leaned a hip against the counter, and her eyes lit up with interest. "Oh, yeah? What kind of mission?"

"Well, we're looking to retrieve a couple missing items from Mr. Larson's original room that might have been left behind."

The woman gave her a doubtful look and chomped on her gum like a cow chewing a cud. "You mean down in 12, the room where his wife was murdered?"

Elise nodded. "He would've come himself, but he had to go into the station this morning."

"I don't know," Harriet said with a skeptical frown. "I thought they let him move his things on Saturday after those CSI folks had swarmed through the room like locusts. I can't imagine they left anything behind."

"I figured as much." Elise sighed and gave the woman a commiserative look. "But the thing is, he's really tied up at the station with Jax, talking about the case and all. Poor man is still not himself after just losing his wife in such a horrible manner."

"Oh my, yes." Harriet shook her head with sadness. "And how do you think we feel that it happened right here at our little motel? We run a clean, safe establishment. Something like this could ruin it all for us."

*Oh yes. By all means, let's make this about you and not the poor man losing his wife in a heinous crime.*

"Anyway, we thought we'd just check it out. You can call Jax to clear it if you need to," Elise said in hopes of getting the woman back on track.

She held her breath as she watched Harriet's face. If the woman called Jackson, he would have Elise's head on a platter by evening for even trying to gain access to his precious crime scene.

But after a long moment, Harriet shrugged. "I guess it don't matter none. I talked to Jax yesterday about when we could get the room back, and he told me it'll be any day now." The woman waved a bejeweled hand in the air. "Good Lord, we're gonna need to completely overhaul that room before we can use it again. Gonna cost us a pretty penny, that's for sure." She rolled her eyes and shook her head, sending her gaudy, dangly earrings swinging back and forth with wild abandon. "And even when we do, who's gonna want to stay in a room where a woman's been murdered, I ask you?"

Elise made a noise of agreement, but didn't actually respond. Then again, with Harriet a response to her ramblings was rarely necessary. "So, is the room unlocked, or do I need a key?" she asked when the woman just stood there chewing her gum and blinking her fake eyelashes at them in a vacant, owlish way.

"Well, of course it's locked!" Harriet bellowed and gave her a look that clearly said she thought Elise was the brainless one. "Don't be goofy, Elise. It's still *technically* a crime scene, after all. Hang on, and I'll get you the key."

Elise glanced over to where Madison stood with a disgusted look on her face.

"Not a word," Elise warned her before she could speak. "Not one word."

Though Madison kept her mouth shut, she shook her head, and Elise could feel her sister's judgment hanging overhead like a black cloud.

Harriet finally came back with the room key, reminding Elise to bring it back the minute they were done. "I don't want to get into hot water with Jackson for not keeping the room secured."

"Don't worry, Harriet," Elise assured the woman as she and Madison headed out the door. "I promise we'll be quick about it. I'll bring the key back just as soon as we've had a quick look around for Mr. Larson's things."

"You're taking the express elevator straight to hell for lying that way. You know that, right?" Madison commented as they left the office and walked back toward the room.

"Oh please, I didn't actually lie," Elise replied over her shoulder. Stopping at the drink machine in the breezeway, she dug a dollar's worth of change from the bottom of her purse and selected a bottle of water. "Besides, Harriet doesn't give a rip one way or the other. She just wants the room freed up so she can charge some unsuspecting traveler an arm and a leg for it as soon as possible."

"You keep telling yourself that, sista," Madison said with a smirk. "But you're just skirting the issue. You gave her the *impression* that Garrett Larson sent you over here *and* that it was okay with Jax."

"Come on, Maddy. You heard her. Jax is going to release the room any day now, anyway. What's it gonna hurt?" Elise grabbed her water out of the dispensing slot and turned, giving Madison the stink-eye.

But her sister just shrugged. "Hell. Express elevator. I'm just sayin'."

"Well, keep it to yourself. My headache is coming back with a vengeance, and you're not helping."

They walked the rest of the way to room twelve in silence. The yellow crime scene tape was still stretched across the door frame, and Elise was careful not to disturb it as she turned the key to unlock the door. She felt like some kind of circus contortionist trying to squeeze underneath the tape to enter the room, which had obviously been shut up tight since the murder and the subsequent scouring by the investigators. The air inside was stuffy and overly-warm, giving the room a slightly claustrophobic feel.

"Can't you leave the door open?" Madison asked as Elise closed it behind her. "It smells like death in here."

"Oh, for the love of mud, it does not. And no, we can't leave the door open. We don't want to draw attention to the fact that we're in here when we shouldn't be."

Madison made a face. "Oh, right. Like us climbing into the room under the crime scene tape wouldn't do that in the first place?"

Elise closed her eyes briefly and prayed for patience. "Let's just look around and get this over with as quickly as we can, okay?"

"Fine," Madison said in a huff as she stepped over the hole in the carpet where the CSIs had removed a piece for evidence. "But what exactly are we looking for, anyway?"

"I don't know, Maddy," Elise said with irritation. "Something, *anything* that might have been missed." Setting her bottle of water down on the dresser, she began to search through her purse for her little pill box and the aspirin it held. She wasn't going to be able to think clearly with a headache brewing.

She finally found it and set her purse next to the water as she opened the container. But before she could remove the much-needed pain medication, Madison startled her with a squeal. The little box went flying, along with her salvation of aspirin tablets.

"Maddy, for crying out loud, what's wrong with you?"

"Sorry." Madison gave her a sheepish look. "I thought I saw a mouse in the closet, but it was only a balled up nylon sock." Turning, she disappeared into the bathroom.

With a shake of her head, Elise knelt down to collect the tablets that had rolled every which way. Several had gone under the credenza, and when she peered under it, she saw not only her wayward pills, but something else as well. Reaching all the way up to her shoulder under the piece of furniture, she felt around until she could locate and get hold of whatever was there.

Pulling her arm back out, she sat back on her haunches and opened her fist to get a look at her prize.

"There's absolutely nothing here, El," Madison said as she came out of the bathroom. "That rolled-up sock in the closet, but nothing else that I can see. What are you doing on the floor?"

Elise pressed her lips together and looked up at Madison with a grim look. "I dropped my pill box when you screeched over the sock mouse, and when I went to pick up the tablets that had flown everywhere, I found this." Elise lifted her open palm.

"So what? It's a button? What kind of clue is that? It could have been there for months."

Elise shook her head. "No, sweetie. I don't think so. I'm pretty sure that I know whose button this is. And if you think about it, you do, too."

"What are you talking about?" Madison frowned. "How would I know who that belongs to? How do you, for that matter? You're always making something out of nothing. For crying out loud, it's just a *button*, El."

Elise stood up and let out an exasperated sigh. "Take a good, close look at it, Maddy. It has a pretty distinctive design that we've both seen before. You even commented on it at dinner last Friday night."

Madison blinked several times in confusion before taking the button out of Elise's hand. She stepped closer to the window and the meager light coming in through the curtains. Elise clearly saw the moment when recognition dawned on her sister's face.

"I'm sorry, Maddy, but that's the button that was missing from Toby's jacket when he got to the restaurant . . . just before Gram called to say his mother was dead."

Madison looked up with shock and disbelief in her eyes. "You can't be suggesting that Toby murdered his own mother, El. I mean, there has to be another explanation. He wouldn't do something like that. I know he wouldn't," she insisted.

Elise's heart went out to her sister; because she knew that Madison and Toby had become a bit more than friends. And it was hard to think of someone you were truly fond of as a cold-blooded killer.

"Give me another explanation that fits." Elise ticked off the facts with her fingers as she continued. "Toby showed up late for dinner the night of the murder, he was distracted and flustered when he arrived, and he was missing a button from his jacket—that button. It puts him in this room sometime before Divia was killed but after the festival closed for the day, because he wasn't wearing that jacket earlier out at the venue."

When Madison didn't respond but continued to stare down at the button in her hand, Elise put her arm around her sister. "I'm sorry, Maddy. I know you two had been hanging out during the festival this year, that you'd gotten closer, but this doesn't look good."

Slowly, Madison nodded. "I know, El. But I just can't believe he would do something so monstrous." She looked up with wide eyes. "To kill his own mother? I mean, Divia was hard on him and treated him poorly at times, but he always spoke of her with respect. And I *saw* his devastation when we got to the motel that night. Her death wrecked him. Now, this? I can't reconcile it with what I've seen and know of him. We've gone out a couple of times. You know, just the two of us. I was really beginning to like him, and I'm telling you I would *know* if he had that kind of evil in him."

"I get it, honey." Elise sighed and hugged her close. "I know exactly how that feels. But sometimes we just have no idea how folks will react to certain things. It could be that he snapped. Maybe all the years of abuse finally caught up to him."

"Maybe," Madison murmured. But when she looked up, Elise read the shock and heartbreak in her eyes. "Can we go now, El? I don't want to be in this room another minute."

"Absolutely, sweetie. Just let me get my things."

Taking the button from her sister, Elise stuck it into her pocket, and then put the pills she'd gathered back into the container, dropping that into her purse.

"Are you going to tell Jax about this?" Madison asked as they left the room, climbing back out under the crime scene tape the same way they'd entered. "Won't he be angry?"

"Oh hell yeah," Elise sighed as she re-locked the door. "Jax is gonna blow a gasket, but he'll get over it when he hears what we found."

"Hello, ladies," a nearby voice snagged their attention and they both turned in that direction.

To her surprise, Elise found the same man she'd seen with Toby the day before standing next to Madison. "Hello. It's Sam, isn't it?" she asked, remembering what Toby had told her when she'd arrived the previous morning. "You were here yesterday. You were just leaving when I pulled in, right?"

"Yes, ma'am. You have a good memory." The man smiled and nodded, though something about his smile didn't seem too awfully friendly to Elise.

"So are you a friend of Toby's or a relative, Sam?"

The man stuck his hands in his jacket pockets and rolled back and forth on the balls of his feet. "You could say that. I'm Sam Raymond."

"*Oh my gosh!* You're Toby's father?" Madison asked with surprise. "How long have you been in town?"

"A while."

Thinking about all the unpleasant things she'd heard in the past about Sam Raymond, Elise felt the greasy fingers of unease slide through her system. And then he turned his attention to her.

"Now, tell me, Elise. What did you and Madison here find in that room that was so fascinating?"

"I beg your pardon?" Elise blinked up at him and tried to keep calm, though she was getting a very nasty vibe. Plus, she was having a hard time getting past the fact that he knew both their names. The note she'd found on her windshield the previous evening flashed through her mind.

"In the room," Sam prompted. "What did you find in the room that you figure on telling Deputy Landry about?"

"I'm sorry, Sam, but that's information regarding an ongoing investigation," Elise said before grabbing Madison's arm and inching toward the car. "I really can't talk about that."

But Sam stepped into the gap between them and the vehicle. "I'm afraid I'm going to have to insist, darlin'."

Madison gasped, and that's when Elise saw the gun in the man's hand.

"What are you doing, Mr. Raymond?" Madison asked. "You can't just go around pointing guns at people in broad daylight and threatening them like this."

Sam took hold of her other arm and pulled her over to his side. Pointing the gun at her rib cage, he looked Elise in the eye and nodded toward the car. "Why don't we take a drive? You can ride shotgun, Elise. Madison will drive, and I'll get in behind her. That way no one will do anything stupid. Now move!"

# TWENTY-THREE

"What do you mean you're pretty sure you know who killed both women?" Jim Stockton asked Toby Raymond with a skeptical look. "That's awfully convenient."

"Look, I don't have any concrete proof, but I think my dad may have killed them both." Raymond looked back and forth between Jackson and Jim, nervously turning the empty water cup around in his hands.

"Toby, Garrett Larson has given us an alibi for the times of both murders. We haven't confirmed those alibis yet, but if what he told us just an hour ago is true, then he couldn't have killed either woman."

"No. You don't understand." Toby shook his head with frustration. "Not Garrett. I'm talking about Sam Raymond, my *biological* father."

"What?" Jim's head popped up from his notepad. "I thought you said you didn't know your biological father. So, how do you know he's here in Delphine?"

Toby sighed and rubbed his eyes as if they burned. "Because I've seen him, talked to him. We've met on several occasions over the last few days. He's staying in an RV park out by the fairgrounds."

Jackson sat back and stared hard at Toby. He wasn't sure if they could believe a word the man had to say, after the way he'd lied before. Plus the guy had embezzled a large amount of money from Garrett Larson's vineyard, which didn't help his cause.

By blaming a phantom, a father he'd never met, he could conceivably be trying to save his own ass. But there was something in Toby's eyes, a fear that had Jackson interested in hearing more.

"Okay, Toby. If that's true, then walk us through it," he said. "When did you find out your dad was in town, and why do you think he killed your mom and Grace?"

"Could I have some more water first?" Toby asked, looking like he might drop at any moment. "And maybe a couple of aspirin? I had kind of a rough night."

"Sure." Jackson waited patiently while Jim retrieved two aspirins and refilled Toby's cup. "Now, take your time and start at the beginning," he said after the man downed the tablets.

Taking a deep breath, Toby launched into his story. "I didn't know my father. I wasn't lying when I said that. I only knew *of* him through the terrible things my mother said about him. So when he approached me late Friday afternoon just before I left the festival and introduced himself, I was stunned, as you might imagine, and a bit leery to talk with him."

"Because of what your mom had told you about him?" Jim asked.

Toby nodded. "Her diatribes regarding my father were always much the same. He had a violent nature; he was a loser who expected her to support the entire family, blah, blah, blah. Sometimes she would say that he wanted to take me away from her, other times it was that he wanted to hurt us.

"Don't get me wrong, I loved my mother, and I think she loved me—as least as much as she *could* love anyone. But the older I got, the more I realized how manipulative and self-serving she was, which made me question all those awful things she said about him."

Jackson sat forward and folded his arms on the table. "I'm assuming Sam Raymond had a very different version?"

"Yes. His story *was* very different—almost the opposite. And a large portion of what he said had the ring of truth to it. It resonated with what I'd seen and heard in recent years. He said that back then Mom was always looking for more. More money, more prestige, more *everything*. He said she'd never been satisfied with what he could give her, and one night when I was about four years old, she took me and disappeared."

"That must have sounded familiar as well," Jim said, leaning back and hooking an arm over the back of his chair. "Grace Vanderhouse had just told you the same kind of story only a few hours beforehand, right?"

Toby stabbed a finger in Jim's direction. "Exactly. He said she'd cleaned out his bank accounts as well. I was starting to see a disturbing pattern in my mom's behavior, which is why I agreed to continue the conversation out at Sam's RV before going back to the motel to get ready for dinner. I wanted to hear more."

"What else did he have to say when you got to the park?" Jackson asked.

"He told me that he'd never forgotten about me and had looked for us for years, hiring private investigators and the like whenever he had the money. He'd received information about our Georgia location at one point, but by the time he got there, we'd already left. Mom must have been tipped off that he was coming."

Toby got up and re-filled his cup from the water dispenser for a third time before continuing. "Anyway, he said that there'd been other close calls, but they were always near misses. He'd show up, but we'd be gone." He sat back down at the table and took a sip of the water. "Anyway, this last time he'd finally tracked us down to the vineyard and found out we were heading up to the festival, so he followed us here."

"That clarifies how he got to Delphine, but it still doesn't explain why you're so sure he killed your mom," Jim said. "I mean, sure, that kind of history and revenge for what she'd done might've given him a reason to want her dead, but it also gives you motive. To find out my mother had lied to me for years, used other people that way? I gotta say that would make me really angry."

Toby's gaze sharpened, and he nodded. "Yes, and I was. I'd just confronted Mom about Grace, and she'd refused to talk about it, told me I'd *misunderstood*. Then I tracked Grace down and actually talked to her. And on the heels of that conversation, my long, lost father shows up and contradicts everything my mother had ever told me. You bet I was pissed. But she was still my mother, Deputy."

"Toby, did you tell your mom about Sam showing up when you argued with her Friday night?" Jackson asked. "And that you'd just talked with him?"

Toby blew out a breath, and his shoulders slumped as if weighed down by guilt. "No. We argued about Grace. I told her all the terrible things Grace had laid on me a few hours before, but I didn't tell her about my father."

He lifted his palms in a plea for understanding. "I will go to my grave regretting I didn't at least give her a heads-up that Sam was nearby. But I was still processing everything that had happened in that one crazy afternoon. Grace, my father ... I was so overwhelmed."

Dropping his hands, his eyes filled with tears as he bowed his head and whispered. "Had I told her, it might've made the difference."

"Toby, I can see why you think he may have killed your mom, but why would he want to kill Grace?" Jackson asked, sliding a box of tissue across the table toward the man. "He'd never even met her, had he?"

Toby took a tissue and blew his nose, struggling to get himself under control. "No," he said after a moment. "But I may have been to blame for that, too."

"How so?" Jim asked with a frown. "Did you introduce them or something?"

Toby shook his head. "Not exactly. Grace came to see me Saturday. Evidently, when I saw her leave my mom's room on Friday night and drive away, she hadn't gone far. She said she'd been angry but decided to come back and finish their conversation, clear the air. She pulled into the parking lot just in time to see me go into Mom's room."

"What does that have to do with Grace's murder?" Jim asked.

"She thought *I'd* killed her. When she came to see me Saturday, she begged me to turn myself in. Said that I'd been pushed past my limits by Mom's past behavior, and the authorities would take that into consideration. She said she'd be a character witness and help in any way she could." He paused and wiped his eyes. "I kept telling her that I didn't kill my mother, but she wouldn't let it go."

"Okay, but how does that make you to blame for her death?" Jackson persisted. "And how is your father involved?"

"Because I told him about the conversation on Sunday morning over breakfast. I made light of the whole thing, but I'm afraid he may have tried to intervene. He told me not to worry about it— that he would take care of things."

"You realize how this whole thing sounds, right?" Jim commented. "You've told us that you were in your mother's room right before her death, and we have no proof that your dad is even here in Delphine. Until we can confirm that he is, and has been since the murders, we only have your word that any of this actually happened. And other than a gut feeling, you have no actual evidence that proves your dad was involved with either murder."

Toby fidgeted in his seat, his eyes darting back and forth. "I know, I know, but what I've told you is the truth. Go out to the RV park. They'll have records of him staying there. You'll see. And as for proof, no, I don't have any, but I know as sure as I'm sitting here that he's responsible."

Jackson ran a hand through his hair and blew out a breath. "All right, hang tight for a few minutes, Toby. Jim and I are gonna step out and make some calls."

"Interview with Toby Raymond suspended," Jim said into the recorder. He added the time and put it on pause before he and Jackson got up and stepped out into the hall.

"So? What do you think of *that* rambling mess?" Jim asked, shoving his hands into his pockets. "I'm having a hard time keeping track of all the craziness."

Jackson smiled and nodded. "I know what you mean, but even though he can't prove any of it, I'm leaning toward believing him.

Although I see where he might have it in him to poison his mother, I just don't picture him strangling Grace—not after just reuniting with her that way."

Jim shook his head in a disgusted manner. "Though it pains me some to say it, I have to agree. I don't like him for either murder. So, where do we go from here? You want to hang onto him until we check out the RV park and can confirm his dad is here?"

Jackson pressed his lips together and crossed his arms over his chest. "I think we'd better, just in case," he said after a moment.

"Then let's get this party started."

They stepped back into the room, and just as they sat down to tell Toby what they'd decided, Jackson's cell phone rang. Pulling out and checking the readout, he was baffled when he saw C.C.'s name on the screen.

"Hang on a second," Jackson told Jim. "I've got to take this. I'll be right back."

He got up and walked back out into the hallway, answering the call as he went out the door. "Hey, C.C., what's up? I'm kind of in the middle of something here."

"Yeah? Well, you better get out of whatever you're doing and hightail it out to the Lost Pines Fairgrounds. And I mean, right this minute."

Jackson frowned. C.C. rarely called him and when she did she never sounded this upset. "What's going on? And what are you doing out at the fairgrounds?"

"I think El and Maddy are in trouble, Jax. Please. You need to come *now!*"

Jackson could hear the near-hysteria in her voice and felt his own concern rise. "Trouble? What kind of trouble? Tell me what's happened?"

"Okay, but don't blow a gasket. Promise?"

"C.C.," he said in a warning tone. "Tell me."

There was a long pause, and Jackson wanted to reach through the phone and shake the woman. Just when he thought he'd lost the connection, she finally spoke up.

"Something had been bothering El about these murders since finding that note on her car the other night, and—"

"Wait, what note?" he asked, interrupting her. "Start from the beginning, and don't leave anything out."

Less than ten minutes later, Jackson had most of the story, and after disconnecting, he raced back into the interview room to get Jim. If C.C. was right, Elise and Madison could be in real peril, maybe even running out of time.

And Toby had been telling the truth.

"What's up, Jax?" Jim asked, his voice holding a hint of concern. "You look like you've had a scare."

"I have. Seems like Toby here may have been right." He turned to Toby. "Elise and Maddy went out to the motel over the lunch hour. It was El's intention to get Harriet Wilson to let them into your mother's room."

"What?" Toby looked horrified. "Why on earth would she want to do that?"

"Who knows why that woman does anything?" Jackson ran a hand over his face in exasperation. "Anyway, C.C. was supposed to meet up with them there but was running late. She arrived just in time to watch Maddy's car turn out of the parking lot and head toward the fairgrounds." He gave Jim a grim look. "And from what she said, they weren't alone. Elise and Maddy were up front, and a man she didn't recognize was in the back seat on the driver's side."

"Oh my God! My dad?"

"I don't know, Toby." Jackson shook his head and dug his car keys out of his pocket. "C.C. followed them at a discreet distance out to the fairgrounds and thinks they may be in trouble. I'm not gonna wait around here to find out."

"I'm right behind you, buddy," Jim said jumping to his feet. "We can be out there in fifteen minutes—less if we push it."

"I'm going with you, too," Toby spoke up, shoving away from the table. "If my dad has taken them out to some secluded spot against their will ... well, I don't want any more death on my conscience. I haven't known him long, but maybe I can talk to him, get him to give himself up without more violence."

It didn't take Jackson but five seconds to come to a decision. "Okay, but you do what I say, when I say. And no heroics."

Toby snorted. "Please. No chance of that. Trust me."

With a confirming nod, Jackson headed for the door. "Then let's do this."

# TWENTY-FOUR

ELISE GLANCED OVER AT her sister as Sam instructed her to pull the car into the back parking lot of the Lost Pines Fairgrounds. They would need to do some fast talking and come up with some sort of a plan—quickly. Because once they got to wherever Sam was taking them, she was pretty sure their time would be up. She had no illusions that he would simply let them go after taking them hostage at gunpoint.

He hadn't said a word since they'd left the motel, and his silence was unnerving. Of course, there was also the fact that he had his gun trained on the back of Madison's head.

"So, Sam, what's this all about?" she asked tightly, in a desperate effort to get him talking.

"Come on, Elise. You're a smart girl. Don't tell me you haven't figured this whole thing out by now. I could see the wheels turning in your head back at the motel."

Sam chuckled, and the sound of it sent a healthy dollop of fear trickling down Elise's spine. She took a deep breath and threw a glance over her shoulder at him. "You were the one who left the threatening note on my windshield, right?"

"Bingo," he acknowledged with a grin.

"Threatening note?" Madison's head snapped in Elise's direction as she slipped the car into a spot and put it in park. "What note? What are you talking about?"

"Sorry. You went to dinner with friends in town last night, so I forgot to tell you. I went to the H-E-B to pick up a few things for Gram before we ate." Elise jerked a thumb toward the back seat. "When I came out, Sam here had left a menacing note on my windshield."

Madison's mouth dropped open. "And you didn't think that was important enough to tell me before you dragged me into your idiotic snooping trip? You didn't think *that* little tidbit would be good for me to know?"

Elise rolled her eyes at her sister's complaint. "Don't be so dramatic, Maddy. I said I was sorry, didn't I? Besides, how was I supposed to know?"

Madison made a growling noise in the back of her throat. "A lot of good sorry does now."

"Go ahead and shut down the engine, Madison. Then hand me the keys, please. We don't want anyone gettin' any crazy ideas," Sam said, tapping her on the shoulder with the barrel of the gun.

"I knew you were digging," he continued, directing his comments to Elise. "Y'all were real subtle about it, but I knew. Toby told me you'd stopped by after I'd left yesterday, told me all about the conversation, though he didn't see it as the fishing expedition that it was." He shrugged. "Not the brightest kid, but he's still my son."

Elise turned in her seat to face him and then put up her hands in surrender when he pushed the gun against the back of Madison's head in response.

"Look, I get it, Sam. He's your son," Elise said. "I was starting to look in his direction, so you had to do something. You were just trying to protect him."

"Yeah, but it didn't seem to discourage you, did it?"

She gave him a sad look. "Actually, it only made me more curious. The note said I was *poking around where I shouldn't*. Since the only thing I'd done was stop by the motel and chat with Toby, I figured it had to have something to do with that ... or perhaps something I'd seen while I was there."

Sam slowly shook his head. "Too smart for your own good, little girl."

"But I was looking at the wrong Raymond, wasn't I?" she asked, tilting her head and giving him a narrow-eyed glance. "Though I didn't know you were here at the time."

"El!" Madison blurted. "For God's sake, don't get us into any more trouble than we already are."

"What did you find in the room, Elise?" Sam asked, ignoring Madison's outburst.

She shrugged. "Nothing much. Just a button."

"A button?" Sam frowned, clearly stumped by her answer.

"That's all."

"Okay, I'll bite. What the hell does that have to do with anything?" His eyebrows descended, and he scowled at her in his confusion. "What kind of button? And why would that be something you'd want to tell the police about?"

"It was a button that told a very specific story, Sam," she told him. "You see, when Toby showed up to dinner on Friday night, he was missing a button on his jacket—a button the CSI folks missed but I found in the room this afternoon."

She pressed her lips together and nodded when she saw understanding dawn in his eyes. "Since he wasn't wearing the jacket earlier at the festival, you can see where my thought process took me."

"Finding the button there meant he'd been in his momma's room," Sam replied. "And it had to have been sometime between leaving the festival for the day and arriving at the restaurant."

"Yes. Toby showed up right before Jackson got the call about Divia's death."

"Clever. And I can see how you would come to the conclusion that Toby had killed her."

Though there was a note of respect in Sam's voice, something in his eyes gave Elise the impression she'd missed something.

"Unfortunately, Divia raised our boy to be a spineless wimp. I'm afraid he ain't got killin' in him."

At his words, the breath backed up in Elise's lungs and her pulse picked up speed. She realized then that she'd gotten the whole thing wrong. Toby hadn't killed his mother.

Sam Raymond had.

Her realization must have been plain to see on her face, because he smiled and nodded. "Yep. I can see you understand now."

"Understand what?" Madison asked and tried to turn around, but Sam shoved the gun against the back of her head again.

"That Toby didn't kill Divia, Maddy," Elise answered, her eyes never leaving his. "Sam did. But why? Was it because she'd run away from you?"

"*Why?*" When he repeated the question, his eyebrows rose and his tone was full of surprise. After a moment, he launched into an explanation. "Toby's momma was a beautiful young woman when we hooked up. But you know what they say about beauty only being skin deep? Well, with Divia that was an understatement. Nothin' I ever did was good enough for Divia Sweeney. And I mean *nothin'*."

He shook his head and his eyes took on a faraway look, a half-smile touching his face. "I was over the moon when we had Toby … a *son*. But that soon turned to shit, too. Whenever she didn't get her way or I refused to buy her the latest thing she had her eye on, she'd use my boy as a bargaining chip."

He turned to Elise with pure hatred flaring in his eyes, in his voice. "A week or so after Toby's fourth birthday she packed him up and disappeared in the middle of the night—taking everything we had with her. At least, everything that meant something to me."

"Ah, Sam. I'm so sorry, but you know you weren't the only one, right?" Elise asked. Evidently, he was the first man Divia had run out on, but he hadn't been the last. And her M.O. hadn't changed over the years.

"Oh, I know. But I've spent twenty years trying to track down my son. Every time I'd get close, she'd grab him up and disappear like smoke on a burn pile. Until last week, that is. I finally caught up to her and saw my son for the first time in two decades."

"So you decided to make sure she'd never run again?" Madison asked, obviously unable to help herself. Elise watched her glance into the rearview mirror. "Or was it revenge?"

"It was *justice*," Sam said with conviction. "That woman left a trail of broken lives wherever she landed. I just evened the score for everyone she'd hurt."

"So, you went to her room after Toby left?" Elise asked, wanting to keep him talking. The longer they could distract him, the longer they would live … and perhaps give help time to arrive.

She'd recognized C.C.'s car pulling into the motel parking lot as they were pulling out. Elise could only hope that her friend had contacted Jackson, and the troops were on their way.

"I saw Toby come out of Divia's room with her yellin' at him from the doorway like a fishwife. I waited for him to get into his car and drive away, and then I made my move." He started to chuckle, and then to laugh out loud. "Boy howdy, you ought to have seen her face when she opened that door and saw me standing there. I'm surprised she didn't pass right out from the shock of it."

"What did she do?" Madison asked, thoroughly sucked into his story. "Did she invite you in?"

"Hell no! At least, not at first, but I can be very persuasive."

"You brought the bottle of wine, right?" Elise asked. "And the cyanide, of course."

"I told her not to worry. That I was only there to bury the hatchet and not to cause her any trouble. Told her that I just wanted to meet my son. I finally talked her into having a glass of wine with me, for old time's sake." The look he sent Elise then was a sly one. "She sat down on the edge of the bed and gave me the same worn, come-hither look that used to work on me so long ago. Well, I just let her think it was still working as I doctored her glass with the poison. Then I sat right there next to her and watched her drink it down."

"Oh my *God*," Madison whispered, and Elise watched her sister's terrified eyes fill with tears.

Reaching out, Elise took her hand and gave it a reassuring squeeze. Showing their fear would do them no good. They had to hold on, keep him talking. Whatever happened, Elise wasn't about to let him see how scared she really was.

"You cleaned up after?" she made herself ask, turning her attention back to Sam. "After …"

"After the poison took her? You bet. I washed out my glass and made sure I hadn't left anything behind. I gotta say you had me worried earlier about what I might've missed." His tone was so matter-of-fact, like he was talking about doing a bit of housekeeping. It turned Elise's stomach.

"Look, I know how this is gonna sound," he continued. "But after over twenty years of searching, of dreaming about finding my son and always just missing out, after every terrible thing that woman did, I *enjoyed* watching her die. I saw the light of understanding come into her eyes at the end, and it made me happy. When she realized what was happening, she grabbed a hold of me so hard she broke off some of her fake fingernails. Do you believe that?"

He shook his head, and Elise tried to look away from the horrible smile on his face and the look of pure evil that had settled in his eyes as he spoke of her death. But she found she couldn't. It was like watching some horrifying yet oddly compelling event.

*Looks like Divia has the last laugh, Sammy-boy. She was spot on in portraying you as the Devil incarnate … and right to be afraid.*

"Anyway," he said, waving the gun around and making her cringe. "We struggled some, and I shoved her away from me. She went down hard and hit her head on the edge of the dresser, and she didn't get up after that." He shrugged. "Then I cleaned up and left. Game over."

Elise hated to ask but couldn't help herself. She had to know. "Sam, did you kill Grace Vanderhouse, too?"

There was a long pause, but after a moment he blew out a breath. "Okay, I'm not proud of that, I'll tell you right now. Where I'd planned out Divia's demise for years—knew exactly how I'd play it if I ever got the chance—I swear as God is my witness, I never meant to harm that girl."

"But . . . then why did you?" Madison asked staring at him in the rearview mirror. "What did she ever do to you? She and her father were as much Divia's victims as you and Toby."

"Yes. Now, that's a true statement." He cleared his throat. "But she gave me no choice. She just wouldn't *listen*."

"What do you mean, Sam?" Elise asked. "Wouldn't listen about what?"

Sam's gaze locked on her and a pained look crossed his face. "She'd come to the same conclusion that you had."

"That Toby had killed his mother?"

"Yep." He gave a brief nod. "She'd seen him goin' into his momma's room that night, and when she'd heard Divia had been killed and when it'd happened, she assumed he'd done it. She tried to get him to turn himself in, even after he swore to her that he hadn't done it."

Sam pointed a finger at Elise. "And she should have known better, mind you. They'd been family for a time. She should have known he wasn't capable of doin' something like that."

He shook his head as if to clear his thoughts. "Anyway, Toby came to me about it, told me he hadn't killed Divia, which of course, I knew, having delivered her to her maker myself. So I went and tried to talk to Grace that afternoon, tried to get her to just walk away, but she wouldn't let it go. Said she was gonna have to tell the police if Toby didn't turn himself in, that it was the right thing to do."

"And so you protected Toby by removing the threat." Elise raised a palm, pleading with the man. "But Sam, adding two more murders by killing us? Where will it end? If you let us go, I promise we won't say anything. You can leave town and no one will ever know what really happened. Toby will be safe."

Sam's heavy sigh filled the air. "I really wish we could do that Elise, truly I do. But I don't know that I can trust you. I need to clean up the field. You understand that, right?"

"But Sam—"

"No, the time for talkin' is over, sweetheart. We're all gonna get out of the car now and head into the fairgrounds." He gave her a hard look, and she knew they'd run out of time. "Just so we're clear, any funny business and I won't hesitate to drop your sister where she stands. You get me?"

This was so not the way she wanted to die, nor was it in her to watch her sister die. She conjured the faces of her family in her mind, and a cold dread filled her heart.

And then there was Jackson. Their timing had never been good, but they'd just begun to find their rhythm. She'd be damned if this was how it was all going to end. She had to find a way out of this mess for both her and her sister.

"Yes, Sam," Elise told him, "I get you."

"Good deal. Now let's move."

# TWENTY-FIVE

THEY GOT OUT OF the car and Sam took Madison by the arm again as they walked toward the fairground's rear gate. He made Elise go ahead of them to keep an eye on her and to ensure that, as he put it, there was no 'funny business'.

When they got to the gate, Elise eyed the thick chain that was wound through the links and the padlock holding it in place. Facing Sam, she raised an eyebrow. "This gate is locked. What do you propose we do? Fly over it?"

"Don't be a smart-ass, El," Madison hissed with a frightened look. "Are you trying to get him to shoot us right here?"

Elise shook her head. "Don't worry, Maddy. Sam's not going to shoot us out here in the open where anyone could drive by and see. Right, Sam?"

The man simply smiled, unfazed by her goading. "Don't tempt me, little girl. We're far enough out of town that it wouldn't be that much of a worry. As for the locked gate? That's not a problem, either. If you look a bit closer, you'll find that I've been out here before—with bolt cutters."

Elise did as he'd suggested, and with growing concern, realized he was right. The lock was just for show, the chain itself having been neatly snipped in two. He may not have meant to harm Grace Vanderhouse, but like Divia's murder, he'd planned ahead to tie off the loose ends that she and Madison presented.

Keeping the gun pressed snuggly against Madison's rib cage, he nodded toward the entrance. "Be quick, girl. Take the chain off and open the gate."

She did as he asked and pushed the gate open wide. When she did, she could have sworn she'd caught movement up on the road. She hadn't heard anything, but wondered if someone or something might be concealed behind the thick brush that grew along the highway. Not wanting to call his attention to what she may have seen, she turned and began walking toward the area that had housed Restaurant Row during the festival.

Though she couldn't be certain what she'd actually seen, or if it had been wishful thinking on her part, her mind went crazy with the possibilities. Of course, the best-case scenario—and the one she was rooting for with every fiber of her being—was that C.C. had contacted Jackson, and the cavalry was about to make their move. She didn't know how much time she and Madison had left, but knew it couldn't be long.

They continued down the thoroughfare and were almost to Restaurant Row when a loud report from the direction of the parking lot startled them all. It sounded like a gun shot, but could've been a car backfiring out on the road. Madison's eyes widened, and she shot a look in Elise's direction before Sam spun around, dragging her with him.

In that split second, Madison surprised them both by taking advantage of the distraction and the momentum, throwing a roundhouse punch that caught Sam square in the nose. It wasn't enough to do lasting damage, but in that moment he grunted in pain and let go of her arm, which gave the women the only opportunity they were going to get.

"Run, El!" Madison yelled over her shoulder as she raced away, disappearing down an aisle before Sam could recover.

Elise didn't waste any time in following her sister's lead and sprinted down Restaurant Row to her right as fast as her legs would take her. Unfortunately, she'd lost sight of Madison, but she prayed that her sister would find a safe place to hide. The good news was that they'd gone down different aisles. At least for the moment, Sam would have to choose only one of them to follow.

At Sam's angry bellow, Elise had the brief hope that Madison's punch had bloodied the creep's nose good. Darting into a booth about halfway up the aisle, she ducked behind the counter and prayed for deliverance.

"Elise, I know you're here somewhere. Do *not* make me look for you."

It seemed like Sam was in the next aisle over, but sound could be deceiving the way it echoed up and down the fairway like a wind-tunnel. For all she knew he could be right at the end of her row.

"You know I took the car keys from Madison," Sam yelled. "Neither one of you can go anywhere, so you're just postponing the inevitable. Might as well come out and face the music, get it over with."

*Yeah, like that's gonna happen. Because we're both just that stupid, you moron.*

She wanted to scream at him to shut his pie hole—that he wasn't going to get away with taking her or Madison from their family and friends. She longed to shout that Jackson would come for them, and then he'd be sorry. But to be honest, she wasn't sure that would happen, at least not in time to save them. Then again, what if Jackson did come and Sam got the drop on him? She wasn't sure she could take that, either.

Her heart was pounding so loud in her ears that she was certain he could hear it and would locate her by that alone. She backed up against the wall of the kiosk underneath the counter, pulling her legs up as close to her body as she could get them in hopes that she couldn't be seen if he glanced into the booth. Terrified to make any sound that might give away her position, she squeezed her eyes shut and listened for anything that might indicate he was near.

As she sat there straining to hear the slightest noise, the loud *bang* when Sam kicked the front panel of a booth on the other side of the aisle was just about her undoing. Slapping her hands over her mouth to keep from screaming, she held her breath, afraid the next booth he checked would be hers.

Just when she was sure he was there just on the other side of the kiosk wall, there was another *bang* and she heard a sound that had her blood running cold. Madison's scream.

Sam had found her sister.

Madison cried out, begging him not to hurt her. By the sound of it, he was dragging her toward the spot where Elise was hiding, and she had to stifle the urge to jump to her sister's aid. That would only get them back to square one.

"All right, Elise," he called after a moment. "It's time to stop this foolishness. I've got Madison, as you can probably hear. Come out now, and I'll make it quick for both of you."

"Don't do it, Elise." Madison yelled, and then screamed again in pain. Elise could only imagine what Sam had done to elicit her sister's agonized cry.

"If you don't come out now, I *will* kill your sister right here. Then I'll hunt you down and make you sorry you caused me so much trouble. And that's a promise."

*Oh, dear God!* She had no choice. If she stayed where she was, she'd have to listen to him killing Madison just yards away from where she was safely hidden. But if she came out they were both dead. Either way, they were screwed.

Elise was so scared she thought she might have a heart attack before Sam could kill her, but she took a deep breath, grabbed hold of her courage, and stood up to face him.

"Elise, *no!*" Madison sobbed.

With her pulse racing, Elise stepped out of the booth into the aisle. Pressing her lips together, she shook her head. "This is my fault, Maddy, and I won't let you die alone because I stuck my nose where it didn't belong."

"Nobody else is going to die here," a voice called from the end of the row.

Taken by surprise, Sam turned with his arm around Madison's neck and dragged her with him back against the nearest booth.

Stunned, Elise looked down the aisle to where Jackson stood, flanked by Jim Stockton.

"Mr. Raymond, I'm going to need you to let go of Madison and drop the gun," Jackson said, putting out a hand.

"That's not going to happen, Deputy. Don't you come any closer, or I'll shoot both of these women," Sam finished, waving the gun back and forth between Madison and Elise, who stood frozen in place a few feet away.

"You don't want to do that," Jackson said, his voice deadly calm. "Because if you harm either of them, Deputy Stockton here will drop you like a stone." He gestured to Jim, who had pulled his service revolver and had it trained in Sam's direction.

Unfortunately, Sam was using Madison as a shield, which would hamper a clear shot. But just when Elise was sure they were at a stalemate, Toby Raymond stepped from around the corner and joined the party.

"Dad? Please do as Jackson says and put down the weapon."

"Toby? What are you doing here, son?"

"What am *I* doing here? Are you kidding me?" Shock chased disbelief across Toby's face. "What are *you* doing?"

Sam licked his lips and his voice took on a quality of uncertainty. "I'm trying to protect you."

"*Protect* me? How?" Toby's eyes went wide with horror. "By killing my mother? Killing Grace?" He gestured toward Madison and then to Elise. "And how does harming two more innocent people protect me? Please don't use me as an excuse to commit murder … again."

"I didn't mean to kill Grace. I swear. That was a mistake. But your momma's death was justice, and not just for us. She deserved what she got. She started the ball rollin' by taking you away from me all those years ago. And she destroyed more than one life along the way as she went. This whole thing is her doing, son."

Toby shook his head. "No, Sam. You're wrong. I've used that excuse for years to justify a lot of bad decisions on my part, but the truth is, I should have made better choices and been accountable for my own actions." He took one step closer and then another. "Did Mom do a lot of terrible things over the years out of greed and vanity? Yes. Did she steal time from us by taking me and running away in the middle of the night? Absolutely. But nobody deserves what you did to her. Nobody."

Elise had been still as a statue while Toby tried to talk his father out of more violence, but when Jackson stepped forward, she gasped. His attention momentarily diverted, Sam swung the gun briefly in her direction before waving it madly over Madison's shoulder at Jackson.

"That's far enough, Deputy. Any closer and I start shooting."

"Come on, Sam." Jackson stopped moving and put up his hands. "You don't want to do this. You start shooting, and it won't end well for anyone."

"Go ahead and test me," the man suggested, pointing the gun directly at Jackson's heart.

Elise could read the resolve in Sam's eyes from where she stood and desperately tried to come up with a plan when Madison went into action surprising them all. The next twenty seconds were a flurry of activity that began with Madison's elbow connecting with Sam's mid-section followed by a heel to his instep, another shot to his nose, and ending with a knee to the groin.

The gun he held went flying, and Sam Raymond dropped to his knees before falling face first into the gravel.

They were all so stunned at the turn of events that no one said a word or made a move for another five seconds, or so. Then Madison leapt over Sam's inert body and made a bee-line to where Jackson stood, with Elise only steps behind. He threw an arm around each of them as Jim collected Sam's discarded gun and pulled out his handcuffs.

"Geez, Maddy. That was incredible … and a little scary," Toby said, a pained look on his face as he watched the deputy cuff his father. "Where did you learn to do *that*?"

"I just remembered to sing," Madison said with a wobbly smile and a wicked gleam in her eyes.

"I beg your pardon?" Jim looked up at her like she was some kind of strange new species. "Did you say *sing*?"

"Uh-huh."

Jackson's eyebrows dropped and he blinked several times. "What the hell does that even *mean*?"

"S-I-N-G. Solar plexus, instep, nose, groin."

Elise burst into laughter at the look on Jackson's face and hugged him up close for a moment. "Let me help you, sweetie. SING is from one of Maddy's favorite movies, where Sandra Bullock plays a female F.B.I. agent who goes undercover in a beauty pageant. For her talent in the competition, she teaches the audience some basic self-defense using the acronym S-I-N-G."

Jackson stared at her for a moment before a smile spread across his face. Soon he was laughing out loud and shaking his head. "Okay, now I've heard everything. And I think I'm going to have to see this movie you're talking about."

Madison smiled in return and then winced when she raised a trembling hand to the bruise beginning to show on the side of her face. "I've got it on DVD at home. You're welcome to it anytime, but I warn you. It's a screwball chick flick."

"I'll keep that in mind. Meanwhile, let's get out of here and get that bruise looked at. I also need to get statements from you two, and C.C.'s probably going a little crazy wondering what's going on." Jackson grinned at Elise. "I made her wait in the car."

"Oh my," Elise exclaimed. "She may never forgive you for making her miss all the excitement."

As she started to walk away, he grabbed her arm and pulled her back into his embrace, holding her tight against his chest for a moment. Then he spoke softly into her ear.

"You gave me a helluva scare, pal. But that's something we're going to have to discuss later when my anxiety level returns to normal."

"Thanks for coming for us, Jax. And I'll be happy to have any conversation you want." She reached up and kissed his cheek. "But right now ... I just want to go home."

# TWENTY-SIX

THE REST OF THE afternoon took forever, and Elise was exhausted by the time she and Maddy had each given their statements and were finally allowed to go home. There were still reports to complete, but Jim volunteered to finish up so Jackson could take her home. And after the harrowing events of the day, Elise was feeling the need to spend some quality time with those closest to her at River Bend.

Madison had rebounded with grace and speed, and after talking to Abigail on the phone, had invited Toby and Garrett back for an additional family dinner before they packed up and headed south in the morning. Elise was surprised at her sister's resilience after their close brush with death and giggled at the re-telling of how Maddy had taken down Sam Raymond with help from a chick flick.

"Isn't that just a hoot?" Abigail cackled and set a basket full of warm rolls on the table before taking a seat next to Garrett. "I'm telling you, my baby girls are nothin' if not resourceful."

"That's all well and good, Mom, but I'd rather have them stay out of trouble in the first place," Laura replied as she took her place at the head of the table. "I just can't take the stress and worry."

"I agree, Miss Laura. And don't get me wrong, I am grateful for Maddy's quick thinking today," Jackson commented, raising an eyebrow in Elise's direction. "But I would also prefer them *not* to get into these kinds of situations at all."

"And like I told you in my statement," Elise countered. "This time it wasn't my fault. All I did was stop by to speak with Toby and see how he was holding up."

"Careful, Pinocchio," Jackson warned with a skeptical grin. "I think there was a tad more to it than just you and your Good Samaritan instincts."

"Whatever. Anyway, how was I supposed to know his dad would go off the rails and target me?" Elise turned to Toby. "No offense."

"Oh, none taken," Toby assured her. "Sam did go a little crazy. Poor guy. I mean, I know what he did was wrong and all, but I can't help feeling sorry for everything he lost."

Madison put a hand over Toby's. "It must have been so hard to watch your father being handcuffed and taken away like that."

He nodded, turning his hand over and giving hers a squeeze. "I have some very conflicted feelings about the whole thing. On one hand, Sam's really a stranger to me, someone I just met a few days ago. I was only four years old when my mom took me and left, so I have no recollection of him." He shrugged. "On the other hand, he *is* my biological father, and I was really hoping to regain that relationship. However, it doesn't negate the fact that he took not only my mother from me and Garrett," he said with a glance at his step-father, "but he took Grace from me as well—and just when we'd reconnected. It's hard to even think about what could have been, had Sam not found us when he did."

Abigail gave Toby a sympathetic look and then turned to Garrett. "I know I've said it before, but my heart goes out to both of you. Though Divia and I had our differences, she didn't deserve to die that way."

"Thanks, Abby," Garrett said with a sad smile. "Divia may not have been the easiest person to be around at times, and she didn't always behave in the most appropriate manner, but that doesn't justify what Sam Raymond did." He sighed and glanced at his stepson. "Toby's agreed to stay on at the winery, and we're going to work at picking up the pieces of our lives and moving on when we get back home."

"Oh, that's wonderful," Abigail replied. "And Toby, I'd only met Grace the one time, but she seemed like a lovely young woman. I'm so sorry for your loss. You, too, C.C., I know you and Grace were friends." She patted C.C.'s hand. "It's just such a waste of life in a short span of time."

Toby gave another nod. "You're right, Miss Abby. I just wish I would've told Elise who Sam was when she asked me about him yesterday. Maybe we could have at least avoided that frightening scene at the fairgrounds this afternoon if I had."

Elise dismissed his comment with a wave of her hand. "I'd actually made a mental note of his license plate before he left, intending to give the information to Jax later. If I'd have followed through with that—" Jackson interrupted her by clearing his throat and giving her a meaningful look. "*And* told him about the threatening note that had been left on my windshield," she continued with a roll of her eyes, "maybe we would've snapped to Sam's involvement sooner."

Jackson closed his eyes briefly and shook his head. "Woman, you try my patience at every turn. There *is* no we, darlin'. Like I keep telling you, leave the investigations to the professionals and keep your pretty little nose out of it."

"Yeah, yeah," she said and then leaned over and kissed his cheek. "I'll try to remember that, Deputy."

He gave her a doubtful glance. "You'll excuse me if I don't hold my breath on that, as I know what an exercise in futility *that's* gonna be for you."

"Hardy-har-har. You're so funny."

"Don't worry, Jax. We have several events planned at Lodge Merlot that Elise has promised to help me with," Madison stated with a smug smile. "I'll keep her busy for sure."

"Yeah, and with the Delphine Opera House restoration finished," Ross added, "she won't have a whole lot of time for nosing around your investigations."

"Oh right, and look who's talking, Mr. 'Let's-Keep-Gram-Out-of-Trouble'. You were right there with me when we started asking questions—though you have no talent for it whatsoever—so zip it."

"Yes," Carolyn spoke up in a stern tone. "Mr. Beckett and I have recently had *that* conversation. His sleuthing days are definitely over. Right, my love?"

Ross didn't even grumble but backed off and clammed up immediately. Elise would have dearly loved to hear how that discussion went. She was pretty sure her sister-in-law had made fast work of her brother, and the look on his face spoke volumes.

"So, what's the deal with the opera house?" Toby asked Elise with a curious look. "I love live theater."

"David Marchant and his partner Robert Taylor are friends of mine from Dallas," Elise told him. "They bought the old building in hopes of restoring it to its previous glory. I've donated some time and a bit of money to help them with the project. They intend to get it up and running before moving back to David's hometown in Oregon."

Ross poured himself some sweet tea from the pitcher on the table. "With the renovation done, they've asked El to sit on the board for the first year."

"Their debut production is scheduled to open in a couple months," Madison said with excitement. "I can't wait to get tickets. I may even get to help with concessions."

"I told David that I'd work the box office for him on several nights," C.C. put in. "I think it's really going to perk up Delphine."

Garrett Larson took some mashed potatoes from the bowl Abigail handed him before passing it on to Toby. "What are they presenting for their first production? I enjoy live theater from time to time as well. Maybe Toby and I could drive up for opening weekend."

"That would be such fun," Abigail agreed. "We could all go together. But I'm not sure what they're performing. Elise, do you know?"

Elise looked around the table at the expectant faces and was hesitant to tell them. "Yes. Unfortunately, I do." Shooting a glance at Jackson, she grinned. "It's called *A Very Country Murder*."

There was a few seconds of silence followed by uproarious laughter.

"Oh my Lord!" Abigail shouted after a moment. "Isn't that just as fitting as it can be?"

"For crying out loud, Mom," Laura said with a shake of her head. "You don't have to sound so gleeful about it. I, for one, have had just about all I can take of real-life murder mysteries."

"Oh, phooey," Abigail replied with a snort and a wave of her hand. "Where's your sense of humor?"

Elise took Jackson's hand and smiled. "And just so you know, I had nothing to do with the choice of material."

Jackson continued to chuckle. "Well, *I* don't mind a good murder mystery. As long as it's performed by actors and is confined to the stage."

"From your mouth to God's ears, darlin'," she replied. "From your mouth to God's ears."

**THE END**

Janet Hanson-Haight

## ABOUT THE AUTHOR

Joni Folger (Tillamook, OR) worked on an airline for twenty-two years. When she's not spending quality time with the characters she creates, Joni enjoys gardening, crafting, and working in local theater. Visit her blog at http://JGSauer.wordpress.com.

# www.MidnightInkBooks.com

From the gritty streets of New York City to sacred tombs in the Middle East, it's always midnight somewhere. Join us online at any hour for fresh new voices in mystery fiction.

At midnightinkbooks.com you'll also find our author blog, new and upcoming books, events, book club questions, excerpts, mystery resources, and more.

## Midnight Ink Ordering Information

### Order Online:
• Visit our website www.midnightinkbooks.com, select your books, and order them on our secure server.

### Order by Phone:
• Call toll-free within the U.S. and Canada at
  1-888-NITE-INK (1-888-648-3465)
• We accept VISA, MasterCard, and American Express

### Order by Mail:
Send the full price of your order (MN residents add 6.875% sales tax) in U.S. funds, plus postage & handling to:

> Midnight Ink
> 2143 Wooddale Drive
> Woodbury, MN 55125-2989

### Postage & Handling:
Standard (U.S. & Canada). If your order is:
> $25.00 and under, add $4.00
> $25.01 and over, FREE STANDARD SHIPPING

AK, HI, PR: $16.00 for one book plus $2.00 for each additional book.

International Orders (airmail only):
> $16.00 for one book plus $3.00 for each additional book

Orders are processed within 12 business days. Please allow for normal shipping time.
Postage and handling rates subject to change.